# No Scars

RENA BOSTON

Copyright © 2014 Rena Boston
Published by Just Writers Publishing Company
Printed in the United States of America
Photography by James Ranger
Cover Design by Gordan Blazevic
Book Layout by Forerunners Ink LLC,
www.forerunnersink.com

All Scriptures cited are taken from the King James Version of the Bible.

ISBN 978-0-9727848-8-7

For licensing/copyright information, for additional copies, or for use in specialized settings, contact:

Just Writers Publishing Company
"Where Fingers Write From The Heart"
Round Lake, Illinois 60073
(847) 494-8420 (telephone)
www.justwriters.com
renaboston@comcast.net
justwriters@comcast.net

# Dedication

*To my loving husband*
James Ranger

*To my daughters*
Le'Trisha Daniel
Jeanine Joe

*To my grandchildren*
Kenneth Daniel Jr.
Kristopher Daniel
Ashley Joe-Fuqua
Kaleb Daniel

I love and appreciate you all!

# Contents

# Foreword

Are you haunted by memories of a former abusive relationship? Does everyone except you believes your current relationship is abusive? Does this concern you?

The emotional damage resulting from an abusive relationship can be long lasting, often affecting the victim for the rest of their life.

Domestic abuse is not readily discussed because of the shame and embarrassment associated with it. Experts in this area say nearly one in four women will suffer some form of domestic abuse in their lifetime.

In *No Scars*, a novel based on a true story, Rena Boston allows us to observe the transition of Raven, from a naïve young girl to a confident woman.

*No Scars* will remind you of the ecstasy of falling in love for the first time as Raven experiences a marriage that is filled with mutual love, trust, joy, and hope for the future. As the relationship progresses, there are signs, some subtle, some overt, that there are major problems on the horizon. Raven is confident however, that as long as they have each other, there is nothing they cannot accomplish…together!

Raven faces a rude awakening as these signs become

hindrances to an otherwise successful marriage. As the marriage deteriorates, she struggles to recapture the attributes which caused them to fall so deeply in love in the first place. How can a marriage transform from joy, happiness, love and respect, to despair, loneliness, shame and abuse?

Raven is flooded with conflicting emotions. All that is within her says divorce is wrong. Should she stay and endure the heartache of what has clearly become an abusive relationship? After all, every now and then, there is a glimmer of hope that things might get better.

Rena Boston allows us to be witnesses as Raven comes to the realization that her trials seem to be pushing her into a deeper and more intimate relationship with God.

One of the most important lessons Raven learns and we are reminded of is, whether you are in the midst of the joys of romantic love, suffering the consequences of mistakes, or enduring the shame of an abusive relationship, if your most important relationship is with God, you will not only emerge victorious, but you will emerge with ...*No Scars*.

I invite you to rejoice with Raven during times of love and romance, shed a tear during periods of sadness and abuse, then give an emphatic, "You-go-girl" as she comes out on the winning side. By the time you finish reading this book, I assure you there will be something acquired which can be applied to your life.

*Elder Edward Jackson, Associate Minister*
*Faith Temple Church of God in Christ, at Evanston*
*Composer and Songwriter*
*Husband and Father*

# Acknowledgments

*Siblings*
Julia Mae Ervin
Patricia Ann Boston
Arthur Boston Jr.
JoAnn England
Sylvester Alexander Boston
Wendy Joyce McClain
Cindy Gaye Burton

*In Memory of*
Arthur Boston Sr.
Virginia Boston
Mary Gardner
Johnny Edward Boston

*Special Thanks*
Dr. Carlis L. Moody Sr.
Mrs. Mary A. Moody
Elder Edward Jackson
Lisa Laudé-Raymond
Rosalyn Dopson
Juliana Taylor
Sandra Ham

*To all who encouraged me, I love you very much.*

# Introduction

At one time or another, most of us have faced the secret battles of "Who am I?," "Why am I here?," and "Where am I going?" These daunting questions disrupted my life until I realized I held the answers!

This book was written with you in mind. The unrevealed, hidden you! You are more than the mirror's reflection. Look deeper! Further than that! There is a better you waiting to come forth. No matter who you are, this book will touch your heart. Come! Experience the comfort in knowing you are not alone. Erase the shame you have carried for so long. Embrace the truth: Our experiences are necessary to bring us to our destiny. Your untapped strength will empower you, your commitment will carry you, your faith will sustain you.

Turn the pages and find hope, encouragement, and inspiration. You can overcome the insurmountable odds. There is a survivor in you.

This novel is a lifeline for those who think there is no hope, for those who want to give up, throw in the towel, and just quit. Don't do it! With your last breath, fight. Something bigger than your problem awaits you.

When I finished my fight, I discovered I had "No Scars"!

This novel is based on a true story.

# 1
# The Awakening

Raven slowly opened her eyes. She raised her head slightly. She pressed her temples to gather her thoughts. *"What happened?"* She avoided sudden movements. She felt weak as she lifted herself from the floor. Confusion overshadowed her. Her mind was racing. *"How did I get here?"* She remembered the bruises on her face. The stinging from the deep cuts over her body. The burning sensation that would not stop. She recalled the pain as a piercing stab in her heart. The pain made her body jerk uncontrollably. The bits and pieces were not coming together. Total recall eluded her. Gingerly, she began rubbing her body. Feeling for scars based on what she remembered, she could not find any. She staggered to the mirror. She needed to see what had happened to her. Raven froze. She was shocked. She beheld a beauty she had never known. She began to laugh, softly at first. Then her laughter caused her body to vibrate. She had no scars!

Her countenance had an unexplainable illumination. Life's battles had groomed her well. It was absolutely amazing! Raven smiled as she remembered the words of her faithful friend Lis. "Every aspect of your life is a voice of hope for someone in trouble." She thought, *The voice of hope can only be heard if I tell my story.* She struggled with the shame she would face if she told her story. Nevertheless, at that moment all the emotions of her life came alive. They bombarded her, intertwining themselves. She felt pain, then healing. She felt sadness, then joy. The message was clear. She knew she had to tell her story. She walked into her bedroom, opened her safe, and pulled out her diary. Next to her Bible, it was her most sacred possession. She left volume one of her diary in the safe and pulled out volume two. She was ready to share her heart. She began reading aloud.

"Here I am. Eighteen-years-old. Trying to make it on my own. So young, so confused, and already bruised by life. I left home filled with hatred, anger, and prejudice. I began my quest to find love and happiness. I desperately needed change. My life was surrounded by obstacles. Wherever I turned, it was painful. Every relationship was the same. My sacrifices resulted in more despair. My hopes and dreams died a little with each failed relationship."

The first entry in Raven's diary was called "The Great Escape."

# 2
# The Great Escape

The year was 1970. The month was June, and as usual, the weather was hot and humid. I made every effort to remain cool, calm, and dry. It wasn't easy, but it was worth it, because this was a special day.

Graduating from high school was the highlight of my life. I had promised myself that at the first opportunity, I was going to get as far away from Darlington, South Carolina, as I possibly could. Here I am, two days after graduation, preparing to board a church-chartered bus filled with other parishioners.

We were on our way to Baltimore, Maryland, to attend our church's annual convention. It was stimulating to know that South Carolina would soon be a distant memory. It was a good thing that there was a bus to take me away, however, I had no money. I was determined that this small detail was not going to hold me captive in South Carolina. We lived and worked on a farm. The owner owned the farm, the house we lived in, and our persons. We were cheap resident laborers, who worked the crops of the farm from dust to dawn. It was routine to work under 105° sun. Some of the crops harvested included tobacco, cotton, soybeans, and corn. The owner assigned an overseer to ensure that all of his crops were harvested timely. The overseer was simply a hound dog, an enforcer. He was responsible for watching and driving us, making sure we did not stop to rest. He accomplished this by slowly riding in his air-conditioned truck, along beside us as we worked. He drove from one end of the row to the next, and he decided when we were tired or thirsty and needed to rest. We were a herd that he was assigned to drive. We were paid less than minimum wage. My siblings and I missed school many days because child labor was mandatory. The more babies my parents birthed, the happier it made the owner; and my parents gave him eleven strong backs to secure his future farming.

I was consistently angry. Bitterness and rebellion controlled me as I became more and more aware of life on the plantation. It enraged me that my parents and grandparents were required to address the owners' teenage sons with "Yes Sir" and "No Sir." Our lives were totally in their control. When a person or family moved from one farm to another, the two farm owners had to agree to the change, and the approved reason usually was due to marriage or other life events. Undoubtedly, you can understand my urgency to leave South Carolina. I went to the plantation owner to borrow $20. His wife said, "Okay." She told me to get it from their overseer. The overseer was a racist and an oppressor. I told him what the Mrs. had said and he began to mock me. He said, "If I lend you this money, will you come back and work on the farm?" I said, "Yes." I knew I was lying and apparently he did too. He said he needed an assurance from my mother. I smirked, thinking, *What kind of assurance is he going to get from my mother? I am grown.* This was a matter of life or death. I was willing to face any consequence and I believe he knew it. He had witnessed years of rebellion from me. He knew that ice water and not warm blood, flowed through my veins. He for certain knew that I hated him. Even as a minor, I refused to say "Yes Sir" to him, but I did to the owners. Once he threatened my life and told my mother if I didn't straightened up, she was going to find me "somewhere"... His threat forced me to become more cunning with my acts of hatred. As he wrote the check, there was a smirk on his face. His smirk seemed much more powerful than mine. At that moment, I believe I hated that man more than he would ever know love. He wrote the $20 check payable to my mother. Then he made it clear that if my mother cashed the check, she was promising I would return to work on the farm. Return to what? The hot sun? The cotton fields? The tobacco fields? The soybean fields? The prejudice? The oppression? The attempted rapes by my uncles on both sides of the family? The rape attempt by my father's friend's son? Not to mention the good 'ole church brothers and deacon... No! Not me. This place would be history. I am out of here for good. I did not have any plans. However, I knew I was not returning, even if I had to live on the streets of Baltimore City.

What happened next caused me to believe God hated me as much as I hated the overseer. It seemed I was destined to be sad and oppressed. I thought the humiliation I endued to get the $20 was the worst. Then, my mother decided she needed a portion of the money, so she offered me $5 of it. Even though I only had twenty-five cents, pride would not allow me to accept the $5. I told my mom, "No, you keep it. Keep all of it." I instantly felt rage towards my mother. *How could she do this to me? What will I do? Where will I go? How will I survive? Doesn't Mama care about me? Can't she look beyond my rebellion and see that I am hurting and scared?*

I felt betrayed. God and my mother deserted me. My

sister, Paula, heard Mama was in Baltimore. She drove from Philadelphia to see her. During Paula's visit, I asked to live with her until I found a job. To my surprise, she said yes.

During the convention I stayed with Aunt Rizzie, my father's sister. When the convention ended, everyone except me boarded the bus to return to South Carolina. This would be my journey of discovery. I was convinced my destiny was waiting, even though I didn't have a clue what it was. As the bus drove away, I felt frightened and alone. This was what I wanted, what I so often dreamt about. Now it was real. Watching the bus depart, I angrily whispered, "They will never see me again."

Greater than the anger was the uncertainty that gripped me. I did not know what I wanted. Part of me said move forward. The other part said go back with your family to the farm. I asked myself questions I could not answer. Fear gripped me so strongly I reasoned, 'Going back doesn't seem so bad. Maybe...'

Years of agony and pain passed before I forgave my mother. Growing older brings insight. It helped me look at the situation differently. My heart said, "Maybe she needed it more than I did." My mind reasoned, "How could that be? I was not going back home. I was going to Philadelphia. I needed those few dollars." My greatest struggle was her keeping every penny just because I would not accept the $5. I began my new life with twenty-five cents, no decent clothes to wear, one pair of shoes, and no job.

Paula took me to Aunt Rizzie's house to get my belongings. I was so excited. I was going to live with my big sister! While living in Philadelphia, I began dying a slow death. It was no one's fault. I was limited because I only knew my immediate family. I did not have a job and there was no one to help me search for one. I was empty inside. Nevertheless, I was not returning home to South Carolina.

I deeply desired a job, but fear paralyzed me. I was afraid to go into the big city alone. I was convinced if I left the house, I would not find my way back. The farm was all I had known my entire life. Now I had to get around in an overpopulated city, deal with bumper-to-bumper traffic, elevated trains, and buses going every direction. Paula's children were too small to help me. Poor Raven! My hopes and dreams were crumbling. Then one day, Paula and her husband decided to move from Philadelphia to Baltimore. This made me very happy because I knew people in Baltimore. I would be able to begin living. Things were looking up.

Unfortunately, even in Baltimore things remained the same. I could not find a job, but this time I had someone to show me around. After a period of hopelessness, I gave up. Periodically, one taunting question kept coming up, "How great is your escape from South Carolina now?"

# 3

# The Unknown Destination

It was early Tuesday evening. I was bravely walking the unfamiliar streets of Baltimore, Maryland. My pace was deliberate and slow because it was hot and I had safety concerns walking through the various neighborhoods. I was meeting a friend named Jessica at her house, so we could walk to church together. Since I arrived late, she had already left. I decided not to go to church because I was not sure of the directions. Yes, I missed church that day, but I met Tony. Tony was Jessica's nephew. When I saw him, my heart skipped a beat. When I heard him speak, my lips smiled. When he laughed, I literally felt like I was floating in the air. He had a hearty laugh that made you laugh even if you didn't know what was funny. His smile was bright and flashy. No doubt, the gold tooth in the front of his mouth enhanced the brightness of his smile. Also, in the center of the gold tooth was the shape of a star. He dressed fashionably and was well-groomed. His hair was filled with waves. He was quite charming. Tony and a group of guys had gathered at Jessica's house and were sitting on the steps. Within minutes, Tony and I were in a controversial conversation regarding men and women roles in marriage. After everyone else had settled their issues, my debate with Tony got stronger. We did not agree on anything. Nevertheless, I thoroughly enjoyed talking with him. I only hoped, it was not obvious that my heart was skipping beats. I knew instantly that I could love Tony. He appealed to me and I'd hoped he felt likewise. One thing I knew, we could never marry each other. Our beliefs were too different.

Tony and I became good friends. One day he picked me up and took me to his job to be interviewed for a cashier's position. He drove a sports car, which to me, validated his persona. It was clean and smelled fresh. It was obvious that he took very good care of it. He was a butcher at a grocery store. On our way to his job, he showed me where I would catch the bus to get back home after the interview. This would be my first time riding the bus alone and I did it. This was a big deal for this country girl. Later that day, Tony accidentally cut his leg while working. He said he was thinking about me when it happened. Even though I did not believe him, I was flattered. I thought, *This wonderful and handsome guy likes me.*

One month later, Tony's cousin, Molly, took me to the federal building to take the civil service examination for a government job. The exam was three hours long. As I waited for the exam results, I landed my first job. I became a cashier at the store where Tony worked. Ten days later, I received notice that I had passed the civil service exam.

Tony was becoming a major part of my life. However, I consistently denied his request to take me out. I did not believe he was a one-woman's man. When I was convinced otherwise, we went on our first date. He took me to a birthday and retirement banquet honoring the president of Morgan State College. I wore a yellow gown with black accessories. My hair was pinned up and I looked rather cute.

After the banquet, Tony took me for a ride in the country. We rode and talked the night away. He showed me sites that were special to him. One of them was the place where his favorite band played. Then he stopped the car and kissed me.

Was this the turning point in my life? Three months later, I became an employee of the federal government. I enjoyed the work. An added benefit was the friends I met. I relaxed, feeling all was well. It was my time. My ship had come in. I was alive. I knew where I was going. I was a girl with a future.

I worked full time and overtime for the government, along with my part time shift as a cashier. Tony and I were getting closer and things were wonderful. Everything was better than any dream I had ever had.

I should have known it wouldn't last. It had been proven time after time. However, this time I was blindsided. I was grateful to Paula for a place to live. I made sure I obeyed her rules. I completed the household chores that were expected of me. I paid my household obligations. I even went to church while the rest of the family stayed home. One night Tony brought me home from work. Paula spoke with me about dating him. She said he was no good for me and I must stop seeing him. I learned she was speaking on behalf of my mother. The conversation escalated to an argument. The argument escalated to an explosion. Before either of us realized it, we had said and done things that caused deep wounds—wounds only time could heal. At the conclusion, I was told I had to comply with her request or leave her home.

I believe Paula thought my compliance meant I respected her and her husband's authority. Likewise, my noncompliance meant disrespect. I believed my position was clear. I respected them and their home. However, this was my life and I refused to give up my right to live. I accepted the option to leave, even though I had no place to go. I called Tony, explained the situation, and asked him to come get me. I began packing my belongings. Paula apologized. She asked me to stay. I said, "No. You will not get another chance to put me out!" When Tony came, he gathered my belongings and we left.

No one knew where we were going, not even us. Tony drove around for hours, asking me what I wanted to do. We agreed I could not stay with him. It was against our upbringing. First, I called Aunt Rizzie and asked if I could temporarily live with her. She responded, "I would rather not. I allowed Sandy to come and she got pregnant. I do not want that to happen to me again. If you cannot find anybody else to take you in, call me back. I will see what I can do." Then I called Uncle Harold, my father's brother, and his wife. They told me they only had enough room for their family. They could not take anybody in. Tony and I stayed in the car until early morning. At daybreak he encouraged me to call Aunt Rizzie again. Even though I was homeless, my pride would not allow me to call her again. Running out of options and the time to go to work nearing, I mustered up enough humility to call Aunt Rizzie back. She told me okay, but it was against her better judgment. If I got pregnant, I would have to leave. It sounded fair and I accepted. Tony took me to her house and he went home.

Our relationship progressed. Then one night at a drive-in movie, things blew up. Tony suggested we become intimate and I became furious. The church taught one should not have sex before marriage. The only sex education Mama gave me was "Keep your dress down and your panties up." That was my sexual training for life. Ironically, it worked. It had sustained me through many years. Now, dealing with Tony was a challenge. During his almost forcible persistence I was scared. I knew I had to fight. I started crying and said, "If you cannot accept me as I am, then we don't belong together." I cried and could not seem to stop. I was still crying on the drive home. He stopped the car. With a painful look on his face, he begged me to stop crying. He apologized again. Since I would not stop crying he started driving again.

When we reached the house, he said he would pick me up, as usual, for work the next morning. I said I would catch the bus. I did not want to see him. The next morning I got up earlier than usual, got dressed, caught the bus, and went to work. When he arrived, I was already there and working. He walked pass me without speaking or looking my way. It hurt, but I knew it was for my best. A short time later, we were back together. Everything was great again. We were very much in love. Nothing else seemed to matter. Love had never hit me so hard before.

A year into our relationship, Tony asked me to marry him. I gladly accepted. Then bigger problems surfaced. First, my mother would not give her consent. Then, one of Tony's ex-girlfriends started harassing me.

# 4
# Choices

Is this what love feels like? Despite its sweetness, the price of love seemed high. I suffered hurts so many times by those who loved me. The effects of my mother's love were the most painful. First, she said Tony was too old for me. Then, he was too experienced and streetwise for me. Next, he already had children. None of the reasons separated our hearts. Finally, we were told there was a possibility of us being fifth or sixth cousins. When that didn't work, I was told it had been rumored that my father and Tony's mother had an affair. Tony could be my father's child. Well, that didn't work either. I was in love and nothing was standing in the way of our love.

When I say, "Suffered for love," I really mean suffered! While working at the grocery store, Tony picked me up at the end of my shift. We would go to his house and watch television. It was innocent. Nothing else happened. His ex-girlfriend Florida had apparently been stalking us. She created havoc. She was fighting to hold onto Tony. She was the mother of one of his sons. One Tuesday night after I got home from work, the doorbell rang. I was downstairs. My nephew answered and told me I had a visitor. I wasn't expecting anyone. Tony and

I were barely speaking. We were in the midst of another misunderstanding. I went upstairs to greet my visitor. To my surprise, it was a woman I had never seen before. She asked, "Are you, Raven Bailey?"

"Yes, I am." I replied with a smile. The moment I responded, she started cursing and calling me every ungodly name she could think of. She called me names I had never heard before. She continued, "I have been dating Tony for over six years and no South Carolina country "@#$^&#!" is coming up here within a few months and take him." Afterwards, she stood silently in the entrance, staring at me with rage. Her body trembled with anger. I didn't know what that crazy woman would do. I never interrupted her. Initially, I was scared stiff and could not respond. Then she began telling my aunt lies. That's when I got angry. She told my aunt she went to Tony's house one night and caught us in bed. To make it juicier, she added, "She opened the door for me." Tony had never touched me, except to kiss. The passion with which she told her lies was quite convincing. It almost sounded truthful to me, even though I knew otherwise.

Florida never knew how big she scored with her next punch. It hurt so badly I wanted to fold over to ease the pain. Nevertheless, I refused to let her see my agony, to give her that level of satisfaction. She continued her rage, saying, "By the way, I spent the night with Tony last night." Shamefully, I believed her. Tony and I had fought the night before. He left my house in anger. So, why shouldn't I believe her? Hiding my hurt helped me to become strong and bold. I responded, "If you are telling the truth, then he's getting from you what he can't get from me. Tony has made a fool out of you. He has gotten what he wanted from you. You are no longer any good for him. Look at you! You are only making a bigger fool of yourself. I feel sorry for you." Whew! It worked! Without responding, she turned and left, cursing and calling me names as she stormed down the steps. I felt sorry for her, but my anger and fear overrode my sympathy.

An emergency alert must have sounded. When Florida left, the telephone rang. It was Tony! I picked up the telephone and told him I didn't ever want to see or hear from him again. I told him not to even speak when we passed each other. Then I hung up. It was over for us. This time was for keeps. Each time he called, I hung up on him. My heart cried, "Tony, I love you." My pride cried, "Forget him!" This continued for a few months. I refused to listen to what he had to say. He started drinking heavily. Even though he had always taken pride in his appearance, it was now unkempt. Aunt Rizzie talked to me. Her mission was to tell me what Tony told her. He told her he loved me and wanted to marry me. He told her the things Florida said were lies. Tony talked with my Uncle Harold. Uncle Harold talked to me. Tony talked with anyone who listened to him. They would tell me what he said. Regardless, my pride always answered, "No." I was hurting as deeply as he was, but I didn't care. I wanted to protect myself by never seeing him again. I tried to hate him, but I couldn't. It seemed impossible to forget him. I didn't know how I would go on without him, but I had to.

Tony's mother preferred Florida, but even she asked Aunt Rizzie to encourage me to reunite with Tony. She feared he would destroy himself or lose his mind. Her selfish intervention made things worst. It was evident her motivation was not her love for me. Her desire was to save her son. I told Aunt Rizzie to remind her that this was what she wanted. She wanted me to leave her son alone and I had obliged. Florida continued harassing me.

She called constantly and said all kinds of mean things. Once she called to tell me she was going to kill me. On other occasions, she had some of her male friends call and threaten me. They told me she had connections. If I knew what was good, I'd better stop messing with Tony. Every day I was afraid of what might happen next.

When the pain and fear subsided, I realized Florida must not have known Tony and I had not seen each other for months. Even at work, when we saw each other, we quickly looked away. The cruelty of life had returned to claim its victim, me. My life was dangling by a thread. Time was moving forward without me. I didn't know what to do. I moped around the house. I did not go anywhere or do anything. I isolated myself. I was in a state of withdrawal. My aunt said I should stop feeling sorry for myself and reunite with Tony. She said, "If you were honest, you would admit you want to reunite." I just couldn't do it.

Months later, the store manager asked what was wrong between Tony and me. I explained it to him. His words illuminated my dark sad world. He said Florida had done the same thing to someone else Tony dated and she won. He said, "Florida believes Tony is hers forever and she is a compulsive liar." I felt bad that I hadn't given Tony a chance to talk. Had she been lying? I really needed to make things right. My heart longed to do so. My desires for Tony came alive. I wanted to run to him. Kiss him and tell him I loved him. I wanted to say, "I apologize for not listening, that I no longer believed the things Florida said." I couldn't do it. I didn't say or do anything.

That night when I got home, I received another call from Florida and her gang. This time, I called Tony and told him I wish he would tell his woman to stop calling me. He became very angry. The following day at work, he told me he was going to her house. He was going to get things straight one last time. His anger was at a level I had never seen. I pretended not to care. Whatever Tony did or said, Florida and her friends stopped harassing me.

The holiday season was just around the corner. Christmas arrived and everyone, except I, went to South Carolina. I stayed home. I had nowhere to go and no one to talk to. I was home alone from Friday until Monday. During that time I never answered the telephone. It rang many times. I was tempted to answer because I was so lonely, but I didn't. I wanted to see Tony. Just a glance of him would have soothed me. I loved him and didn't want to admit it. I also knew that he loved me. I could see it in his eyes. His actions and his words revealed it. Sometimes, I would sneak a peek at him when we were at work. Nothing had ever gripped me as hard as the love I felt for Tony. I didn't know what to do. Things weren't working out and I needed to accept it.

One night around 3:00 a.m., the doorbell rang. We were all asleep. Aunt Rizzie answered the door. She came downstairs and said it was for me. I went upstairs where Tony was waiting. He reeked of alcohol. His clothes were dirty and hanging off him. He needed a shave. He looked terrible, but I loved him. It was my Tony. The one I loved. The one I wanted and belonged to.

He started talking, and for the first time I listened. He went on and on. I believed he was telling the truth. I loved him and felt sorry I was so stubborn. It was difficult to look at a 'self-destructive' man who'd always had it together. The next thing I knew, we were in each other's arms. Drunk as he was, we clung to each other. We kissed and told each other of our love. That night we promised we would never let anything come between us again.

We were back on track. Things went smoothly for

a while. Then more challenges developed. My mother's concerns surfaced again. When we were dealing with his ex-girlfriend, my mother constantly tried getting me to cut ties. She said and did things to show me I needed to end it. Hurtful things were said. Tony and I wanted to handle it in the right manner. However, there seemed to be no right solution. Someone was going to be hurt by our decision. Tony drove to South Carolina to talk with my mother and her pastor. Nothing changed. My mother was determined to end the relationship. I couldn't believe some of the allegations. Things regressed so badly that Tony and I broke up again. This time it was for our benefit. We separated to think things through. Things were really tough. He was constantly asking me to marry him. I still didn't know what to do.

Day after day I heard my aunt's opinion, whether I wanted it or not. She often said, "If you marry Tony, it would probably kill your mother." Fear and guilt of possibly hurting my mother held me captive. I knew even a good marriage could not bear certain weights. I cried because I loved Tony and wanted to marry him. I also cried because I loved my mother and she did not want me to marry him. I was in the midst of a crisis filled with confusion. I prayed. I cried. I talked with myself. Yet, I found no solution. Even God didn't seem to care. Things were getting tough. When I didn't see Tony, he was in my every thought. I felt I was losing my mind. I couldn't allow that to happen. I had to fight for my survival. Things kept going backwards. I started moping around again. I stayed home. I avoided most of the visitors who came to the house.

One Saturday night Aunt Rizzie, Sandy, and some family friends went to a Cabaret. I was home alone. I didn't know Tony was going to the Cabaret also. They all attended as planned. Around 10:00 p.m. the doorbell rang. I was listening to my music and singing loudly to block out my issues of life. I went to the door, happy that someone had dropped by. I opened the door and there stood Tony. Big and handsome as ever. I invited him in. Lowered the stereo so we could talk.

He said, "I thought you were going to be at the Cabaret." I said, "You know I don't attend parties." The conversation turned serious. We talked a long time. We remembered the vow we had made to each other to never allow anyone to come between us. It seemed futile, but each time we were more determined than the time before.

We resolved that no one had the right to stand in our way, not even our parents. Our determination grew stronger as our endurance grew weaker. I realized I was placing my mom ahead of the man who wanted to marry me. Yet, I couldn't say yes to him until I received my mother's approval. As I reminisced over my mother's reaction to my high school sweethearts, the burdens of my choice lessened. When I dated Ronald, she loved him. She was convinced he was the right young man for me. We broke up and I started dating Chuck. She disliked him because she was sure Ronald was God sent. Ronald proved to be a cheat. She finally accepted Chuck. He became "the one."

Chuck and I stopped writing each other. My mother's heart was broken, and she made sure I knew it. Nevertheless, Chuck and I had an understanding. We agreed to always be friends. We agreed we were not meant for each other. Our love relationship ended in a friendship. Almost everyone blamed me for our broken relationship. They didn't know Chuck and I agreed we didn't belong together. He had another girl whom he loved; and I had Tony, whom I loved. It was best for all involved if we remained just friends.

# 5
# The Choices Get Harder

Months passed and we were still stagnated at the same crossroad, facing my mother's resistance. She totally disagreed with my choice of Tony instead of Chuck. She encouraged me to write Chuck and keep in touch. She believed if I wrote him we would get back together. I knew it was not possible. I loved my man. He loved his woman. We were both very happy. I only hoped my mother would understand that I had to love whom my heart loved. I couldn't just arbitrarily change it. One night, I told Tony I would marry him whenever he desired. We departed that night with our hearts filled with joy. Tony and I began to grow together. We grew closer and our love grew stronger. We had endured so many difficulties. It was time for us to be happy and free to love.

I was a virgin and planned to remain celibate until marriage. Tony was eight years older than me. He had much more experience regarding life. I allowed him to teach me. During our abstinence, Tony talked with me as a parent should to a child. He explained the facts of life to this innocent, naïve country girl. I learned later he told me what my naïve mind would accept as truth. Tony told me if I agreed to make love, I could do so without getting pregnant.

He further explained that a woman only gets pregnant if "getting pregnant" is on her mind while she is having sex. I feel stupid writing this. Yet, I accepted everything he said as truth. He was very patient with me. He did not rush with his instructions or his demonstrations. He even questioned me to make sure I understood what he was telling me. This naïve country girl did not know any better. Babies today know more than I knew in my twenties. When it was time for hands-on practice, I couldn't go through with it. He waited and then explained some more. I tried to believe him enough, to let myself go, but I couldn't. We started, I cried and fought, he gave up. To my surprise, this was only the beginning. I thought we would never try again. Boy was I wrong.

As time passed we were consistently happy and loving each other. One night while watching television and kissing heavily, I tried to fight the feelings but my body was not cooperating. I was afraid. I had not been taught about sex. I knew it was something dirty if it occurred before marriage. It was made for marriage only. Our love overtook us. In the heat of a moment, it grew too strong too quickly, and we did not stop. Then it happened! The jewel I had treasured for twenty years was gone in a matter of minutes. Even though my body was weak, I chose to ignore the "No" screaming from my heart and soul. We had controlled our temptations for such a long time. Now, it meant nothing. In one moment we yielded to our heated desires. I immediately knew I had made a big mistake—one that could not be reversed.

Afterwards, as I thought about the whole process, I decided it was not even worth it. During our sexual act, my body was in pain. There was no enjoyment. The only enjoyment was the foreplay. I kept thinking, *This man doesn't know what he's doing.* The pain told me he did not know what he was doing. Regardless of my thoughts of

Tony, I was the pathetic one. I was so naïve. Until this day, I thought sexual intercourse was when the man laid his penis on top of the woman's vagina and that was all there was to it. Surprise! My painful surprise! It happened a couple more times, but it was not a regular routine. The guilt was too much to endure. The little pleasure could not erase the memory of the pain.

Guilt consumed me. I consoled myself by saying, "At least I'm grown." My conscious responded, *So what? Many 20-year-old virgins still exist.* I deceived myself, thinking it was almost acceptable since I loved him. No excuse erased the guilt. Finally, I told myself, *After all, we are going to get married.* No points! The fact remained that we were not married. I gave up a priceless jewel for one moment's desire.

For a long time, we had no sexual contact. Feeling safe, I visited him for his birthday. I prepared dinner for him and gave him a bedspread and a sheet and pillowcase set for a present. Afterwards we began watching television. Then it happened. This time it was different. I felt something more than the act of sexual intercourse had occurred. I was not surprised when I missed my menstrual cycle. I knew a seed had been planted. I was carrying a life within me. Despite Tony's teaching, it happened even though I was not thinking about getting pregnant while we engaged in sex. I was pregnant and scared.

Although it was our secret, I felt everybody could see it. I tried to hide it. I wore girdles, belts, and dresses that covered the obvious. My only consolation was Tony loving me and wanting to marry me. The biggest problem had yet to be faced. I had to tell Mama and Aunt Rizzie. I knew eventually I had to face the fact, I was pregnant!

Tony started going to church with me. He wanted to dedicate his life to Jesus. I needed restoration and forgiveness of my sin. Tony gave his heart to Jesus. No matter how hard I tried, I didn't feel forgiven. I doubted whether God wanted me back. I had failed Him and my mother. I was in my third month of pregnancy when Tony received the Baptism in the Holy Spirit. Afterwards, he completely separated himself from me. We never engaged in premarital sex again. I'm not saying it didn't bother us being together, because it did. We controlled ourselves, and Tony led the way. I experienced some emotional ups and downs, almost anger. Tony was living his commitment to Jesus whether I wanted to or not. Yet, when I had the same opportunity, I failed the test. I tried blaming Tony, but that was of no use.

I was growing before my eyes. Yet, I was in denial. I delayed going to a doctor. Finally, I went and my pregnancy was confirmed. The doctor asked me what I had planned to do. He talked as if he expected me to abort the life, which had formed in my body. I left irritated. Whatever else I appeared to be, I was not a murderer.

Here I was, the dreamer! Great ambition and goals that will never be realized. The enlarging stomach would change the course of my life. Tony and I kept postponing our marriage. We desperately wanted my mother's approval. However, by all indications, we were not going to get it. The question remained, "What are we going to do?'"

The more time passed, the more uncertainties crept in. I began questioning Tony's reasons for wanting to marry me. I became uneasy about every little thing. Tony tried reassuring me of his love and desire to marry me. He comforted me. Telling me my pregnancy was not the basis of our marriage. He reminded me he had three children by two other women and never desired to marry either of them. He asked me to go to the courthouse and obtain the marriage license. I did it, but I was scared and began having second thoughts. I was preparing to experience what should have been the happiest day of my life, yet I was scared! Thank God we couldn't get marriage immediately. There was a two-day waiting period, and the license was valid for six months. My life was on the brink of being complete. This was the best day God had ever made, it was glorious. The sun was shining brightly. I thought, *Any day now, I might be married.* So I sat down and wrote my mother a letter:

*Dear Mama:*

*I am very sorry I failed you as a daughter. I am very sorry I couldn't be the ideal daughter you wanted me to be. If you so terribly want me to give Tony up, then I guess I will end up on the losing end again. If things work the way you want them to, it means they are not working the way I want them to.*

*I will be losing, like I have been doing all my life. I've never been the lucky one in the family. No matter what the competition was, I didn't come out the winner. I have always been the ugly duckling of the family. I've always felt like 'the throwaway'! You know how that is. It's like the fish that was thrown back into the pond when we went fishing on Saturday mornings. It was good for nothing but to be thrown back. That's how I view my life, 'the throwaway'! The one who is only important when someone else needs her!*

*For the first time in my life, I have someone who I really love and who loves me. Yet everyone seems to ignore that fact. I have only one life to live. It seems everyone is trying to destroy it. I can't even make plans for my life.*

*For once, Mama, I've found true love. I've found someone to trust, someone who does not take me for granted. Mama, I have tried to help you financially.*

*Whether I marry Tony or not, one day I will get married and won't be able to help as much. So, if this is why we are not getting your blessings, please think about it. Consider the life we have ahead of us.*

*Mama, I love you, my father, and all my sisters and brothers. If I end up regretting the decision not to marry Tony, I will hold it against you and the others who interfered in our life. So Mama please, if I make a mistake, please let it be my decision, my mistake.*

*Love, Raven*

I never received a response to my letter. So I called her and made another plea. Her resistance was still very strong. We decided to postpone marriage until we won her over. Tony drove to South Carolina again to talk with her. She didn't consent, but her resistance was not as strong.

Meanwhile, I was dealing with a terrible pregnancy. I was sick night and day, 24 hours, 7 days a week. The constant sickness caused my aunt to become suspicious. One day she pointedly asked, "Are you pregnant?" I answered, "Yes." I knew she would call her sister and niece in South Carolina right away. However, she would not call my mother, who was often mistreated by the family.

Knowing this, I decided it was time for me to tell my mother. I took the easy route. I wrote her a letter. No matter which way it came, I knew it would break her heart. So I put my heart into the letter. Everything I said had to be right. It also had to be in the right manner. About a week later, my mother called me. Every time she attempted to mention the pregnancy, I changed the subject. It was difficult for me to discuss it with my mother. I was so uncomfortable. Finally, she said, "If this is what you want, then go ahead and get married." I was happy. Everything within me began to dance.

Tony and I had our marriage license. However, we never discussed when or where we would get married. My attention was solely on my pregnancy. I was constantly sick and it was hard to be cheerful. My friends assured me that my hard pregnancy meant I would have an easy delivery. At least I had something better to look forward to.

My friends at work gave me a surprise baby shower. Ella Lawler, Rita Summerall, and Nadine Larue sponsored it. It was the nicest thing anyone had ever done for me. It was one of the happiest days of my life.

When I started my maternity leave, I wasn't looking forward to staying home. Things were not the best at my aunt's house. There were strong disagreements. She required me to do almost all of the housework. It was too much work for me to do at my stage of pregnancy. The list goes on. Aunt Rizzie's house became a place where I was an outcast. She constantly mumbled and grumbled about not having enough room for all these children. She routinely made nasty remarks directed at me. Sandy told Aunt Rizzie she would take her son and find an apartment. My aunt told her she wasn't talking about her and her son. That meant her anger was towards my unborn child and me. It was comforting to know I wasn't imagining things. Nevertheless, I couldn't blame her. She gave me a fair warning up front. It was the spiteful things that came later that hurt. Since I was home all day, I was expected to do everything in the house, including cook. Yet, I was still expected to pay the same household obligations as when I was working.

I told Tony I was getting an apartment. This time he wasn't going to talk me out of it as he had done before. I was determined to find peace, even if it meant being alone. I wanted to live where I would not be humiliated, abused, or rejected. Tony won again. So, I stayed and tolerated the turmoil. However, most nights it got the best of me.

When I went to bed, I cried myself to sleep. I decided to withdraw from my aunt and cousin. My routine became cooking dinner for them, going downstairs, taking a bath, getting in bed, and watching my television. They soon realized I was avoiding them and asked why. I said, "I don't have anything to say." I was having a very difficult time. I thought everything would be okay if I isolated myself. That didn't work either. One night in her irritated state, my aunt demanded I turn my television off. It wasn't disturbing anyone. I had completed my housework, paid her my portion of the rent, and cooked dinner. She was deliberately hurting me. It may have been her method of releasing her anger regarding my pregnancy.

One night, I was in the bathroom dressing for church. Suddenly, everything seemed extremely quiet. With curiosity, I went close to the door to listen. I heard Aunt Rizzie say to Sandy, "It just doesn't make any sense for anybody to be so doggish. You know Raven ate four eggs, a half pack of bacon, and bread. When I returned from taking Henry to school, there was nothing for Jerry and me. She also eats Kelly's cornflakes and milk. Then she gives him canned milk." Sandy responded, "I'm not going to buy things for somebody else to eat while Kelly is not getting anything." Aunt Rizzie continued, "After she ate all that food, she went into the bathroom and started vomiting. I didn't ask her a thing. Because I didn't even care whether she was sick or not." The lies pierced my heart. Nevertheless, I continued to listen. It was most disappointing to hear my cousin respond to obvious lies. She and I often discussed how easily Aunt Rizzie lied. For a brief moment I hated my aunt. I thought about the lies and all the other things I had opted to ignore in the past.

The fresh hurts caused other things to surface. A battle began in my mind, memory after memory. She expected me to pay her an all-inclusive rental fee, cook food for everybody, and clean the house. However, I had limited freedom. It was okay for her son to cook three or four times a day, and eat again when everyone else ate. Yet, I couldn't touch anything I didn't personally bring into the house. I never ate breakfast previously, even though the rent covered it. I was only eating it now because I was on maternity leave. However, from that moment forward, I never ate anything else at my aunt's house that I didn't personally buy. Nevertheless, I continued cooking for them. Every Friday I went to the grocery store to buy my food for the week. One night my aunt jokingly said, "Boy, when you go on a diet, you really go on one." I offered no response. They began asking why I didn't talk with them anymore. I said, "I don't have anything to say." When they asked why I didn't stay up I said, "I want to get to bed early." I knew they did not believe me. I really didn't care. I was fed up with the hypocrisy. The entire living arrangement stunk. I was so consumed with the turmoil, I didn't realize Tony was making preparations for us to get married.

On February 23, 1972, Tony picked me up from the hairdresser. After I got into the car, he said, "I had planned for us to go and get married tonight, but since it is snowing so badly, we'd better get in off the streets." I was too happy to think about what he had just said. How could he had planned it without talking with me? Some surprise! I was so happy that being excluded really didn't matter. I smiled from that night until we got married two nights later. I was the happiest human being alive. We didn't get married the night following the snowstorm because Pastor Newson wanted to get my mother's approval. My mother worked at night, so it took her another day to reach her. *What's one more day to freedom?* I thought.

# 6
# I'm So Excited

It was February 25, 1972. Baltimore, Maryland, was facing one of its worst snowstorms mixed with sleet and fog. Nevertheless, Tony, the man I loved—the man of my dreams— picked me up from home. He said, "We are going to get married." An argument? Not from me. Despite the hazardous weather watch, this was our night. The night we would become one. Around 7:30 p.m. we arrived at Pastor Newson's house. She performed our ceremony. Elder Ransom was present as a witness. I wore a pink pleated maternity dress. Tony wore a black sports jacket with black pants. I was experiencing the jitters as if I were having a large church wedding. My dream was unfolding and I did not want to be awakened.

During the ceremony, Tony held my hands as if he thought I was going to fall. I did likewise. Our hands were clutched together so tightly they were sweating. As we were leaving, Tony gently placed his arms around me to keep me from falling. The streets were covered with snow. How could this snowy night bring the brightest sunshine into my life?

Marriage was wonderful. Every day was filled with love, hugs, and kisses. Surprises and dates also came with

Tony's marriage package. I was a very happy woman. My dream finally came true. I had reached my destiny.

We knew things would not be easy, but we made a commitment. We promised, despite the obstacles, that we would stick together, standing side-by-side and not allowing anyone or anything to separate us. We embraced the commitment that was needed to keep us together. Tony and I were compatible in many areas. If our goals were different, we merged them into one. We achieved things rapidly because we were unified.

On Monday, two weeks later, the contractions started. I endured them until Tony came home. We called the doctor. My contractions were five to ten minutes apart. He told us to go to the hospital. There would be a doctor waiting. The doctor examined me and said it was false labor. I sensed he was wrong, yet I returned home. Later that night the contractions got so bad I felt I was dying. I cried and prayed but no relief came. I tried to endure the pain. When I couldn't bear it any longer, I got up and dressed. We were on our way back to the hospital. We followed the same procedures and received the same conclusion. The doctor insisted I was having false labor. Without any medical experience, even I knew this was not false labor. The examining doctor called my doctor and told him everything was the same. There were no signs childbirth had started. He said the opening was the size of a fingertip. He also said I was tense and tightened up each time he touched me. My doctor told him to keep me in the hospital and call him when the real labor started. Either way, I was to stay until he arrived at ten o'clock the next morning.

I called downstairs and told Tony to go home. I would call if I needed him. The pains continued with no sign of a baby. Some of the assigned nurses were kind and some were not so very kind. Nurse Selena Bruno was gentle, kind, and patient. She did everything to comfort me. Although I never saw her again, she has been a friend in my heart for the last forty years.

I was in labor for three days. The pains were so bad I cried, screamed, and prayed constantly. Each contraction came with a greater punch than the one before. During Tony's visits, I tried hiding the pain. His presence comforted me, but the tears still gushed out. He stayed as long as permitted. Nurse Bruno let him listen to the baby's heartbeat.

The pain made me feel like I was losing my mind. I begged to sit up but was made to lie down. Hopelessness gripped me. I had never experienced these types of feelings. I never thought there were greater pains than menstrual pains. Another strange thing happened. I began hallucinating. It was as if I had lived the event before. I saw images and reached into the scenes and touched the people. It was weird. It was like a rerun movie of my life. I can't explain it, but I was reliving my life again. The things that were happening to me had happened during my first life. However, I didn't know about it until that moment, as if it had been suppressed. It was so mixed up, yet so real.

I fought with the doctor and nurses because they refused to give me pain medication. Around 11:30 p.m. my water broke and my spirit lifted, but not for long. Even though the water had broken, nothing changed. I was in so much pain. I felt like I was about to die. Tony would have to raise our new baby alone. The doctor must have eventually given me pain medication because I blacked out. I slept until approximately 3:30 p.m. when I was awakened by pain. In my dazed state, I heard the doctor say, "The baby's heartbeat is getting slower and weaker." That confirmed my baby was going to die. If my baby died, I wanted to die also. After those thoughts, I blacked out again. I felt someone lightly shaking and tapping me. The doctor was trying to wake me. They told me they had called Tony and gotten permission to operate. The reason? They finally realized I wasn't able to give birth. The opening was the same as it was the first night when they said it was false labor.

I woke up in the operating room with an oxygen mask on my face. I began hyperventilating. I pulled the mask off my face and threw it to the floor. Two doctors, one on each side, grabbed me under the arms and bent me over. I thought they were deliberately hurting me. I could feel needlepoints in my back. Someone was sticking me repeatedly all over my back. I wanted to get up and run but couldn't. Afterwards, they placed another oxygen mask over my face. This one was heavier and much tighter. I tried to pull it off, but I couldn't. Then they tied my hands down. I fought, but it did no good. I promised the doctor if he untied me I would not pull it off again. No one responded. I felt like I was suffocating. Things began to fade and I blacked out again. I regained consciousness during the operation. I woke up but was unable to see anything. There was a big white sheet in front of me. I begged them to take it down. I was told to go back to sleep. I told him I wasn't sleepy, and I was out again. Around 4:00 a.m. the third day, I heard the nurse telling me to roll onto the bed next to the one I was in.

When I finally woke up, Dr. Appitiz was standing at my bedside. He said, "You have a beautiful baby girl." I was still heavily sedated; however, I saw the small package in his arms. Then I was out again. When I woke up the next time, I saw the friendly face of Nurse Bruno. I appreciated her so much. She had the sweetest personality, and her presence comforted me. With a smile, she told me I had given birth to a girl. The news made it all worthwhile because I wanted a girl badly. She said Tony came earlier and saw the baby and me. I was in the recovery room. Ms. Bruno was washing and preparing me for my room.

When I got into my room, all I wanted was to sleep and drink water. The nurses were instructed to limit my water intake. I was only given ice cubes to suck and sips of water at specific intervals. This did nothing for my thirst. So I tricked the nurses into giving me as much water as I wanted. I told one a sad story and I pleaded with another; each time it worked. By the end of the day my thirst was quenched.

I had not eaten anything since the banana I'd had four days earlier. I was quite disappointed when they served me liquids for lunch. I couldn't trick them about lunch. When I started walking the halls to strengthen my body, the nurses called me "The walking dead woman." They said both my baby and I almost died during delivery. I had given birth to a beautiful baby girl. I named her Tina. She was born with yellow jaundice. When I was discharged from the hospital, I had to leave her there for almost another week. That was very difficult for me. When my man, my baby, and I were finally in our own home, the pieces of my life had come together. We were living in our own little perfect world, and what a perfect world it was!

About three months later, I went to the park with Tony and his baseball team. We returned home, ate dinner, and I began talking with him. Tony had two bad habits. He ignored you. Then asked what you said even if he heard what you said. It was nerve wrecking. It was not a personal attack against me. It was just his way. His justification was, "I've been doing this all my life, as long as I can remember. You can't expect me to change now." As I talked to him, he would watch television and not respond as if I wasn't even there. I was so irritated. I decided to talk with him only as needed.

Around 12:00 a.m., my mother called and said my four-year-old nephew shot himself through the hand. I became extremely upset because I thought she said, "Head." When I asked, "Head?" She said, "No, hand." I didn't know what to do. My nephew was Paula's son. He and his sister lived with Mama. I didn't have a telephone number for Paula. When I hung up with my mother, I thanked God the shooting was not worse. I went back to bed but could not rest. I got up and called Jessica to get Irene's telephone number. Irene was one of Paula's close friends. I knew Irene would know how to contact her. I called, but she only had part of the number. I called 411 and requested a number for Paula's brother-in-law, who also lived in Philadelphia. Certainly, he would know where they were staying. He did and gave me the number. I finally reached Paula. Before I told her my reason for calling, I felt she needed to know that I disapproved of Mama raising her children. Mama had raised her eleven children. It was unfair for her to be responsible for raising her grandchildren too.

My conversation with Paula and her husband was totally insensitive. It was judgmental and degrading. My brother-in-law came to the telephone first and I jumped on him. "If you are interested, I'm calling to tell you about your son. Yesterday, Jonathan shot himself through the hand. How? Earl got the rifle and put a bullet in it. He was going outside to shoot across the field. Earl sat the rifle down. Jonathan picked it up and pulled the trigger. His other hand must have been over the barrel. Anyway, it doesn't make sense. They should have been living with you and this wouldn't have happened."

Without a word, my brother-in-law handed the telephone to Paula. He told her what he thought I'd said. When Paula came to the telephone, there was a crack in her voice. "Raven, what did you say?" I repeated everything to her. When she realized it was the hand and not the head, she calmed down. I told her that Mama called me because she didn't have any contact information for them. I continued, "Anyway, I just called to let you know about your child, in case you are interested." She asked, "What do you mean about that?" "I mean just what I said." Then she cursed. With a "holier-than-thou" attitude, I said, "You should be thanking God instead of cursing." Then she said, "I'm going to get ready and leave tonight." She said thanks and goodbye. I felt terrible. I was in pain dealing with Tony, and I willfully inflicted pain on them when they needed compassion.

While this was happening, Tony never said a word to me. Nor did he offer any comfort. After a while, he said, "Do you think the Holy Spirit was working in you? You received an emergency telephone call. You called all those other people and have not said a word to me." My floodgate opened and I quickly responded, "I wanted to say something to you, but talking to you is impossible. You can hear me and still not answer. That disturbs me. It gets on my nerves. It upsets my mind. Sometimes I feel like I'm going crazy. I walk around the house talking and not getting any response. Anyway, why couldn't you ask me what was wrong? If you had the least bit of concern, you would've asked me. Why couldn't you do that? Huh?" Oh My God, here we go again! He didn't answer. He didn't say a word. Not a sound or a movement, nothing. I was so upset, I just couldn't control it any longer. I took my fists and started beating on the bed, crying, "Don't answer! Don't say a word! Just forget it." I got up, took Tina out of her crib, got the alarm clock and her bottle, and was on my way into the other bedroom. Then he speaks. "Put that baby back in her bed." I kept walking and crying. He repeated, "Put Tina back in her bed. I bought the crib for her to sleep in." When I reached the other bedroom, he was still saying, "Put Tina back in her bed." One thing about Tony, he didn't lose his temper very often. He was as calm and controlled as ever, but demanding. After a period of restlessness, I was tempted to go back into our bedroom, but I couldn't, and I didn't. Tina and I eventually fell asleep.

The next morning, I got up, placed Tina in her crib, made my bed, and got dressed for work. Usually I woke Tony when I was finished in the bathroom. However, that morning I didn't have to. As I came out of the bathroom, he went in. Neither of us said a word. He didn't speak to me and I didn't speak to him. The tension was thick. When we passed each other, we made sure we didn't touch. The only sounds were our movements and our individual conversations with Tina. This continued until we left for work.

We took Tina to the babysitter. We were halfway to my job when he said, "Do you think the Holy Spirit was working in you?" For a moment I didn't say a word. I didn't want to talk to him. Nevertheless, I couldn't resist. I said, "Do you think the Holy Spirit was working in you?" I continued. "I'm tired of talking to you and not getting a response." He recited the same old reason he always used whenever the subject came up. "I've been like this since I've known myself." Then I said, "Why do you think I'm supposed to live with your faults and you can't bear mine?" I went on to say, "What you really mean is, you've been this way all your life and nothing or no one is going to cause you to change it. So I should plan either to live with it or live without you." He responded, "I didn't say that. I mean, do you expect me to change a habit I've had all my life at this late age, after twenty-eight years?" "It's okay. Forget I said anything about it." We didn't exchange another word. When we reached my job, I was a little hesitant about kissing him goodbye, but I did. I quickly brushed my lips against his and got out of the car. It took a lot for me to do that because I tend to withdraw when I'm hurt.

All day at work I was crying inside. I wanted to call and apologize. However, I wasn't convinced I was wrong. I told a few people about the situation. I asked them if they would have expected someone to ask them what was wrong or for them to volunteer the information. Everyone I asked said they would have expected the person to ask them what was wrong. At that point, I was convinced I was right.

Even if I was right, I couldn't bear being angry with my husband. When I left work, I went to the store and bought Tony a coconut pie. This was his favorite dessert. When we arrived home, I went downstairs to cook dinner. When I finished setting the table, I went back upstairs. Tony had polished two pairs of my shoes. It was apparent we were trying to make up in our individual ways. I smiled, told him dinner was ready, and we went downstairs to eat. After I cleaned up the kitchen, we did something we had not done since Tina was born. We stayed downstairs and watched television together. Tina was upstairs sleeping. While watching television, it wasn't long before I was lying in his arms. We stayed downstairs until about ten o'clock. I apologized for the way I'd acted the previous night. I made it clear I was not apologizing for not volunteering the information. I still believed he was supposed to ask me what was wrong. Even then, he insisted he was right and I was wrong. We decided to drop the subject. This was our first big disagreement since marriage. I was glad it was behind us.

During the next three years we experienced some bumps, bruises, and growing pains. However, none were insurmountable. Each time we learned a little more about each other. During those years we bought our first home, a second car, and whatever else we agreed on. Despite the growing pains, my marriage to Tony was absolutely wonderful. I was head-over-heels in love. Some of our friends would mimic the way I said, "My husband" and the way we showed our love to each other. If Tony said, "Jump," without a word I said, "How High?" No one could have paid me to believe I would face deadly struggles in this "Happily Ever After" marriage, my little perfect world. Tony and I did most things together and our church attendance led the list. Whatever came our way, we worked it out.

From the time Tina turned two years old, I had been asking Tony to have another baby. He always said no. I never knew his reason. I simply accepted it and moved on. When I got pregnant the second time, I was so happy. Then Tony told me why he was afraid of having another baby. Since Tina and I almost died during childbirth, he didn't want to take the risk. I always wanted four children. My ideal family would be two girls and two boys. It looked like I was on my way!

It's Sunday, four years later. I arrived home from church and began changing the bed linen. I wanted to finish my housework before being hospitalized. I was scheduled for a c-section delivery Monday morning. Suddenly, sharp pains raced through my stomach. Mild pains started at church earlier. I ignored them since I was going into the hospital the next day. Contractions were the last thing on my mind. I called my friend Carolyn, told her what was happening, and asked her advice. She said call the doctor. Sure enough, I had gone into labor. Panic! This is not supposed to happen. No labor! They promised me no labor. This should not be happening. The doctor told me to rush to the hospital. I did. Another surprise. There was no anesthesiologist on duty to prepare me for surgery. In addition, none could be located to come on duty. Whether we were ready or not, the baby was coming.

I gave birth to my second baby girl. I named her Joni. She was born with major complications. She required an immediate blood transfusion. She was kept in an incubator in the Intensive Care Unit. I was not allowed to hold her. Along with all that, she had a birth mark on her face that appeared to cover half of her beautiful round face. I hated it and cried when I first saw it. Hindsight, the baby's face was so small and the birth mark looked humongous. Despite all of her complications, I was allowed to take her home when I was discharged from the hospital. Although I took only six weeks off from work when I gave birth to Tina, I wanted to enjoy what might be my last birth, so I stayed home for six months.

Tony loved his girls. He played with them. He took them to the babysitter and I picked them up. During his talks, he gave them good fatherly advice. We were his girls! I admired Tony for his perseverance. As an adult he obtained his GED. He also took courses at a trade school and learned to work with his hands. He maintained the household. I believed Tony was a good man. I prayed he would be a man of endurance. We'd mastered the small challenges, but what about the big ones?

A few years passed. Our family was growing beautifully. The three girls in Tony's life would climb all over him, playfully fighting for his attention. He would pretend it was too much. We were developing into a happy Christian family. Suddenly, a curve in the road tilted our home. Tony's mind began playing tricks on him. He believed and said things that left me speechless. Knowing it was in his head didn't make it easier to bear. He started accusing me of things that never occurred. I tried to override the lies in his head with truth. I did and said things to give him an assurance of my love and commitment. Nothing helped! In his mind, I was a filthy, cheating whore one day. The next day I was the submissive, loving wife. The third day I was a disgusting lesbian.

Tony was a countryman from the South. As his wife, I was expected to cook every day, clean and maintain the house, care for the children, handle the bills, and satisfy his needs, while he simply took out the trash and mowed the lawn. I met all of my requirements. I was naïve and submissive. If Tony said to do it, I did it. No questions asked and no opinion of my own. Because he was older than me, I mistakenly believed he was also wiser.

Outside activities pulled Tony in many directions. His heart left the marriage, his children, and God. We were a Christian family, but he started condemning the church. Later in our marriage, he joined a secret order occult.

I tried to rationalize things. I tried to recall things we talked about, which would explain what was happening. One specific thing came to mind. During our dating and marriage, Tony constantly spoke of his dad losing his mind. He told the same story often of how one day his dad stood face-to-face talking with him and did not remember who Tony was, how he allowed his dad to walk away at the end of the conversation without telling him that he was his son. He pretended it didn't matter. The pain on his face and in his voice said otherwise. He spoke of his independence. How he'd been taking care of himself since age thirteen. He never had anybody to depend upon. Tony was fighting a lifelong battle with an invisible opponent. He lived in fear, always proclaiming he would not lose his mind like his dad. Yet, each day I witnessed what I believed was schizophrenic behavior. This was never diagnosed, but all the telltale signs were present. Tony was no longer the man I had married.

I was helpless and afraid. I reached out to him. Sometimes he received it and other times it backfired. If I called him at work just to talk, it was translated into a cover up. I had done something with whomever he tied me to that day. He started refusing to eat the food I cooked and to touch me intimately. He would move out of the bedroom into the basement one week, then, without a word, return to the bedroom. My life had become a roller-coaster ride with bends, dips, and blackness. Nevertheless, I was still willing to fight for my marriage. It was an investment. I knew there would be great returns if I just rode out the storm. I committed to do so.

# 7

# The Thrill Is Gone

The thread that was holding my marriage together was getting thinner. I wasn't sure how much longer it could sustain us. At work one day, a young lady asked to talk with me regarding her depression. Even though I had talked with her frequently regarding it, she wanted to talk away from work. I told her what I said would be the same whether at work or at my house. She pleaded to come anyway. I consented and she came. When Tony saw her, he immediately said she was my lesbian lover. Everything turned upside down. Tony was never the same after that young lady came to our house. It was as if an "evil" presence came with her and stayed. The accusations intensified. I almost collapsed mentally under the pressure.

For the next year and a half, living with Tony was hell on earth. It was already bad, but it got worse. It started long before the young lady's visit. After ten years of marriage, I had been unsuccessful in persuading Tony to take a vacation, so I decided to take one alone. That year, I went to Ontario, Canada, on a weekend bus trip with a local community church. When I returned three days later, I was accused of being a lesbian, participating in oral sex, and having orgies. He accused me of sleeping with every Mary,

Jane, and Sue one moment and with Tom, Dick, and Harry the next. He accused me of filthy sexual acts I had never heard of.

I returned to work. The days that followed were the beginning of an even greater hell. Every day, every hour of the day, he called to tell me what a good-for-nothing whore I was. He told me whom I was laying around with. He said he knew what I was doing at that moment and all during the day. He cut off my outside connections. My friends were forbidden to come over or call our house. In pursuit of peace, I complied. I asked my friends not to call or visit. All during the night, he would walk very softly through the house in the dark. Sometimes, I caught him standing over my bed. Fear gripped me. I was sleeping a maximum of two to three hours nightly.

Accusations continued daily. My girls were constantly told about their good-for-nothing-whoring mother. They were told filthy lies of their mother's activities. The children were becoming a nervous wreck. I felt helpless and could do nothing about it. At age seven, our youngest daughter, Joni, wrote this letter after Tony and I had a fight:

*Dear Lord,*
*My family is falling apart. My mother and father are going to get a divorce. That is going to be hard for me. It is going to be tough saying good-bye. I know it's going to be me saying good-bye to my father. My mother loves me too much to let us go. I'm not saying I don't love my father and he doesn't love me, I do. I just think that I would be better off with my mother. Speaking of my health, it's not very good, I would say that my mother gives me the healthiest food. My father gives me foods like eggs, bacon, etc. I love it when he gives me that kind of food, but some*

*of it is not good for my health. Sometimes they talk in a considerably loud tone about my sister and me. They fight about who is going to keep us when they separate. I don't like them to fight and argue. It scares and frightens me. I hope everything works out for the best. I love them both and want the best for them. There is going to be lots of changes. When my father leaves I think that my mother will calm down more about the situation. I don't want this situation to end up in death. Lord, pray with me that everything will be all right in Jesus' name. Amen.*

*Joni*

I don't know what she was illustrating, but on the back of her letter to God, Joni drew a black house with black clouds over it, green grass beneath it, three flowers on one side of it and a tree on the other side.

During some of his awkward conversations, Tony told me everybody knew what I was. He was the last to find out. I later learned he had called almost all the people we knew in South Carolina and Maryland, telling everyone what a whore I had become. For the longest time, no one told me anything. Then one day while I was visiting my mother, she asked me, "Raven, what is going on with you and Tony?" I said, "Nothing. Why?" She said, "He called me and said he caught you and one of your women friends having sex in the house and on the front lawn." It crushed me that my mother was told such filth. However, it encouraged me when she said that she told him: "You can't tell me that kind of stuff about Raven and expect me to believe it, because I don't." I knew she meant what she said. She had never asked me about it, even though Tony told her a long time prior. Surprise! Surprise! I thought I was protecting Tony by not telling my family what was going on in our marriage.

Hallelujah, he unveiled himself!

I began accepting the fact that Tony was no longer the man I had married. For every accusation he made, there was a negative change in him. His attitude, habits, likes, dislikes, routines, conversation—almost everything changed. It was so scary. Whenever he was around, I would shiver as if a cold breeze filled the atmosphere.

One sunny Saturday afternoon, Tony came home unexpectedly early. As he came in, my girlfriend Ella, her two children, my two girls, and I were leaving to get her hair done. When I opened the door, the young lady who previously came to the house seeking help with her depression was coming up the walkway. I had not invited her over, she just showed up unexpectedly. Her first visit had sent Tony over the edge. Now, her showing up like this was going to make things even worse for me. I told her to leave and never come to my house again. I had given her all the help I could. Tony's accusations continued for months, sea-sawing back and forth. His mind was almost gone.

I called Olivia, one of Tony's ex-girlfriends. She had two children by him. I wanted to explain to her the stress Tony was experiencing. I only called because I thought we had a mutual respect for each other. I welcomed her children into our home. My girls accepted her children as their older siblings. They received everything they asked Tony for, with my help. These perks were along with his child support payments. Her children were living the life of luxury, receiving love and support from both families. My girls were living in hell with me. When I called, I only asked her to tell the children to stop asking for things he could not afford. I asked them to wait until he could handle things better. I even explained we were going through an extreme situation. What I thought was an amiable request caused me greater problems. Olivia complained to Tony, and he came after me. I was shocked. I was only trying to help. We had the worst fight we'd ever had. This time it became physical. Tony hit me in the face with his fist. Unbelievably, I felt I had provoked it. I believed it was my fault.

Four months later on Thanksgiving Day, my family came from South Carolina to visit us. During their visit, Tony held a meeting. He told them how he had tried to make the marriage work, but I continued to destroy it. He said I did not clean the house and only did it this time because they were coming. He said I left my panties all over the house. He was forced to live in my filth. The day after Thanksgiving, after my family left, he moved back into the basement. He remained there permanently. We had no dealings with each other. He wouldn't eat anything I cooked because I was not clean enough. He stopped buying food. He stopped helping to pay the monthly household bills. However, I blindly trusted he was still paying the mortgage and his car payment.

# 8

# Can It Get Any Worse?

Enough is enough! My life was already filled with pain. Now the doctors are predicting that my mother is dying. It's a day no one is ever prepared to face, the day when sickness touches death. Mama was never sick. She was strong; she had no time to be sick. She was Super Mom. Despite what the doctors said, I knew it was just a matter of time before she got up. No obstacle had ever stopped her before. She had to get up. She was entering the prime years of her life. I was told of the sickness that had gripped Mama. However, I didn't believe she would leave me when I needed her most. She'd just recently paid me the greatest compliment of my life. She believed in me and stood up for me when Tony tried to mar my name. You can't buy that type of compliment. It was something I had waited a lifetime for. That one compliment healed many of my childhood scars. Daily, my siblings called to report, "Mama is sick. She is no better than she was yesterday. She is getting worse." Each day the reports were more frightening than the day before.

When Mama first became ill, I was told the hospital would not admit her. She had an outstanding bill. My mother had given her life serving others. Now, when she needed it most, no one came to her aide. No one! Not even the church. She was slowly dying in her bed, a bed bought with her own sweat, with no one to help her. I went to South Carolina to see what I could do. When I arrived, I found her freezing on her bed. She was curled up, trying to get warm. The house was ice cold. There were windows missing. No wood to start a fire. No food. No husband committed to taking care of her. I don't think anyone expected anything from my father. All of his time was dedicated to his younger women, who had no problem being mistresses.

After settling in, my family told me of the suspicious details surrounding her illness. I was told she ate a poisonous sandwich intended for my drunken father. He was given the sandwich to eat. Instead, he brought it home and gave it to my mother. She ate it. This was not unusual. During my childhood years, when my father came home drunk with a sandwich or anything edible, we raced to get it. It didn't matter where it came from, who made it, or what was in it. We were hungry. We ate whatever we could get. I asked who told them about the poisonous sandwich. They said the information came from a fortune teller. Unbelievable! My Christian family went to a reader on behalf of my Christian mother!

Mama had begun hallucinating. She fought everything and everyone who came near her, except Samson, my baby brother. Some of the family wanted to take her back to the reader to determine who placed the curse on her. Then we could have it removed. I objected. My mother had lived a Christian life and that was a total contradiction to her belief. My goal was to get her into the hospital.

My cousin Diana and I made many telephone calls trying to get Mama into the hospital. Finally, swallowing my pride, I called Mama's pastor for assistance. After giving us a long, unnecessary lecture, her pastor agreed to help us. That night he came to the house with his monetary assistance. I don't know whether I was grateful or angry. He sat and counted over one hundred one-dollar bills into my hand. It was so demeaning. I saw red as he counted. Nevertheless, I was not going to refuse the help. Tony sent what he could to help get Mama into the hospital. Finally, we were able to do so. I was relieved. She could now receive the care she needed. Shortly after Mama was admitted into the hospital, I returned home. Home is such a warm word for what I feared facing upon my return.

My life continued in an upheaval. However, my primary focus was my mother and my girls. I could not afford to be distracted.

For months, she laid in those hospital beds in a coma. She was transferred from one hospital to another as doctors tried to find the source of her illness, all to no avail. The best specialists had examined her. She was transferred to the best hospital in the capitol of South Carolina. My spirit was broken. My heart ached. I decided I had to do something. Since I had no vacation time at work, I requested one-month leave without pay. I went to South Carolina. Nothing was more important than being by Mama's side. I was told to rush home because she could die at any time. This was a pre-death visit. The doctors said she was dying. My mom, who was once over 260 pounds, was now just a little over ninety pounds. She was wearing pampers. Her long beautiful soft silvery hair was gone. Only roots remained on her head. Her fingernails had prematurely started turning green. They said she was surely dying.

As I visited Mama, I walked into her hospital room with my head straightforward. I walked directly to the window. I never turned my head in the direction of her bed. I sat on the windowsill looking out the window. Then I left. I wanted to. God knows I wanted to. Still, I couldn't even look at her, talk to her, or touch her. I cried quietly as I left her room. I could have stayed home if that was the best comfort I could give.

The hospital kept pressing us for money. They wanted a guarantee of payment. Every agency we visited for assistance said she did not qualify, either because she didn't pay into the system or my father made too much money. Her lifetime of slave labor was still robbing her. Raging anger gripped me. My sense of reasoning left. I could not bear anymore. I had to find an answer. The pressures of life were winning. I fought, but it seemed I was destined to lose. I blamed my father for my mother's illness. I cursed him for her not being able to get help. He suddenly wanted to be the "big man," telling the agencies he made amounts of money that never came into the house. I was irate and blurted out threats to kill the overseer of the farm. I wanted to burn the $20 in his face that I'd borrowed when I left home. I wanted to beat him for only paying the minimum Social Security taxes for Mama. All those years she slaved in those fields, and it was nothing for him to cheat her. He was an evil man. Regardless, she couldn't receive Social Security benefits now when she needed them because there was a waiting period. I condemned everything and everybody to hell because they did not help my mother. In my heart, I even cursed the church where she had been a lifetime member. My family walked softly around me. They were unsure of what I might do.

Anger consumed me. My rational thinking departed. Nothing had value anymore, not even life. I locked myself in one of my sister's bedrooms. I considered knocking my head against the windowpane in hopes it would stop the pressure. I fell to my knees and cried out to God. "GOD, OH GOD, please let me die! GOD, don't you understand, I want to die! Why would you force someone to live who does not want to live? God, please, just let me die. I can't take the brokenness of my marriage anymore. I can't deal with losing my mother. I can't endure the pains of life. I just don't think it is worth it." I thought it was simple! I just wanted to die. What's the big deal that God wouldn't answer me? Little did I know, before I called, He had answered.

I was in the bedroom having my tantrum. The telephone rang and it was for me. It was Ella and Penny, my friends from Maryland. They said they had visited a church on the south side of Baltimore. The church was having a revival. The special guest speaker was a minister from Africa. While speaking, the minister asked did anyone know someone named Raven? This man did not know me. He further stated, "She is in trouble. God said we must intercede for her right now." My friends both yelled out, "Yes, we have a friend name Raven, whose mother is dying and she's in South Carolina with her." The minister interceded for me. My friends were calling to encourage me. They emphasized the concern God had shown towards me. That specific telephone call, on that specific night, helped me keep my sanity. I cried and collapsed to the floor. I repented to God. My friends prayed with me before they said goodbye. I cried myself to sleep. I experienced a relief from the pressure. Later, I apologized to my father because I hurt him deeply. Because every time he got drunk, he talked about my cursing him. I apologized every time he mentioned it. It was apparent that he was having difficulty processing what I had done. I had never done anything like that before, but I could not take it back.

The month was ending. I would soon return home to the stranger I was married to. Mama remained in a coma.

# 9
# Ah, Home Sweet Home

Since I knew Tony was not the man I'd married, I began my search to find him again. I placed love notes in his shoes, pants, and shirts. I called him from work to tell him I loved him. I walked in front of him naked. I encouraged him to return to the bedroom. He started doing nice things. He returned to the bedroom. He talked to me in a conversational tone. However, every time we had sex, he would ask me revolting questions, comparing his sexual moves with those of my lesbian lover. I would lay still and weep silently, waiting for him to finish getting his relief. The filthy accusations started again. The fragments of hope were being destroyed. I felt sick from his statements. I became even sicker as he performed on me what he believed my lesbian lover had done. Sex was revolting, but I had to fulfill my wifely duty.

Here we go! Browbeating is back in session. The new approach was my filthiness. Nothing was ever clean enough. I spent most of my time on Wednesday and Saturday cleaning the house, washing clothes, dusting, polishing, and ironing. It meant nothing to him. He was still dissatisfied. By his account, I didn't do anything. He said the washing machine washed the clothes. The vacuum cleaner vacuumed the floor. These duties did not include my daily routine. I went to work, picked up the girls from school, cooked, washed dishes, checked homework, got clothes ready for the next day, gave the girls their baths, and everything else defined as woman's work. He did nothing inside unless it was to repair something, or things classified as masculine duties.

# 10
# It Could've Been Different

You have probably heard the saying, "If only I could turn back the hands of time, I would change this or that and make things better." I'm glad the hands of time cannot be turned back. I might make the same choices. Nevertheless, I am grateful for second chances.

I was a trainer on my job. I was standing in front of the class teaching when I received a telephone call. It was my mortgage company. The caller, Mrs. Hammond, gently asked, "Mrs. Jordan, what's wrong?" Not understanding her question, I asked her what she meant. She began, "I don't understand. Your account has always been current and timely. I've sent repeated notices about the delinquent payments. Neither you nor your husband has responded. Recently, I sent a final notice informing you that your house was being auctioned off next week. I still haven't gotten a response. What's going on?" I told Mrs. Hammond I would call her right back.

I told the class to take a break. I went to the telephone booth and called Mrs. Hammond. I explained our life to her. My husband had separated himself from our marriage. However, he had not moved out of the house. He was living in the basement. I continued. He buys food for himself only. He eats steak, lamb, chicken, and pork chops, while we barely eat at all. He forbade me to touch his food, even when the children were hungry. Mrs. Hammond was so gentle that the floodgate to my heart opened wide. I told her everything. She shared some information with me. It helped me understand some unexplainable things that had been happening. I told her Tony had been receiving calls from a real estate broker concerning a house he was buying. I didn't know it was going to cost my girls and me our home. It didn't seem to matter to him that our home was being auctioned off because his sight was on a new home for himself.

I explained to Mrs. Hammond that I paid the tuition for our two girls to attend a Christian school. I drove them to and from school, or paid someone to do it for me. The school was a long way from our house. It was beyond where I worked. I added that I paid all the gas and electric bills. Tony refused to pay them. I explained that I had to pay four months of gas and electric bills to keep the utility companies from cutting off the services. I told her since Tony had the telephone cut off, I had to pay to get a telephone in my name. I paid the water bill. I choked as I heard myself list all of those things aloud. I told her I just learned Tony had cancelled my car insurance without a word to me. I continued. All the charge cards for everything we owned were in my name. I paid those bills also. I also bought all the food for the children. I thought my husband was at least paying the mortgage. She said the mortgage had not been paid for over three months. The house was scheduled to be sold on Thursday of the upcoming week. I told her I didn't have any money. I did not have anyone I could borrow it from. I didn't know what to do.

The things I shared with Mrs. Hammond were things Tony had done over a period of time, but I'd just recently found out about them. One day I visited the bank. I was told I could not make a withdrawal. The account was established as "Tony Jordan and Raven Jordan Subject to Tony Jordan." Tony could withdraw. Raven could only withdraw with Tony's approval. I felt stupid. I mean really stupid. How could I not know the joint bank account we established was not a joint account at all? I was naïve—the country, churchgoing girl who was taught the man was the head. He was the one in authority. I was to be submissive, and so I was. No one imparted the real wisdom of God in these teachings. No one explained what to do when you found out too late your trust had been violated. No one told me it would be like this. I was paying for this lesson with my life.

Mrs. Hammond wanted to help me, so she devised a plan. First, she wanted to know what time Tony usually came home. I told her, then added, "Sometimes he stays out all night." She said she would call at a certain time. We didn't have caller ID. We agreed on the hour. She told me not to answer the telephone. She wanted him to answer. She wanted to confront him and apply pressure. She would demand payment in full. She didn't want him to know she had talked with me.

Mrs. Hammond called at the appointed time. Tony was not answering the telephone, so I answered it. She asked whether he was at home. I told her he was but was not answering. I asked her to call again. I would go into the bathroom. When the telephone rings, I'll ask him to answer it. She agreed. However, she advised me to try getting the money just in case Tony didn't agree to pay it. If he agreed, she would call back and let me know. God had given me favor with this woman whom I had never met. She was the answer to my problem. After talking with Tony, she called me back. She assured me he would bring the money to her.

She promised to keep me informed.

Late Friday evening, Mrs. Hammond called to give me an update. She didn't want me to worry the entire weekend regarding what would happen the following week. She said the mortgage was current. She had gotten all the delinquent mortgage payments from Tony. She encouraged me to save money for the future mortgages. To be prepared to pay, just in case Tony didn't pay. I assured her I would secretly pay the mortgage if Tony didn't. I repeatedly thanked her for helping me and for her kindness. She was truly an angel sent by God.

I was grateful God had worked for me, but I still needed answers. It was one thing to discover my marriage was over before I realized it. However, it was a totally different thing to find out the person you loved was strategically planning your destruction. Words can't describe the pain and confusion I suffered. Standing in front of my class to train was getting more difficult as the days passed. On Monday, I decided to stay home from work. I had so many unanswered questions. Why didn't I see the mail Mrs. Hammond referenced? It's true: I was a poor naïve and trusting wife. Yet, I was more than that—I was a victim! It troubled me not knowing what would happen to my girls and me. Without knowing it, I was in the midst of a battle, had suffered a blow, and was out for the count. Not even Mama could have prepared me for this war.

Since I stayed home from work, I received the mail that day. I noticed only mail solely addressed to me was delivered. I also noticed one of my letters had a post office box number annotated on it, then scratched off. I visited our local post office and explained I never received several pieces of important mail which was sent to me. I was told Tony had bought a post office box. Any mail with his name on it, with or without my name, was placed in the post office box. I asked about my rights to my mail. I argued that my name was also on the mail, which was placed in a post office box where I had no access. I stressed my rights were being violated. The postal clerk made it clear that it was simply not their problem. I returned home, searched through Tony's things and found all the letters that were sent. He knew the house was being auctioned off. He didn't care because he was buying himself a new house. I even knew his specifications for his new house because the realtor regularly called leaving update messages.

I needed money desperately. I looked for the savings bonds and could not find them. They were gone without a trace. When I signed up for savings bonds, I made Tony the co-owner. He had cashed all my bonds and taken the money. I checked every possible avenue. I contacted my life insurance agent to obtain the available cash from our policies. The policies had been surrendered for cash over a year and a half earlier. Imagine my surprise. If anything had happened to either of us, there was nothing. He had taken it all, and I was running out of options.

After my shocking discovery, I decided I needed to move quickly. I contacted the bank again. I was seeking an appointment to discuss my access to our bank account. My heart sunk as I was told the account was closed. Too many issues crowded my mind. Why hadn't I seen these things? Was it trust or stupidity? What will I do?

Tony was a butcher for over twenty-five years at a local grocery store. I worked there as a cashier. The store manager was a friend. I decided to call him seeking answers. After a brief conversation with the manager, I realized the problems were deeper than I thought. The manager told me Tony had not worked there for over six months. He said one day Tony became irrational. He began throwing knives around the store and making crazy statements, some of which were true. He spoke of being overworked and underpaid. Then he walked off the job and never returned. By the time I finished my inquiries, my head was spinning. I was on a roller coaster searching for the truth, but the twists and turns were too much. All my peace was gone. It was a good thing Tony did not come home that night.

The next day after work, I came home and Tony was downstairs. I went downstairs to confront him. As I reached the sitting area I felt the aura in the room. I became red with fury. He was lying in bed with his head propped up on his folded arms and fingers locked together. The television was turned in the direction of the bed for his comfortable viewing. The look on his face said he had not a care in the world.

Through clenched teeth, I began speaking softly, almost in a whisper. I didn't expect a response to anything I said. With each statement, my anger escalated. "You are lying in my bed all day. Running electricity I'm paying for. Cooking with gas I'm paying for. Eating your steaks, lamb, chicken, and pork chops that we are forbidden to touch. Redirecting my mail. Cashing my bonds. Canceling my car insurance. Cashing in our life insurance policies. Taking all of our life's savings out of the bank. Quitting your job. Staying out all night, and having my house up for auction!"

I was walking slowly towards him with intensified anger. He began to rise up. He felt my fury. He clamped his teeth over his bottom lip and formed a fist with his right hand. He leaned forward slightly. Before I realized it, my entire body swung around and my right hand scooped up a letter opener off the dresser behind me. The letter opener was like an ice pick, very pointed and sharp as a knife. I had apparently seen it in my peripheral vision. I began to challenge him. I begged him to come after me. I pleaded with him to swing at me. I beckoned him with my fingers.

I pleaded for him to raise his fist against me. Still through clenched teeth, I said, "I'm going to gut you today and see what color blood flows through your veins. I can almost taste your blood." Then I moved rapidly towards him, almost running, and yelled, "You are a dead man!" With all of my might, I swung backward and then forward, aiming directly for his head. As my hand came down towards his head, he jumped. He moved just in time for me to stab the pillow. I missed his head by a few inches.

He jumped up yelling for the girls to come and see what I had done. He told them I had gone crazy. I had completely lost my mind and tried to kill him. He yelled for them to come downstairs to see the knife in my hand. I hid the letter opener and my rage from the girls. I instantly became calm. To the girls he looked like the crazy one. I sent them back upstairs. As I was leaving, I gave him a final warning. I told him to get out while he could. I was determined to see the color of his blood. I didn't accomplish anything that could be seen, but you can be assured he treaded lightly the days following.

I am not making excuses or justifying my actions, but when I mentally rehearsed what happened, I knew temporary insanity was real. No longer did I doubt such theory. You can lose your mental grip in a split second without realizing it. Regardless of other things that cause temporary insanity, I know pain can do it. When pain surpasses your tolerance level, you begin to operate in a whole new arena. You forget who you are and what you represent. Survival is the only thing that matters. I had been to hell and back so many times in my marriage that I couldn't take any more.

When we started experiencing trouble in our marriage, I attributed it to Tony having mental issues. I remember when my girls were eight and four years old, Tony did the unforgivable. One day, I picked up my girls from the day care and Tina said, "Ma, I need to tell you something, but I can't tell you in front of Joni. She shouldn't hear things like this." I said, "Okay, baby, wait until we get home." When we arrived home, Tina said her dad told her I asked him to have oral sex with me. When she didn't understand what oral sex was, he explained it to her. Then my little girl said, "Ma, I don't believe that about you. I know Daddy is sick. It's okay. We'll pray for him." It was a good thing she had a praying spirit, because I did not!

I was outraged. What sane thirty-six-year old father would tell a filthy lie like that to his eight-year-old daughter? I was twenty-eight-years old and could not believe what I was hearing, so how could an eight-year-old child process that? I felt it was a verbal form of child pornography. It was disgusting, and ironically, I didn't know anything about oral sex. I was a virgin to my husband and everything I had learned, he taught me. He had never approached me for oral sex. In my outrage, my thoughts were erratic and my actions scary. I called my girlfriend Ella, who was Tina's godmother. I asked her to promise she would take care of my girls and keep them together if anything happened to me. She wanted to know why I was talking that way. I said, "This kind of life must end. It can't continue like this. It ain't worth it." She pressed, so I told her what Tina told me. Then I swore I was going to kill Tony. I was frightened by the person I had become. That was my second decision to kill him. It became painfully clear "murder" was in my heart.

I was determined to put Tony out of his misery. I told Ella if it took all night, I was going to stand by the front door with the butcher knife. When he turned his key in the door, I was going to cut and stab him. I didn't even see the irony of killing the butcher with a butcher knife! I promised Ella I would get the girls to bed early so they would not witness it. Ella became gravely concerned. I could hear the crack in her voice. The sound of sobs was between her words. She could feel my pain. Even though her situation was different, over the years she had also suffered deeply. She tried to encourage me from the Bible. Then she tried to pray with me. She asked me challenging questions, to which I had no answers. Finally, she said, "Okay, Raven," and hung up.

While Tina did her homework, I sat by the door waiting for my prey. Within half an hour, my doorbell rang. It was Brenda. Brenda was a mutual friend of Ella and mine. She was not a professional hairdresser, but she could create an exceptional masterpiece with anyone's hair. She periodically did our hair. However, we had to catch her at the right time, and the right time had not occurred in almost a year. Now, all of a sudden, she shows up at my door telling me she came to pick me up so she could do my hair. I told her I didn't want a hairdo. I was busy and wanted her to leave. She refused to leave. She started packing my girls' things so they could go with her. She packed school clothes and nightclothes. She insisted I get my things together and come with her. The more I refused, the more she insisted. To know Brenda was to know she would not give up easily. Also, she was the friend you wanted everyone to know you had because she was beautiful. However, at that moment I wanted her out of my house, but she wouldn't leave. Brenda didn't need to be in the middle of my mess. Her life had been a storybook drama too. Somehow I sensed she knew my state of mind. Then it registered. Since Brenda was so insistent that we leave my house, I realized Ella must have called her.

Ella lived on the east side and I lived on the west side. She knew she could not reach me in time to stop me. So she called Brenda, who lived on my side of town. When Brenda realized I had figured it out, she began to quote Bible verses to me. For years, Ella and I had been trying to get Brenda to commit her life to Christ. Here she stood giving our words back to me. After a while, I decided if they cared about me this much, I wanted to show them I appreciated their love. I packed and left the house with my girls. We stayed the night at Brenda's house. Things always look different in the morning.

I didn't understand, but I knew someone somewhere had an explanation. There had to be answers to my questions. Why had a good marriage gone bad? How did two people with one dream drift apart? What can be said when two lovers stop speaking, stop understanding, and stop desiring? Why live in the same house, yet live so separate and far apart? Why the slander and the attack on the character of one you loved?

I recall the many times Tony told me we had grown apart. He said our desires in life were different. Our goals no longer agreed. He said the best thing for both of us was to go our separate ways. I was no longer the type of woman he desired. He had moved out of our bedroom into the basement. He got involved with many extracurricular activities. He joined the baseball team, bowling league, partnership in a men's club, and became a member of a secret order occult. He spent less and less time with the girls and me, he rarely went to church, and he was practically never home. He became devoted to the sect. His life was consumed by it. Everything he did and said, and everywhere he went, was governed by the bylaws in that little black book. I wanted to know the driving force behind Tony. I secretly took his little black book and read it. It was not surprising that his mind was all confused. I tried to rationalize and understand his behavior. I even tried to console myself thinking it might be a midlife crisis.

So much had happened, yet I was still willing to fight for my marriage. I feared the scars of divorce. No one in my family had been divorced. I didn't want to be the first. Couldn't I deal with the pain until Tony got himself together? Pondering this question caused me to recall one haunting memory after another.

One night while asleep, I felt a cold breeze in my room. It was an unwelcome breeze. It was eerie. The presence in the room caused me to open my eyes. I saw Tony standing over my bed in the dark. He had a pair of 12-inch scissors in his hand. He was just standing there. I started praying. After a little while he turned and walked away without a word. I was terrified. I didn't sleep the remainder of that night. Every night afterwards, I closed the girls' and my bedroom doors. I also became a very light sleeper.

I hated every minute of it, but many nights I made myself sensuous to be sexually appealing to Tony. I did it for my marriage and the fear of divorce. It worked. It enticed him, but in the midst of making love he would touch my body and ask, "Is this how your lesbian lover did it? Am I as good as your man?" It was nauseating. I did not want him to touch me. It made me sick. It was degrading. Even though I was married, I felt so dirty. After living in this hell for years, praying and crying, trusting God, and talking to my friends, I said enough was enough.

One day during prayer at work, I told my girlfriend Deedie I believed Tony's accusations resulted from his own guilt. I didn't know what he had gotten himself into, but it must be serious. I further stated I was going home to confront him. She told me to make sure I was ready for the answers. I assured her I was ready. After work, I got into my car, but it would not start. I stopped a friend and asked for help. After checking the car inside and out, he said, "You left your lights on. I'll give you a jump." I thanked him. I immediately had an uneasy feeling. I sensed Tony had been in my car and turned on the lights. Fear gripped me. I was certain I did not leave my lights on. Questions flooded my mind. How did Tony find my car? There were hundreds of cars and numerous parking lots. How would he know where to begin? I never showed him where I parked. I didn't always park in the same parking lot. Even though I had a parking sticker, it was first come, first serve. If my assigned lot was full, there were specific overflow lots. What led Tony to the location of my car? I started analyzing one fact after the other. I did not need lights when I came to work that morning. I didn't recall turning them on. Was God trying to tell me something? Again, I felt a strong premonition that it was Tony. I was afraid, but I knew what I had to do when I arrived home.

It was the middle of December. The weather was cold and rainy. The forecast predicted it would get worse by evening. There was nothing, not even bad weather, worse than what I was suffering. From the time I got into my car, until I reached home, I experienced an irregular heartbeat. My life was already broken into pieces. Now the pieces were being reduced to crumbs. I picked up my girls from day care. When I arrived home, Tony was upstairs. I sent the girls downstairs to play.

There was no time to waste. I went upstairs and said, "Tony, do you know what God told me? He said you have been accusing me of all types of infidelities because of your own guilt. All of these years, you were the one guilty of the false accusations you've made against me." He stood motionless. His eyes stretched to the maximum. He stared at me. He was wearing a sweater. He'd gotten dressed to go out for the evening. I could see his rapid breathing through his sweater. Each inhale and exhale became shorter and faster. It sent a guilty message loud and clear. He didn't have to verbalize anything. I knew he was committing adultery. The shocked expression on his face told me God had indeed spoken to me.

Having received an unspoken confirmation, I continued. "Tony, do you know what else God told me? He said you came to my job today and sabotaged my car. You got in my car, searched inside of it, turned on the lights, and then you left." His very expression revealed his guilt. I stared at him and did not utter another word. Suddenly he blurted out. "If you hadn't started messing with that bull-dike, then I wouldn't have had to do any of those things." I didn't allow him to go any further. I said, "I'm not taking another accusation from you. Now, I'm the reason you've committed adultery and only God knows what else. No, not tonight! We both know you are the whore here. I guess I should thank you for having the decency to move out of the bedroom. Tell me, why would you sabotage my car? What satisfaction did it give you? I want you out of here. Get out and don't come back." He responded, saying the house was his too and he was not going anywhere. I responded, "You don't have to leave, but be assured, starting tonight we will both be doing the same things. To show you I mean business, I'm going out tonight and I'm going to screw the first person who hits on me." I left him standing stunned and looking stupid.

I may have fooled Tony into believing I was big, bad, and strong; however, the truth was, I was ready to crumble to the floor. Why was I so shocked? So devastated? He'd spent night after night away from home. Did I think he was attending Sunday school? I strengthened myself. This was not the time to crumble. I couldn't let him see he had destroyed everything I had ever lived for. I got dressed. I called his Aunt Jessica, who lived down the street. I asked her to watch the girls for a little while. She agreed. I told her

I would bring them down shortly. When we left, Tony was still at the house. He sat looking as if he had lost his best friend. As I left, I said, "Thanks for teaching me that what's good for the goose is also good for the gander."

It was dark and dreary. The rain was mixed with fog and icy road conditions. As we walked to the car, the streetlights illuminated my girls' faces. There was a look that said it all! On their faces I saw desertion and pain. As we got into the car, Tina kept asking, "Ma, are you coming back for us?" Despite answering yes, she continued asking me the same question over and over. She even asked if I was sure I was coming back. When we reached Jessica's house, Tina said, "Ma, promise us you are coming back for us tonight, no matter what time it is." I said, "Okay, Tina ... I promise." I knew I was lying, but I wanted to comfort her heart. I thought, *There is no way this child knows what I have planned. How did she know I wasn't planning to come back?* My heart was filled with pain and my eyes with tears. I hated to leave my girls without a mother. The selfishness of my plan never entered my mind. I just wanted to be free. To encourage myself, I thought, *Even if Tina felt my pain, she still had no way of knowing what I'd planned.* I lied to Tony also. What did I know about screwing the first person who hit on me? I didn't even know where to go. Tony was the only man I had known sexually, and all I knew he taught me. My entire body, soul, and spirit were one big ball of pain. I wanted to die. I had lived for the love of my husband and daughters. Losing one half of my foundation devastated me. I was 28 years old and couldn't understand how so few years could bring so much pain. Life had not been kind to me. I'd planned to kill myself after my girls were safe and secure.

The girls got out of the car. I waited until they were inside the house. I didn't want them to see how fast I drove away. They stood in the doorway, waving goodbye. After Jessica closed the door, I pressed the accelerator to the floor. The street we lived on contained a high incline followed by a deep decline, with a stop sign at the bottom. One of two things would stop me: colliding with the oncoming traffic or crashing into the house across the street directly in front of the stop sign. The distance from Jessica's house to the stop sign was only one and a half blocks, but I didn't care. I wanted it to be over quick. As my car hydroplaned, I reconsidered and slowed down. I knew if I didn't stop, I would go straight through the house. I didn't want to hurt anyone else just because I was hurting. So, I decided to go to one of the main streets to kill myself.

I left home to balance the "adultery" scale. Then I thought, *Why prolong the pain?* I decided to forego balancing the scale and go directly to suicide. My attempts began. I ran every red light hoping someone would hit the side of my car and kill me. I sped up and down Liberty Heights Avenue slamming on brakes, trying to skid on the ice. I was hoping an accident would kill me. Since running red lights didn't work, I tried the green lights. I drove slowly and waited until the light was yellow for a while, then rushed through the changing light. A collision with another car traveling the opposite direction would be ideal. All of my attempts failed. I couldn't even commit suicide successfully. Since I had already failed as a wife, this convinced me that I was destined for "failure."

I drove around aimlessly. Then a miracle happened. I ended up at a church on the south side. During break time at work, a group of Christians met in the stairwell every day to pray. During prayer on this specific day, someone mentioned a revival. They told us how to get there if we were interested in attending. I didn't pay close attention because I knew I wasn't going. Despite that discussion,

I cannot explain how I got there. I had never been there before. I did not frequent that side of town. Yet, that night, I drove directly to the place.

Broken and weak, I entered a worship service with a prophetic anointing in operation. The church was an old movie theater that seated thousands. The place was packed. I didn't see anyone I knew. I was seated in the middle section. I was in the middle of the row and midway from the back. Still, God saw me. The minister called me into the aisle. He did not know me, so he used the color of my clothes to call me. I was wearing a dark green velvet suit with a light green blouse. When I reached the aisle, the preacher said, "God said the devil desires to destroy you. Many ditches have been dug all around you. But God said if you would turn your face like flint towards Him, He will cause your enemies to fall into the ditches that were dug to destroy you. You are at a crossroad of decisions. You are facing some major decisions that will affect you for a lifetime. People you've trusted have turned their backs on you..."

He continued for a long time. He talked and I cried. Everything he said was specific to me and my situations. The more he talked, the more I cried—until I was crying uncontrollably. No one but God knew my situations, and He had come to speak to me. God had spoken to me through the prophet. Little old insignificant me! There was comfort in knowing God saw me and was concerned about me.

The preacher had no way of knowing I just learned my husband was committing adultery. I felt alone, hurt, and scared. When the service ended, my girlfriend Roxie came to me. I didn't even know she was there. Roxie had been where I was. She had suffered for many years, but God was with her. There couldn't have been a better person to encourage me. I explained to Roxie what had happened.

I told her I didn't want to go home. I knew the Lord had spoken. I was strengthened, but I was not ready to face my problem. Roxie stayed with me. She ministered to me. She cried with me. She reminded me of the promise from God, spoken by the preacher. She told me the prophecy was scriptural. She picked up her Bible, turned to Isaiah Chapter 50, Verse 7 and read it to me: *For the Lord God will help me; therefore shall I not be confounded: therefore have I set my face like a flint, and I know that I shall not be ashamed.*

That Scripture encouraged me for many years. As we sat, she continued ministering to me. Providing Scripture after Scripture, with an explanation of hope. The Scripture in Isaiah cross-referenced to Romans Chapter 8 and Verse 31: *What shall we then say to these things? If God be for us, who can be against us?*

God was plainly telling me He was with me and He was the one I needed.

# 11
# A Suspended Life

It was called progression when we learned to pause a video, place a telephone call on hold, freeze a picture, and delete and restore data on our computers. Yet, a life on hold is destructive to its captive. It is like a death without a burial. I was committed to my marriage. I was not perfect, but I was committed. What do you do when only one person wants to be married? How long do you wait for them to get it together? I was taught marriage was until death. So, I decided I had all the time in the world to wait. The majority of my life was ahead of me.

I knew Tony didn't want to be married to me anymore. I also knew he was struggling to maintain his sanity; therefore, I was willing to wait for him to get himself together. I didn't know how costly it would be. One year passed. Then another and another. Six years passed and nothing had improved. Things got worse. Still, I was not willing to entertain a divorce. I looked back over our life. We were not divorced, but we had not lived as husband and wife for some years. Tony lived in the basement, while the girls and I lived upstairs. My wooing didn't work anymore. The energy I spent writing love notes that I placed in his drawers, shoes, jacket pockets, on his dresser, under the bedspread, and on top of his pillow was wasted. I couldn't forget the many times I reached out to him, to help him snap out of his apparent trance. The calls telling him I loved him. The surprise visits to his job. The food offered him and his refusal. None of these things brought a positive change. So, why was I still trying to fix that which could not be fixed? I was stuck between "Then" and "Now."

I didn't know Tony's girlfriend, but Jessica made sure I knew there was one. One day she came to my house just to tell me she had seen Tony and a woman in the grocery store shopping together. I showed no reaction. I was not giving her the satisfaction of seeing my pain.

It took years for me to accept the facts. Time was not waiting for me. I was not living. I was barely existing. There was love all around me. My friends were dating and marrying. Other people seemed to be enjoying life. I decided it was time for me to live again. I threw my head back, pressed my chest forward, and said, "World, here I come."

I started doing things and visiting places I enjoyed. I felt myself reviving. I could smell the fragrance of flowers again. I saw the beauty of the trees in autumn. The green lawns looked like soft, plush carpet. Life was warm. Everywhere I went, I thanked people for their courtesy. It's amazing how important courtesy becomes when you have been verbally and mentally abused. There were no clouds in my sky. I was content. I enjoyed my presence. Life was beautiful. I had two beautiful daughters. I was not alone. I had a good job. Things were tough, but I was making it. Despite having the bare necessities, I woke up one day and said, "I'm going to take a trip."

I'd never traveled anywhere on an airplane. Every year our family vacation was a drive to South Carolina, visiting my family. This time it was going to be different. I was now in charge of my life and my destiny. I could do whatever my heart desired. Mentally, I had removed Tony from my world. I stopped trying to make our marriage work. I stopped chasing him. I no longer attempted to woo him or entertain ways of reaching him. I revoked my commitment and was moving forward.

My strength didn't produce this change of attitude. One night I dreamt Tony had died. He was handsomely dressed, lying in a casket. The casket was in the middle of my living room. I never left his side. My girls were not in the dream. The room was creepy. A dark-blue blind covered each window. No one was able to see that we were home. No sunlight seeped through. The house was very dark. The doorbell rang. I stood still and remained quiet until the person at the door left. Multiple days passed. The same dream repeated itself day after day. The telephone rang. I answered it, but I didn't know who was calling. The voice on the other end said I needed to call the police and the morgue to report the death. I refused and hung up.

I prayed to understand the dream. The revelation hit me hard. I arose with a determination to change my life. I kept my bad marriage a secret from everyone, except my close friends. When I left home I gave the appearance that all was well. I didn't want anyone to know we were having marital problems. I had to portray the wholesome, happy family until my prayers were answered. My friends and I had been fasting and praying, night and day, but nothing changed. The dream revealed that my marriage was dead. I was protecting a dead corpse. Realizing it helped me move forward.

I called my girlfriend, Roxie, who had remarried her ex-husband and moved to Illinois. I asked could I come for a visit. She readily welcomed me. My plans went smoothly. I arrived in Chicago not wanting, looking, or hoping for anything. I definitely was not ever planning to get involved with anyone. I had been in captivity long enough. My main desire was to relax and enjoy my vacation. Roxie was unable to show me around. I didn't mind staying in the house. Sleeping was a hobby. Yet, she apologized and made arrangements for her uncle to show me around.

Roxie was eager for me to meet her uncle. He was her uncle by marriage. His name was Roland Hackman. Her excitement about introducing us intrigued me. She told me how wonderful he was. She said he was handsome but not conceited. She mentioned he had been in two bad marriages and he deserved to meet someone who would appreciate him. When I met Roland, I saw he was not particularly my type. However, he was all that Roxie had said—and more. He was a special man, a gentleman and extremely sensitive. My type or not, I didn't entertain the thought of rejecting a "gentleman." From childhood, I always dreamt that my Prince Charming was tall, dark, and handsome; with a bright flashy smile. Roland was extremely light skinned, but he was tall and had a very nice smile. So, I decided I could enjoy his company for two weeks.

# 12
# New Beginnings

Roland became my tour guide, my transportation, my escort, and my date. I spent most of my waking hours with him. Before long, we were interested in each other. It was happening. I was being smitten by love and didn't even realize it. Love was slowly flowing through my veins. Time flew by. My two-week vacation seemed like two days.

When I left Chicago, we exchanged telephone numbers with a promise to keep in touch. I explained that Tony and I were living in the same house. He lived downstairs and my daughters and I lived upstairs. All utilities remained the same as when we were married. I assured him there was no problem calling the house. One day he called and Tony answered. When Roland asked for me, Tony said, "This is her husband, who's calling?" Roland said, "I'll call back." Later that evening Roland told me what transpired. After all the years I sat and waited for him to be my husband, he decided to instantly be MY HUSBAND when I received a call from a man. I had been there, done that, and I wasn't looking back. Life with Tony was forever over.

I had contacted a lawyer several times thinking I was ready for a divorce. Each time I could not go through with it. The lawyer told me not to return until I knew what I wanted. One day after Tina's tenth birthday and two weeks before Joni's sixth birthday, I knew. Therefore, I wrote the attorney a letter,

> *Being of a sound mind, I, Mrs. Raven Jordan, on this ninth day of March 1982 request a legal separation from Mr. Tony Jordan pending divorce proceedings. This decision is made for the welfare and sanity of all parties involved, namely Joni Jordan (age 5), Tina Jordan (age 10), Tony Jordan, and myself, Raven Jordan. The marriage has created an unsuitable environment and living conditions to properly raise the children. During and after this legal separation, I desire custody of my above named children.*

Our legal separation was approved. For the next two years, Tony refused to pay child support. We had a child support hearing pending. He tried manipulating me. My mom died in June 1984, more than seven years longer than the doctors had predicted. During my bereavement, Tony said he would attend my mother's funeral if I waived his child support debt. I promised him that he would be in "hell" a lifetime before I waived his obligation.

On September 25, 1985, the love, marriage, and baby carriage that Tony and I shared for thirteen and a half years ended. We were divorced. Everything was final, or so I thought!

My two girls were my life. They were my reason for living. They were the only good things left from my marriage to Tony. After giving Tony the divorce he wanted, he returned with a vengeance. He went to court and charged me as an unfit mother. He was planning to take my girls away from me. I found out about this at work. I received a call from the court clerk. She was rude and spoke as if she knew everything Tony alleged was true. She said I was expected to attend a court hearing the upcoming week. I asked sisters at my church to be character witnesses. None of them were willing to testify. They said they did not want to get in the middle. However, I knew it was because they were all Tony's relatives. I decided not to ask any of my friends. I prayed to God. I felt so alone. No one wanted to stand with me. I was almost despondent. Later that evening, a quiet calmness rested upon me. I called Tony and said I was not going to fight him. He could do whatever he wanted to. I was not coming to court. He could have the girls to raise. Two days later the court clerk called. She said Tony had dropped the charges. She warned me. They will be monitoring my case. Mr. Jordan can reopen it at any future date. I called Tony's bluff and he caved!

I hated Tony. I longed for him to reap what he had sown. The desire to see him suffer consumed me. I told God I thought Tony should die and go to hell so that he could feel what he had put me through. I sincerely believed hell was the only thing compatible to my years of suffering. I didn't realize I was digging a hole, which would grip me in its claws. My unforgiveness distanced me from God. It left me feeling stuck. I was unable to move forward or backwards. Then I dreamt I was in a deep pit struggling to get out. I was unable to do so. I prayed, but my prayer was just words. My heart was cold. I felt nothing. I was numb. My Christian walk became a facade because only a shell remained. Years passed before I forgave Tony. During those years of anger, God taught me the benefits of forgiving.

Meeting Roland was so timely. He was everything a woman desired. Every moment with him was heavenly. He treated me so tenderly and so special. It didn't seem real. Roland said the right words. Did the right things. He made me feel like the woman I had fantasized about for so long.

Roland, my Roland, what a wonderful man he was.

After leaving Illinois and returning to Maryland, Roland took our relationship to another level. He called me every day, sometimes two or three times. He sent me Helen Steiner Rice cards every day for weeks. He systematically mailed them. The message of each card would sequentially follow the one he intended. He even numbered the cards to ensure I knew the order to read them in. If the words on the card were not exactly what he wanted to say, he would modify it. This continued throughout our three-year long-distance dating.

Then, there was our special song. "I Just Called to Say I Love You" by Stevie Wonder. I had never heard it. From the day he declared it our special song, it was so. He told me the words of the song. He sang it to me. My knees weakened and my heart raced, not because he could sing. Rather, because he was singing to me. Roland, just being Roland, took it to the next level. Each time he heard the song on the radio, he called me long distance for me to hear it. Long distance telephone packages were not as they are now. Our long-distance relationship cost much money. Besides the telephone bills, there were the airline fares, gas, hotel charges, food, and entertainment. Things were more expensive being girlfriend and boyfriend than husband and wife, because we still had to maintain our homes. None of those things mattered when we were together. Sometimes we were at a restaurant when our special song came on. We stopped whatever we were doing and just looked into each other's eyes, singing along until the song ended.

On any given day at work, I would receive a telephone call from the lobby, the security guard telling me I had a package at the receptionist desk. I would go get it and there would be a dozen red roses from Roland. After this happened a few times, whenever I received a call from the lobby, I would suspect it was something from Roland. One day I received one of those routine calls and went downstairs as I normally would. To my amazement, the dozen of roses were there being handed to me by Roland. I almost fainted. I ran to him, hugged and kissed him. The employees in the lobby began cheering and clapping. The story traveled throughout the building like a wildfire. This man knew how to treat a woman. I wondered, *Is there another man anywhere who knows how to treat a woman better than this?* The women at work and those in my personal circle were telling me they were jealous of the jewel I had found.

Whenever I visited Roland, his nephew and niece would invite us on a double date. We usually attended a stage play. It was a special bond we shared. I really appreciated them including us into their fun time. It enhanced our relationship. I'd hoped it would become a tradition we would share for many years to come.

During one of my visits to Illinois, Roland took me to Wisconsin. He surprised me with an engagement ring and marriage proposal. I didn't dream of saying no to such a perfect man. When he proposed, we discussed going to the justice of the peace. However, my friends decided I was going to have a wedding since I never had one. In one week, they planned a wedding that was very special.

A year earlier I bought the dress I wanted to get married in if Roland asked. The dress was in my closet waiting to be worn. Now that I had a proposal, I could wear my dress— and I did.

The dress was a light beige color. It had a high collar with a wide sash. The sleeves were puff with a strip of lace going down the sides of the arms. Three pearl buttons stood high on the cuff. The wide waistline was also designed with a sash.

The time had finally arrived for us to be married. The

cue was made for me to march in. I was scared. I froze and would not come out of the bathroom. My girlfriend Sandra pulled me out and pushed me towards the aisle. After I made it past the first two rows, a big bright smile formed on my lips. I began to walk with a bounce. I was just short of skipping. I raised my head and got a glance of the anticipation in Roland's eyes. His look of expectancy and pride made me want to hurry. It seemed the aisle was growing. I wanted to make it to the front without falling. At that moment, as though it was rehearsed, Roland walked back to the first pew to meet me. Our guests began to laugh and so did I.

The assistant pastor, Mother Eve Francisco, officiated the wedding. My daughters were my bridesmaids. Roland's nephew was his best man. Only close friends were invited. Sandra made my bouquet with cream and pink flowers. Roland wore a double-breasted gray-striped suit, a light gray shirt with faint blue stripes, with a royal blue tie. My girls wore pink dresses. The best man wore a black suit, white shirt, with a black bow tie. This was our day. The day that would not end, "till death do us part!"

Our wedding was so special. My girlfriend CC sang during the wedding. I knew she could sing, but the way she sang that day sent chills up my spine. My friend Margie spoke words of inspiration. It encouraged my guests in their relationships. Evelyn worked diligently preparing the food for the reception. Two friends from work gave us our wedding album as a gift. The photographers, also friends from work, donated their service as a gift. Everything was wonderful!

When it was time to kiss, my girls were embarrassed. They dropped their heads and looked down at the floor. Roland kissed me so passionately he pulled my head covering off. I carried it in my right hand as we marched out. Roland held onto my left hand with the bouquet.

When Mother Francisco gave Roland the marriage certificate, his smile was one of the biggest I had ever seen from him. He seemed so relaxed, so comfortable! So very sure! During the reception, Roland smiled when I smiled. He sat warmly watching me. My friend Carlin made us a beautiful homemade three-tier wedding cake. It was delicious! Janet, who was already secretly married, caught the bouquet.

Some of our guests said our wedding was the most intimate wedding they had ever attended. That's encouraging! What a great sign of the happiness awaiting me, as Roland and I would grow old together. I was enjoying myself so much that I didn't realize Roland was ready to leave. He became irritated. Sarcastically, he asked whether I had planned to leave and go home any time that night. Was this just anticipation?

*New Beginnings*
*by Raven Bailey*

*In your garden of new beginnings, fruits of mystery await you.*
*It's a garden designed for those who no longer exist as two.*
*This garden is known for its oneness of heart,*
*Wherein lies the strength to keep you from tearing apart.*
*Enter your garden as friends, as well as mates.*
*Treat each day together as your very first date.*
*The foundation of the new does not agree with the old.*
*You must give yourself to each other, spirit, body and soul.*
*Priorities must change; it's not family and friends anymore.*
*A new life began when you walked through the "New Beginnings" door.*
*So, walk into your future and close the doors to the past.*
*Commit to do everything possible to make your love last!*
*Wrap yourself in each other's love, and security will prevail.*

*Don't let selfishness or strife cause your relationship to fail.*
*Create new horizons and new heights for you to enjoy.*
*Let the kid in you come forth, that little girl and little boy.*
*If you trust your heart to cover each other, love will serve you well.*
*And soon, in your new beginnings, you'll have love stories to tell.*
*Be encouraged to have a new beginning, each and every day.*
*Committing yourselves to each other in every possible way.*
*Sing a new song, dance a new dance, and make each other smile.*
*Play games, "hide-and-seek," always going the extra mile.*
*This "New Beginning" can be the best thing for each of you,*
*as you honor your Covenant, living as one, and not two!*

Our marriage was good. We shared some very special moments. We kept our marriage alive. Roland and I dressed alike. When you saw him, you saw me. We rode together. We did everything but work together. Roland had a great sense of humor. He was quite witty. He was a very smart man. He was a mechanic. I admired the way he could break down a car and put it back together again. He was physically strong, yet emotionally tender. He opened doors for me. He held my hand as we crossed the street. He dated me regularly. We went shopping together, even if I was the only one shopping. He went with me to the hairdresser and waited for me. Roland gave me baths and rubbed lotion on my body. He gave me massages, pedicures, and manicures. Roland was the man. He periodically did my perms, washed, blow dried, and curled my hair. At one point and without warning, my body began treating the "normal" process of hair growth as something "foreign," and rejected it. This resulted in hair loss. I had bald spots throughout my head. I decided to oil my scalp with vitamin E and brushed it at least a hundred strokes each night. Roland willingly brushed my hair every night until it grew back. Periodically, he took me to work and picked me up. My desire was to make him a happy husband for the rest of his life, because this man needed to be cloned.

We made it to our first-year anniversary! Saturday evening we took our wedding cake out of the freezer so that it would defrost. We'd planned to celebrate on Sunday after church. Since none of his family attended our wedding, we shared the cake with them.

On our third anniversary, I stayed home from work and planned a romantic evening with a candlelight dinner: a five-course dinner of steak, corn, greens, potato salad, macaroni and cheese, and corn bread, with Pepsi and Welch's grape juice.

I set up the table in our bedroom. I took a shower and slipped into a black lace negligee. Roland came home, showered, and we entered our bedroom for an undisturbed evening. My daughter took pictures for us. The evening was quite romantic, and it was cute watching Roland struggle to open the grape juice. I enjoyed the simplest things about Roland. It was another fun thing we laughed about. During the evening we reviewed our marriage certificate. We had always disagreed on the date we were married. I wasn't sure whether Roland was serious or just kidding. Either way, I had the certificate at the table for discussion.

At the end of each anniversary celebration, I looked forward to the next one.

# 13

# One Thing Was Lacking

Roland loved me and I loved him. A reflection of our love could be seen in the things we did and the words spoken. Despite the reflection, a deep concern lingered in my heart. Roland's heart was divided. It was frightening. Uncertainty triggered so many questions about this good man. He fulfilled what he viewed as his obligations. He paid the mortgage. The other areas I felt were important were not important to him. A major ingredient was missing from our marriage: total commitment!

It was wonderful to love and be loved. However, love is not love without commitment. It's like loving with your mind, with no attachment to your heart. When I married Roland, I was fully committed. Sadly, I was slowly learning Roland was afraid to fully commit.

The center of Roland's heart remained in his past. His ex-girlfriend, ex-wives, children, ex-girlfriend's children, family, and ex in-laws possessed the core of his heart. Before long, I found myself at the mercy of his insurmountable past. My storybook marriage had begun to produce pain on a daily basis. The handsome prince had transformed into a beast. Every decision we made was influenced by Roland's past. Each attempt to advance was crippled by his lack of commitment. His outside influences had the final word. They decided when he came home, went out of town, or purchased items. Everybody's opinion and their selfishness shaped and strengthened Roland's stubbornness. He boldly justified his refusal to totally commit. He said his children will always be his children. His family will always be his family. However, there was no guarantee I would always be his wife.

We were simply playing house. Marriage was not supposed to function like this. We had separate bank accounts. Roland wanted it that way. After my experience with Tony, I should have welcomed this decision, but I didn't. Roland said, "Nobody is going to say a woman paid my debts." Our lives were so mixed up. He even made his children the beneficiaries on his life insurance policy. I didn't matter. One day I asked Roland could we pull together and pay off our bills. I wanted to stop working. He said, "If you stop working, you must plan to eat beans for the rest of your life." I dismissed the idea because this apparently was not going to happen.

Time passed and the non-commitment grew more intense. I had become an outcast with his family. Roland had very little contact with me outside of the home. It appeared he didn't want the family to know we periodically had good times. Most new members at our church didn't even know I was married. They never saw me with anyone. However, he was a great behind-closed-doors husband. He was considerate. He nurtured and caressed me. I became content with his non-commitment. Then I had the audacity to blame God for my unhappiness. I told Him, "You don't want me to be happy. You think if I am happy with a husband, I will love him more than I love you." After my one-on-one with God, I was left speechless. Who do I blame for Roland's Christmas list? Every year, his ex-girlfriend and her entire family was on his Christmas list whether we could afford it or not. Roland offered no reason, excuse, or apology for his actions. He was bold and intentional.

The unanswered question remained, "Will our marriage survive without full commitment?"

# 14
## Graveyard Cruelty

I should have seen it coming. It was obvious while we were dating. It was present after marriage. I was blinded by love.

Roland gave jealousy a new meaning. He was convinced every man I met wanted me. Sometimes I caught him watching me from a distance. They were not looks of admiration. Accusation and suspicion were on his face. Each time I prepared myself to hear about it later. He saw things that did not exist. He believed things that were not true. I tried convincing him no one was pursuing me. I told him I was not God's gift to men. I wrestled with how to change his belief. I did nothing to encourage his negative thinking. I enjoyed being me. I've always loved people and communicating openly with them. I treated my male and female friends alike. Sometimes I found myself talking to a male friend, saying, "Girl, such and such." To solve Roland's jealousy problem, I decided to change me. I separated myself from people. I spoke briefly and continued on my way. I left church immediately after the benediction. This was totally out of character. I wanted to be happily married, so I had to change who I was. I was willing to do whatever it took. It wasn't long before I realized I was becoming someone I didn't want to be. I no longer knew the person in the mirror. The price was too high. I didn't want to change who I was. I had no assurance of a worthwhile return. I decided to take a different approach. I tried seeing myself through Roland's eyes. I could not see what he saw. I didn't see a beautiful, sensual, desirable woman. I merely saw a woman who wanted to be happy. High self-esteem was never one of my strong characteristics. I would look into the mirror and see all the things I would change. Even the things I liked about myself needed some modifications.

Often in frustration, Roland would say, "You are so naïve. You pretend not to see how he looks at you, how he is always in your face," and so on. Other times in anger, he would only say, "I don't believe you are that naïve!" I was neither pretending nor playing games. I accepted people at face value. I found out later Roland was correct in some of his observations. I never told him because I knew he could not handle it. I believed an acknowledgement would have intensified his jealousy. My belief was later proven. The next time it happened, I told Roland and he did exactly what I had anticipated. He assumed the one incident validated all of his suspicions. I decided to handle any future situations myself. I rebuked the lustful brother and distanced myself. I still knew it was not every male. Talking with Roland confirmed I could not be myself or be open with him. It was rough dealing with his jealousy. Nevertheless, I loved him. I recognized his insecurities. I wanted to help him. I worked extremely hard reinforcing that I was his. Nothing changed his thinking.

His jealousy was very degrading and humiliating. A person living a clean life doesn't want to be made to feel like dirt. A virtuous wife faithful to her husband doesn't want to be made to feel like an adulteress. Those were the emotional whirlwinds I experienced daily.

Once while dating, Roland gave me a surprise visit. He drove all the way from Illinois to Maryland alone. My weekend began as usual, cleaning the house. It had been a joke among my neighbors that I spent my entire Saturday, every weekend, cleaning my house. So I decided to make a change. I decided to clean on Friday evening. Then I would be free on Saturday. I began my household chores. I was mopping, vacuuming, washing clothes, playing my music, and making sure the children were doing their homework.

The entry doors in the front and back of the house were opened. However, the screen doors were locked. I often did this so fresh air could circulate through the house. Roland came to the house and rang the doorbell. There was no answer. He waited and rang a few more times, still no answer. He left and went to his hotel room. After settling in, he fell asleep. He was tired. He had driven over thirteen hours to see me.

The next morning Roland called. He said he was calling from his hotel room in Woodlawn. I was excited to hear his voice. When he said he was in town, I did not believe him. He tried convincing me, but it didn't work. How could he be here and I not know it? Our conversation went around and around. Finally, he said he had been to my house. The door was open, but I wouldn't let him in. I was so excited I couldn't think straight. I wanted to see him as badly as he wanted to see me. The feeling was wonderful. No one had ever surprised me with anything. With him, surprises were becoming the norm, which was intriguing. I was floating on the wings of love. Later that day, my wings were broken and I fell flat. Reality kicked in. Roland came back to the house. We sat talking, kissing, and enjoying one another … *until* he shared his thoughts regarding Friday night. He swore the reason I didn't answer the doorbell was because my boyfriend was inside when he arrived. Therefore, I had no way of letting my boyfriend out without the two of them meeting. His suspicions totally ruined the essence of his surprise. Throughout our marriage, he "kidded" that my reason for not opening the door was because my boyfriend was in the house.

Hindsight is truly 20/20! When we were getting to know each other, I voluntarily told Roland about my childhood, school days, and family life. Little did I realize he would later use the information against me to support his suspicions. He was threatened by my old high-school sweethearts. Any visits to my hometown were suspect. I learned very little about his life and his past. He answered my specific questions, but little information was volunteered. During disagreements, he brought up names of old boyfriends whom I should have married.

His jealousy brought challenges. One episode occurred at church. It was a celebration honoring our pastor and his wife. Our special guest speaker was a visiting preacher. I was seated in the audience when the preacher asked me to come to the platform to read the Scriptures. I felt honored and did as requested. It was such an encouragement for me.

I glanced at Roland. His face was red, and fury was in his eyes. I could tell he was angry. However, I didn't know with whom or about what. After church, he walked up to me and said, with anger and sarcasm, "I'm sick of this. Everybody likes Raven. You always have to be in the limelight. Why did you have to read the Scriptures? His wife was there. The preachers were there. Why did you have to read them?" I was taken aback. I whispered, "Roland, he asked me to read and it was an honor." He continued, "If we ever work things out, there's going to be a lot of changes. You don't have to be involved in everything." I walked away in tears.

Challenges were always present. It was coincidental that I worked on several committees with the same brother,

Brother Sam. We became friends. Whenever we talked or worked on a committee, Roland became enraged. When we were alone, Roland said abusive things about Brother Sam and his wife. Brother Sam had done absolutely nothing to Roland. His kindest words towards Brother Sam were, "I can't stand him." Since Brother Sam was my friend and mentor, I told him of Roland's insecurities. Brother Sam and I agreed to love Roland into God's secure love. He made deliberate efforts to greet Roland. He talked to him and regularly embraced him. Once he even forcefully kissed Roland on the cheek, saying, "Hi, my friend." Brother Sam began including Roland on the committees. He even gave Roland specific assignments. Roland gladly completed each assignment. Despite all that was done, Roland's heart was never touched enough to change.

Even my doctor's visits became increasingly difficult. I didn't like doctors, especially male doctors. My doctor-patient relationship was terrible. I was never comfortable with male doctors, but I dealt with it. Roland had problems with male doctors looking at my body. After returning from a doctor's visit, he asked me questions about the procedures. Then he would get his small pocket flashlight and play his "Doctor Game." The "Doctor Game" was his own creation. The game allowed him to be my doctor and examine me. I thought it was for fun, another way to keep our love fire burning. He caressed my body as he examined it. I soon realized it was not a game at all. He reenacted the examination to address his suspicions. The game began to bother me. A short time later, I requested a change to a female doctor.

Although Roland's jealousy was his war within, it became my battle on the outside because there was constant confusion. Jealousy and the other negative influences were destroying pieces of our marriage daily, destroying our future together.

# 15
# The Bull

Ithought I understood stubbornness. I had met many stubborn people. Even I was one of them. However, I'd never met anyone as stubborn as Roland. As a matter of fact, if I thought I had suffered with Tony, I was in for a rude awakening.

Along with his stubbornness, Roland seldom forgot the negative things. He refused to forgive the smallest offenses. He held unbelievable grudges. If I didn't know better I would say there were two of him: the "Mister Nice Guy" and the "Evil as Sin Guy"! "Hindsight is 20/20" constantly rang in my ears. Each enlightenment reminded me that it was there all the time.

Roland lived in the "middle of the road." He did things that made everybody happy. Unfortunately, I wasn't a part of the "everybody." Anyone in his good graces basked in his kindness. God help those who were not. His grudges became a family affair. If you were out of his good graces, it also applied to his children and the family. If the anger of one family member didn't sting you, the anger of another was waiting in the wings.

When dating, I anticipated our double dating with his niece and nephew, Peggy and Paul, would continue.

I quickly learned not to make long-term plans in "The Family." Shortly after our marriage, I became an outcast of "The Family." Our double dating came to a screeching halt. Roland's niece and nephew would visit him. If he wasn't at home, they would sit in their car and wait for him. They refused to come inside where I was. After their visit, they left without a word to me. The hurt was deep because I thought we had connected.

Roland was as warm as a sunny afternoon one moment, and as cold as ice the next. He seldom admitted being wrong in situations. I can barely remember an apology for his wrong doings. It was frustrating always being the one to apologize. Whether right or wrong, I didn't want my heart to harden like it did with Tony.

In situations where I was wrong, I asked for forgiveness. Roland would simply say, "Okay." Nevertheless, each time something new happened, the old things surfaced. I reminded him I'd asked for forgiveness. So, I really didn't want to hear it.

Roland had a depository. He deposited things about me until the opportune time to use them, over and over. In his depository were unfair judgments. Indictments involving situations I knew nothing about. Old things he did not like but had never said anything about. So many times I couldn't even remember the details surrounding the situation he referenced. It was rough. I was the one who apologized most of the time. I apologized so much he would angrily say, "You are always asking to be forgiven." My apologies meant nothing. I told him I would rather ask for forgiveness too much than not enough. I believed each time I asked for forgiveness, my slate was wiped clean. I couldn't begin to imagine the magnitude of Roland's unforgiveness for so many people, because he would not let things go!

# 16
# You Should Have

I wanted Roland to know everything about me. So, I talked and talked some more. The more I shared, the more information he stored in his memory. I told him about myself before meeting him. I described my storybook ideas about romance.

Roland began telling me what kind of man I should have married. Those words "you should have" were as routine as my daily meal. The walls could probably echo those words of their own accord. *You should have married Sam because he is a preacher. You should have married Tom because he is tall and dark. You should have married Dan because he is handsome. You should have married Ben because he has a gorgeous smile. You should have, you should have...* Some of the men he said I should have married were even husbands of my friends. It was sick insecurity.

If I talked with a man, he was a candidate for my "should have" list. If I walked past a man and we spoke, he became qualified. I appreciated Roland thinking I was attractive. However, I knew I was not the answer to every man's prayer or the image in every man's dream. I told him his confidence should be great since he had what other men could only desire. My encouragement made no difference.

Roland had low self-esteem. He could not see how valuable he was to me. I tried telling him how important he was in my life. I explained that just as he chose me, I chose him. Therefore, there was no one else I "should have" married. I told him how much smarter he was than I. Anything I did not know politically or educationally, I would ask him. I tried convincing him he was a handsome, kind, and gentle man. He responded, "You're just saying that." I was proud to be his wife. Proud to say, "This is my husband." I felt we complemented each other and belonged together.

Roland was color-blind. So, I shopped for his clothing. I wanted to boost his confidence to encourage him. I regularly mailed cards and wrote love letters to him. We called each other several times a day. I did all I knew to do. Yet, he regularly ended our conversation either jokingly or seriously, "You should have married so and so."

# 17
# Those Baltimore Women

"Those Baltimore Women!" Are those words complimentary? Should we smile or frown? What does it mean and where did it come from?

I was one of three women who fell in love with one of three men from Illinois. I was one of three women who married one of three men from the same family. I was one of three women who lived in Baltimore, Maryland, and relocated to Evanston, Illinois. I was one of three women who uprooted herself and, in trust, left Baltimore to spend the rest of her life with the man she loved in Illinois. The three women became friends while living in Baltimore. One by one we relocated to Illinois to be with the men we loved. The soul-ties began with my girlfriend Roxie, who was married to Brad. Her goddaughter, Sophie, married Brad's first cousin. Then I married their uncle. All three men were blood relatives and members of "The Family." Our survival in this family was doomed from the beginning. Although Roxie and Sophie had many more years of marriage than I, their marriages in "The Family" also ended. Over the years, "The Family" branded us, and we became known as "Those Baltimore Women."

Acceptance into "The Family" was based solely on their terms: become who they wanted you to; submit when they wanted; be available when they required your presence; graciously accept their rejection when they didn't want you in their presence; accept their judgment whether it was right or wrong; and accept all the exes as "Family." We had to grin and bear whatever was thrown at us. Fortunately, I was never one who needed people to accept me in order for me to function. I loved people, but I also loved spending time alone. There was no permanent void in my life that needed others to fill, in order for me to feel complete. I rarely visited anyone without purpose. I was not pretentious, cliquish, or manipulative. So, my acceptance into the "Family" was short-lived. Tina inherited my professional traits, so she could take you or leave you. Joni inherited my personality traits; she was lovable and loved people. Joni was accepted and loved. Tina and I were tolerated. When we first moved to Illinois, my girls and I were the pies, and "The Family" was the ice cream. We blended well, *until* I crossed the line by maintaining my own identity.

"Those Baltimore Women!" These three words spoken by "The Family" were clearly negative. Each time they were spoken, they carried a different message: ridicule, disgrace, humiliation, false accusations, and unjust judgments. There was disdain for the Baltimore Women who were once loved and accepted. Without the bloodline our acceptance was easily revoked, especially if we resisted the family rules.

How could three women who knew and loved God find themselves branded by "The Family" as "Those Baltimore Women?" After a while, people outside "The Family" were using those words. Implications were made without a reason. People were convinced we were different. We were the cause of things going wrong in our relationships.

Everything about us was judged, specifically our

personality, our dress, our appearance, our walk, our talk, the way we praised God, our testimony, and our prayers. Something was always wrong because we did not fit the mold.

Then one day we graduated from being "Those Baltimore Women" to "Who Do They Think They Are?" It was the same course with a different title. It provided the same results, pain, and agony. It caused me to question my value.

Despite what happened to me, I affirm that if you didn't do or say things that displeased "The Family," there was nothing to worry about. They would love you eternally.

"The Family" gave a new meaning to the adage, "The ties that bind." It could have been admired if it wasn't so frightening. The pain and agony it produced were not godly. Yet, most of "The Family" were godly people. It was eerie.

# 18
# Lark, Dooley and Jetway

Roland and I frequently visited three houses. They were unfamiliar to me. I was never invited in. Two of the houses were in Evanston. One was a brown-and-white house on Lark Street and the other a brick house with an enclosed porch on Dooley Avenue. The third was an apartment on Jetway Terrace in Chicago. Although I was with Roland when he visited these places, he never told me who lived there. Neither did I ask any questions. When we arrived at each place, Roland said, "I'll be right back." I said, "Okay," and waited patiently in the car until he returned.

The frequency of the visits increased. It became apparent that the people at these places had a significant influence in our lives. I needed to know who, what, when, and where, so I started asking questions. I learned each house was associated with his children in one way or another. Everything seemed acceptable, except the house on Dooley.

The visits continued. One day, while visiting the brown and white house, I was unexpectedly invited in. As I entered the door, I realized the blessedness of not having been invited in before. Roland's first ex-wife, his older children, and his grandchildren lived there. I didn't know who changed the rule that allowed me to come in, but I felt privileged. I was Roland's wife. I wanted to be part of everything that involved him. Once inside, courtesies were exchanged. I remained standing. I was afraid something might bite me or crawl up my clothes. I just wanted to get out as fast as I could. I was not used to that type of living condition. It was filthy. I grew up in poverty, but the little we had was clean. I could see Roland's embarrassment. I lightheartedly laughed and talked with the smaller children. The interaction helped with my discomfort in the surroundings. When we left, I resolved I would never visit again.

Then there was the apartment building. Roland's second ex-wife and his two youngest children lived there. The rules changed here also. I was invited in. Once inside, I knew I would never visit again. It was one hundred percent cleaner than the brown-and-white house, but cats and kittens ran freely. They jumped on top of everything, including the counters and sofa. When she offered us something to drink, I almost choked. My stomach felt queasy. However, I made it through the visit.

I was never invited into the house on Dooley. As much as I tried, I could not make the connection. My questions were evaded. My brain worked overtime trying to figure out how this house fitted in the family puzzle. Roland's explanations regarding this house were always very vague. He and his family were playing games. I was the brunt of their joke. One morning, I attended prayer at church with his sister, Esther. Unknown to me, the woman from the house on Dooley was also present. She was holding a cute little girl in her arms. This woman and child were characters in the deep dark secrets of Dooley Avenue. Esther knew them and they knew me. I was at a disadvantage. I greeted them as I would anyone else in church. I kissed the woman and the little girl on their cheeks. I held a brief conversation with her, as I played with the little girl. I noticed Esther standing to the side watching us with a smile on her lips. I did not have a clue regarding what was happening. When the woman walked away, Esther smiled and said, "Do you know who that is?" I said, "No." She said, "That was Miss Jezzy, Roland's ex-girlfriend. That's her little girl who calls Roland Daddy, but she is not Roland's child." I was irritated by Esther's amusement.

If I didn't remember anything else, I should have remembered those three houses. Yet, I did not! I was new to the city and had a poor sense of direction. I never made a correlation of their locations when we began our search to buy a house. I recall certain things that happened when I thought we had found the perfect house. At first view the house was unattractive, but I fell in love with it. I saw its' potential. For each positive thing I noted, Roland noted a negative thing. He provided multiple reasons why we should not buy that house. I could tell he did not want to buy it, but I did not understand his resistance. Finally, he agreed to buy it. Surprise! I didn't know at the time, but we'd just bought a house around the corner from his ex-girlfriend on Dooley Avenue. I asked why he did not tell me. He said it didn't matter. Oh, how it *did* matter in the days that followed.

The house on Dooley Avenue was the only place where there was not a legitimate reason for Roland to visit. It was reasonable for me to expect visits to that house to stop.

Although it was ugly, the puzzle of Lark Street, Dooley Avenue, and Jetway Terrace was finally complete. I recognized the players, the pieces of the puzzle, and where they fit.

# 19
# How Much Is Enough?

All I wanted was a little common courtesy. Was I expecting too much from my newly constructed family? Did I create an environment impossible to survive?

When Roland and I got married, I left my daughters in Baltimore with my pastor and her family. I would return for them in June at the end of the school year.

In the meantime, new drama developed each day. There was one surprise after the other. I only had five months to get ready for my girls' arrival. Within the first month of our marriage and without a word to me, Roland's oldest daughter, Viola, and her three children were moving in with us. Viola was from his first ex-wife. She was in her late twenties and her children ranged from infancy to nine years old. A house designed to accommodate two or three people now housed seven people, soon to be nine. Nothing was discussed with me. I was told they were coming on the day they moved in. Viola and Jezzy were close friends. With Viola living with us, Jezzy would be privy to our personal and private lives. Viola's moving in also gave Jezzy a freedom to call our house whenever she desired. I had no voice in the matter. I was told even if she called Roland, it was only to talk to him regarding his children. My problem was, his children were not her children. So, why did she need to call our house?

Jezzy went to the extreme trying to buy Roland's and his children's love. She took care of Viola's children. She regularly gave Viola, Claudia, and James gifts. Claudia and James were Roland's two younger children by his second ex-wife. She would invite Claudia and James to her house and cook their favorite foods. She taught Claudia how to make brownies. I knew these things because they were the topic of conversation when they came to our house. Roland told me I had no reason to complain since I didn't do those things with Claudia. It did not matter that I didn't even do those things with my own girls. It was made clear I had nothing to do with how much time Jezzy spent with his kids.

Viola's presence in our home created extreme tension. Although Roland did not agree, I felt Viola should have been self-sufficient and on her own. I understood periodic emergencies, but I could never accept parasites. Nevertheless, my views were not accepted and I was not liked very much for expressing them.

My mother always told us that it doesn't matter how little you have, just take care of it and keep it clean, and it will serve you well. Viola did not know cleanliness; therefore, she did not teach it to her children. Things got so filthy I didn't want to go home after work. I started going out with Roxie. Sometimes we went shopping and other times we just went downtown to buy some popcorn. Whatever I could do to delay going home to a filthy house, I did. Old habits die hard! I spent all day on Saturdays cleaning and sterilizing the house to no avail. By Sunday it was filthy again. Dirty clothes covered the floor. Soiled baby diapers were left throughout the house. The bathroom was always filthy. A stench developed in the house. It was the kind that stayed in your clothes long after you'd left the house. Then came the straw, you've heard of it, the one that broke the camel's back. I became ill when I found her baby's feces smeared all over the kitchen floor, on the cabinets, refrigerator, stove, and in the dish towels. Sobbing uncontrollably, I told Roland I could not live like this. Something had to give. He angrily reminded me Viola would not be there much longer. Then he said, "If it was your daughter who needed help, you would do the same thing." He missed the whole point. I needed someone to tell him it was the filth.

What did he want from me? I had already made costly sacrifices. Leaving my girls in Baltimore was the most self-serving thing I had ever done. Viola left shortly before my daughters arrived. She moved in with her mother.

Our move to Evanston seemed like the right thing to do. Since I worked for the Federal Government, I could possibly be transferred. Roland worked for the City of Evanston and a move to Baltimore meant he would have to find a new job. It didn't matter what was required. I was willing to make the adjustment. So here we were, my daughters and I, living in a place we'd never even heard of. It was a place where we had no family. We didn't know where or how we would fit in. We were blindly trusting Roland to take care of our concerns by covering us.

One of my first major mistakes was to move into the house Roland owned with his second ex-wife. The house was too small, but it did not matter because I was with Roland. I loved him, and as long as we were together, everything else could be worked out.

There were two bedrooms. A room or enclosed porch was next to the kitchen. It was partially completed. It was packed from floor to ceiling with stuff. Roland kept things that would never be used again but were too good to be thrown away. The exterior and interior of the house were painted white. The living and dining room floors were covered with a royal blue carpet and no padding. It was so worn that the floor could be seen through the carpeting. The kitchen and bathroom desperately needed a thorough cleaning. The whole house needed a woman's touch.

Roland and I shared his bedroom. The bedroom was so small it could only accommodate a twin size bed. Again, it didn't matter. We had each other and our love. In the past, I'd regularly slept on my stomach. However, we had to sleep on our sides for both of us to fit on the bed. That was okay too. It provided a cozy night's sleep. His dresser drawers were filled to capacity and the one small closet overflowed.

Most of my belongings remained in boxes, except a few dresses. I hung them in the coat closet behind the front door. Next to our bedroom was the bathroom. The bathroom was so small that two people could not be in it at the same time. Even that didn't matter when we wanted to be romantic and take showers together. His son Robert had the larger bedroom. This was not surprising because Roland was self-sacrificing. Robert was indeed a bachelor. He was not required to clean anything, and he didn't. His room reeked of a foul odor. Tina and Joni were given the partially completed back room. We made it livable; however, there was no ventilation in their room. I felt guilty. The heat in the summer and the cold in the winter were unbearable. We had to make the best of what hopefully was a temporary situation. My daughters appeared to have adjusted, but I constantly battled with guilt.

Then I noticed Tina was having her own issues. She regularly asked for money to buy stamps. She was constantly writing letters. Roland would give her the stamps without hesitation. Her requests for stamps increased. The more stamps she received, the more she needed. When it appeared out of control, I intervened. I talked with Tina.

She began to cry. She missed her friends in Baltimore. I tried to be sympathetic to her feeling of loss. It was difficult. I was fighting my own monsters of guilt. It saddened me knowing I was the reason for her void. She had just graduated from junior high school. She was "in love" with her first boyfriend. More importantly, she was on her way to high school. Soon she'd enter a high school, in a strange city, where she had no friends. It was terrible. I desperately tried to prepare them in advance.

Before marrying Roland, I asked the girls how they felt about my remarrying. They said they wanted to see me happy and if that was what I wanted, they were happy too. I told them not to give me the answer they thought I wanted to hear. I told them if I remarried, we would have to move from Maryland to Illinois. I talked about the changes in their schools, church, friends, and new home life. They assured me they understood. They even said they loved Mr. Roland because he treated them special.

We discussed the facts of our life. Roland was not their father. I did not expect them to call him Daddy. I expected them to respect him as my husband. They were expected to obey the house rules. They would obey Roland and not talk back to him like his children. They were required to treat him as they treated me. I also asked them to do the best they could to get along with Roland's children. They said they understood and accepted my instructions. They tried calling Roland Dad, Pop, and Daddy Roland, but it was too awkward. They finally resorted to Mr. Roland. Even though they said Mister, it was still filled with love and respect. From the day of our marriage until this day, they kept their word. They never disrespected Roland. There were times when they despised some of the things he did and allowed his children to do. Yet, they still respected him as my husband. There were times they said if Mr. Roland's children disrespected me again, they were going to beat them up. They were angry that strangers were allowed to do things to me they would never dream of doing. Even after preparing them for relocation, unexpected challenges still arose.

Roland never required his children to respect me. I continuously sought their cooperation and respect, but to no avail. Each one of them, from the youngest to the one next to the eldest, disrespected me. His eldest son, Roland Jr., was the only one who never disrespected me.

Since Robert lived with Roland and my girls lived with me, it was understood our reconstructed household would include the five of us. It was also understood that both of his ex-wives had minor children who financially depended on him. He was paying child support to both families. Often his support was above the court's requirement. His first ex-wife had teenagers and adults. Rona had his two youngest children, Claudia and James. Before our marriage, Rona denied Roland visitation even though he supported them.

Things changed rapidly. I was headed for one of life's greatest roller-coaster experiences. Suddenly, Claudia and James were calling daily and coming over every weekend. Roland's visitation rights were expanding. Initially, I had no problem with it. It was an opportunity to merge two of our three families. Problems developed, which changed everything. All rules vanished. Everything we did or ate, every place we visited—all was based on what Claudia and James wanted. Sadly, Roland allowed it all to happen. Claudia was the same age as Joni. If things were different, this could have worked well for us.

Claudia was the most disrespectful child I had ever met. She was arrogant and self-centered, demanding and disobedient, jealous and hateful. She wouldn't have recognized a child's place if it were attached to her body.

In contrast, James was mild mannered and pleasant. There was a level of comfort between us immediately. As long as Claudia was not around to influence him, he was like any other child. Her influence was like poison. He became a different child when Claudia was around. It seemed he was afraid of her knowing he liked us. Years later, I found out that the waters flowed even deeper than I realized.

I was learning some hard life lessons. Yet, I was getting to know the love God had for me. I learned to believe God was working things out, whether I could see it or not. I also believed when people plot to do evil against you, God would use it to accomplish His purpose for you. Rona had become quite insistent on Roland selling the house. They owned the house together and she wanted her share of the proceeds. She told Roland, she did not want his "bitch and her children" living in her house. What she didn't realize was I didn't want to be there. When the proceedings started, the bank required so many repairs to the house that most of Roland's profit was absorbed in repairs. After the repairs were completed, Rona told Roland she did not want me at the closing. Naturally, Roland was going to comply and I was considering it. Until one day the potential buyers came by the house. They wanted to bid on some of the antique items Roland owned. As we talked, I mentioned I would not be at the closing. I explained the marriage and housing situations. They disagreed and encouraged me to come to the closing. They said, "You are Roland's wife. You are one. You need to be there to make your statement, without saying a word." So I decided to attend. They were right. Without saying a word, I became a thorn in Rona's side. It made my day. I could not have made a better decision. Throughout the closing, she made sarcastic remarks with smirks across her lips. I returned her grace by looking coldly at her, extending smirks of my own.

Leaving that house meant leaving Rona's control and Roland's past behind. Viola and her children were gone. With excitement I thought, *Surely, things could only get better.* Since we had not found a place, I thought I would get a temporary relief from Claudia and James. That did not happen. Tina went to live with Roxie. Joni went to live with Esther. Robert went to his mom's. My friends, Charlene and Roger, allowed Roland and I to move into their basement. Even while in their basement, Rona made sure Claudia and James called constantly, made constant demands, and took Roland away from me often.

We finally settled on a house. The week of our closing, Rona sent Claudia and James for the weekend. My girls were still at Roxie's and Esther's houses. Roland and I were barely in the house. We didn't have one single night alone to celebrate. We were sleeping on the floor. Our furniture was still in storage. Rona made sure we did not have time to ourselves. When the children were not at the house, they were constantly calling. When they called, I usually answered. Without even a "hello," Claudia would say, "I want to speak to my daddy." Each time I spoke to Roland about the rude and disrespectful behavior, he got angry. He said I was always looking for fault in his children. He failed to realize I didn't have to search. It was consistently slapping me in the face.

Finally, we settled into our new home. The light at the end of the tunnel gave me hope. I thought things would improve. Wrong again! Rona kept James and gave Roland full custody of Claudia. She was coming to live with us. Their custody battle was my lifetime war. Claudia used the custody dispute to manipulate them. When she was angry with Roland, she returned to live with Rona. When she became dissatisfied with Rona, she returned to Roland. If she was upset with both of them, she went around the corner and stayed with Jezzy. When she realized she could not manipulate me, she would go to Jezzy's house and have Roland come with her.

I knew Roland would do whatever she wanted. I was tired of my home being subjected to the different elements from the other houses. I told him all of our homes were governed differently. Claudia was transporting evil spirits from those mixed settings into our home. He usually got angry. Then he and Claudia would spend their days and evenings at Jezzy's house until bedtime. They came home when they were good and ready. Sometimes, Claudia stayed overnight. Roland offered no explanations for his actions and I didn't request any.

There was no limit to the evil that possessed Claudia's soul. It was her innate nature to be contrary. One day I came home from work to find Claudia and five other girls in our house. They were not just visiting. They were in the kitchen cooking. I became ballistic. I reminded her that the rule governing the house was that no one comes into this house when Roland or I was not at home. I also told her no one enters my kitchen to cook and mess over food we had to eat. The kitchen was a mess. I told them to clean up their mess and leave. Fortunately, she left with them. She went around the corner to Jezzy's house to wait for her dad. Again, Roland felt I was wrong. I was just picking on his daughter. I learned all too quickly that if Claudia didn't want to, there was no rule or law anywhere she had to obey. Everyone needed to know she was the exception to every rule, no matter whose or where the rule applied, especially if you wanted Roland's acceptance.

Claudia was allowed to curse me and call me a black b---- from Baltimore. She was allowed to use black markers and write messages to my girls and me on boxes of cereal. The last one was in all caps, "DO NOT TOUCH. DO NOT

PUT YOUR HANDS ON IT. IT DOESN'T BELONG TO YOU." She did those things because Roland began buying foods that were solely for her. During the good times, and there were some, whenever Roland and I were in our bedroom laughing and having fun, Claudia stood outside the door calling him, demanding he come to her. Yes, he consistently obeyed. At a point, I thought I was becoming paranoid until Roxie witnessed it.

One day, Claudia was really beside herself. As we watched her behavior and interaction with Roland, we were appalled. We decided to give her a taste of her own medicine. We cornered her and begin to repeatedly say, "You know, everybody is talking about you. Nobody likes you. They are saying things we can't even repeat. They said you think you are cute, but you are not." Her evil attitude instantly changed. A look of disbelief came across her face. Roxie and I were making those things up. We hadn't heard anything. We wanted to penetrate the evil that was in her. Sad to say, next to Rona at the closing, this was one of the best moments of my married life with Roland.

Household chores were to be shared by all the children. They were assigned on a rotational basis. Each time it was Claudia's turn to do the chores, Roland did them for her. If she was assigned to wash dishes, Roland washed them. If she was assigned to vacuum the carpet, Roland vacuumed. If she was assigned to clean the bathroom, Roland did that too. He even washed the tub and ran her bath water the nights she bathed rather than showered. It was a luxury I no longer received. Every exception was hers. This left her clueless about cleanliness. She didn't know how to and didn't care to learn, and forcing her was not an option. She kept her hair looking good, but she was a nasty child. Periodically, there was a lingering stench in the bathroom. At first I couldn't tell where it was coming from. The odor was stifling. Finally, I sniffed until I figured out it came from Claudia's washcloth hanging above the heat vent. So, when our small bathroom got hot, the smell intensified. I spoke to Claudia regarding my discovery. She smelled her washcloth and acknowledged that the offensive smell came from it. I explained the necessary steps of personal hygiene. She listened and took immediate corrective action; unfortunately, it didn't last very long.

This family I had married into was unique. It was one-of-a-kind! I used to welcome the challenge of getting to know people. However, this family added a new meaning to "getting to know you." They turned joyous events of life into alarming pain.

Esther was a Christian and a prayer intercessor. However, if she wasn't pleased with you, you knew it without her saying a word directly to you. When we were not in her good graces, she would call the house and if one of my girls answered she would say, "This is Sister Peterson, is my brother there?" If I answered she would say, "May I speak to my brother?" If we were in her good graces, my girls would hear, "This is Auntie Esther, is Roland there?" I would hear, "Hi Squirt, is your husband home?" I have been accused of being militant-at-heart. I don't agree or disagree. However, what I would say to this is, count your losses and move on! I told my daughters they should always call her Sister Peterson. I told them, "When we are in her good graces again, I don't want you to go back to Auntie Esther." Children are forgiving. They could not do it. They continued calling her Auntie Esther. I'm glad God covered my girls' heart against my wrong, revengeful teaching.

Then there were the family gatherings. Oh, how I hated those gatherings. Not because I didn't feel welcome but because I felt disrespected. The family had a saying regarding the ex-wives, "We didn't divorce you, so you are still a part of the family." During the family gatherings, all the wives, ex-wives, girlfriends, ex-girlfriends—everybody—were invited. It was one big "happy" family affair. It was distasteful, but who was I to complain? After all, Roland's family was the only family I had in Illinois. Esther's husband, who supposedly was not a Christian, was the only one sensitive to me. He would call me before a gathering to find out whether I'd planned to attend. If I was going to attend, he told me who to expect, whether they were invited or not. He also said he wanted to make sure I knew where he stood. If I was not going to attend, he would invite all the exes.

At the end of each gathering, I questioned why I exposed myself to this unnecessary humiliation. Every time I thought I had it figured out, things backfired. Little by little, I stopped attending. I didn't need or want the crumbs that were being offered to me. I opted to enjoy my daughters and have fun with my friends.

The family gatherings were just the beginning of the torment I would face within the next few years.

# 20
# Well, Shut My Mouth

I knew the solution. Why wasn't I applying it? I should have shut my mouth and prayed; but no, I had to express myself! No one was going to think I was stupid. I knew what was going on. Roland was going to know that I knew, because I was going to tell him.

I didn't have a clue regarding this family I was marrying into. I didn't know Roland had not prepared his family, children, ex-wives, or ex-girlfriend for our marriage. I did all I knew to prepare my girls for our new life. It was reasonable for me to believe Roland had done the same. My move to Illinois was blind trust. I had an immediate rude awakening. I had never in my entire life met children like Roland's children, children so filled with hatred, selfishness, and jealousy. They routinely cursed me. They cursed my children. They refused to do anything I asked. They were too good to help with housework. They made selfish demands and demanded compliance. They did not respect my property. They did not respect my right to privacy. The list goes on. However, the bottom line rested with how I dealt with it. I admit I did not deal with these things lovingly.

It was never spoken, but it was understood that no rules

were established for Roland's children. No expectations were made of them. His children were not required to respect me as an adult, much less as his wife. How could I have been so blind? So deceived? Regardless of how I got here or what I found after I arrived, I could have handled it differently. All I wanted was some changes. I regularly reminded Roland of the things his children did and did not do. I regularly reminded him of not requiring them to respect me. I reminded him of the things they said and did not say. Justifiably, I only gave reminders when incidents occurred. My method did not work to my advantage. It made him judge me more harshly. He was absolutely convinced my complaints meant I hated his children. I tried convincing him that I did not hate his children. However, I disagreed with most of their actions and attitudes. My upbringing wouldn't allow me to accept certain things from children, no matter whose they were. There were things we were not allowed to do or say and ways we were not allowed to act as children. I applied the same principles when raising my children. However, there were no rules that governed Roland's children.

Almost everything I said to him was twisted to mean something I had not said or meant. I should have learned that words could not solve this situation. Nevertheless, I tried daily to get Roland to understand my emotional, physical, and spiritual needs. He was an introvert. It was hard for him to communicate. I was a communicator, but I apparently talked too much because it seemed he never understood what I was saying. I never stopped trying to explain myself, hoping to be understood. I talked and talked and talked! I often asked myself, "Why didn't I just leave it alone? Why didn't I pray? Why didn't I shut my mouth?"

I knew timing could have made the difference between a peaceful environment and a hostile one. I also knew there was a particular manner in which I should have approached him, least of all when I was upset. Nevertheless, I did it anyway. I was driven by the pain in my heart. I had to be heard. Nothing else seemed to matter. I didn't shut my mouth.

# 21
# That's My Husband

That's my husband! The Lord told me he is my husband. Nothing else matters. The Lord said he is my husband and I'm going to marry him." Those were the words of Jezzy, my husband's ex-girlfriend.

On January 10, I got married and then I woke up. From the first day of our marriage, my husband never closed the doors to his past relationships. His ex-girlfriend manipulated him. She used his children to convince him of her undying love and devotion. She bought his children gifts to prove her love for them. Every day after work, Roland stopped at Esther's house, then Jezzy's house, where his children conveniently congregated, and finally came home. When he arrived home, I was supposed to be happy he came. Of course, he and his actions were always innocent to him! I was just too suspicious. Nothing was going on. He simply went to Jezzy's house to get some peace and rest. It was a clear case of mistrust on my part. It was rumored that Jezzy practiced witchcraft. Roland was playing with raging fire.

He could never say he was totally tricked into anything. His eyes were wide opened. When they were not opened, I enlightened him. Esther even told him Jezzy said she loved him so much she would go to hell for him. Everything that occurred, he encouraged and allowed. When I told him he was being manipulated, I was always wrong. When I told him he was being used, I was always stupid. When I told him it was a plot, I was so mistrusting.

I witnessed lust in a way I had not seen before. Jezzy was determined to get my husband. It didn't matter the cost. She was willing to do whatever was necessary. She gladly waited as long as necessary. She used whomever and trampled on whatever was in her path. My neighbors told me every day they witnessed her coming to our house and walking around it, and afterwards just standing in front of it. They didn't know what she was doing, but she did it every day. She even used one of the teenagers from the church who frequented our house to bring news back to her. She would have the teenager call our house and ask for Mr. Roland. When he came to the telephone, Jezzy would come on. When I discovered the game, I told the child's mother. The child was not allowed in our home ever again. It seemed Jezzy would have sold her soul to the devil to get Roland. Nothing mattered but to get him and make him hers. When Esther told me she had said, "I'll go to hell for him." I could only reply, "It's sad, but that just might be the fate that awaits her."

The way Roland dealt with relationships was frightening. His actions could have been scripted for *The Twilight Zone*. They were scary. Yet, he blamed me for his lack of peace.

Jezzy's lust for my husband increased so much, that I wrote her a letter. Just in case she said I wrote things I did not, I kept a copy of the letter. It simply stated she needed to release her obsession for my husband and move on with her life. She didn't have to bypass me at church as if I was her enemy. I said Roland made a choice that she must learn to live with it.

# 22
# Flashback

We've all had good dreams, bad dreams, and nightmares. Likewise, we have good or bad memories and flashbacks. The flashbacks bring to mind things we thought we had forgotten. Flashbacks can cause us to react in a manner that surprises us.

I lived with the shame of Roland's constant visits to Jezzy's house. I was mocked for enduring the shame.

Roland was a mechanic. He used his skills to earn extra money when he was off duty. He had regular customers whose cars he repaired. Yet, he refused to repair my car. He changed my oil twice and my brake pads once during our five-year, nine-month marriage. When I needed a repair, he told me to take it to the dealership. Since I had an extended warranty, I did. Nevertheless, when Roland worked on his customers' cars, he always used Jezzy's garage during the winter. He said Jezzy told him he could use her garage. He justified using her garage because hers was heated and ours was not. Our garage was electrically wired and a heater could have been used. This continued year after year.

Jezzy's house was a haven for his children, an escape from their wicked old stepmother. Roland constantly reminded me that Jezzy loved his children and wanted them around. If she loved his children, she cared about him. Likewise, his indictment against me was, I hated his children; therefore, I couldn't love him. Allegedly, his frequent visits to her house were to visit or pick up his children.

Jezzy's house was en route to our house. I couldn't begin to count the number of days I passed Jezzy's house and Roland's car was parked out front. Periodically, he was walking in or out of her house as I passed. Each time I was gripped by rage and helplessness. The pain I experienced was almost unbearable. After church on Sundays was no different. By the time I'd come from church to Dooley Avenue, Roland was already there, walking towards the front door. It was as if that was his home. Sometimes, when he was walking out, I would slow down and stare at him, eye-to-eye, thinking it would make him feel guilty. I'd hoped the guilt would make him change, but he was not moved by my stares. Instead, he stared back at me, in an almost daring manner.

Jezzy's house was also used as an escape for Roland, a place where fantasy replaced reality. It was a place where he could go and find "so-called" peace, a place where he could lay his head and rest. One night during a heated argument, Roland yelled, "You want to know why I go to Jezzy's house? I go there because I can find peace there. There is no peace in this house. I go there and lie down and take a nap. I don't care what you think, but nothing is going on."

One night my mind was tortured by Roland's absence. I suspected where he was. I got into my car to drive around the block. However, as I began to make a U-turn in the alleyway, my headlights flashed on a car, which looked like Roland's. It was parked in the alley behind Jezzy's garage. I drove through the alley to confirm that it was Roland's car. I got out of my car and checked the doors on Roland's car.

They were locked. I peeped into the garage, but it was dark. I climbed into my car to get a piece of paper and a pen. I wrote a note: *I hope you and your whore are having a good time.* I signed it, placed it under his windshield wipers, and drove away. When I returned home I was sick. I was sick and in severe pain. I didn't know what I would do. I figured the next move was his, since I left the note.

When Roland came home he said nothing. I waited until the next day, and he still didn't say anything. I was on the verge of losing my mind. I needed to yell and scream. I needed a fight. I waited as long as I could. Finally, I said, "Did you get my note the other night?" He questioned what note. I told him I'd left a note on his car when it was parked behind his whore's house, while they were inside screwing each other. I could have died when he said there was no note on his car. I was stripped of all satisfaction. The discussion elevated into another useless fight.

This was only one of many episodes. However, this was the one that caused the flashback. It occurred a few years after the incident. One day the memory of his car in the alley tormented me. It was a bright sunny day that turned instantly black for me. I drove to the same alley to make a U-turn. Suddenly, the rage of Roland's car parked behind Jezzy's garage overwhelmed me. It was as if I were looking at it. I relived every fact and every emotion. I had transformed from the present to the past without realizing it. As the emotions of the incident gripped me, I began to cry. I was crying because I wanted revenge badly. I felt an inner rage, which made me feel like I could change how I handled the situation. I should not have written a note. I should have busted his windows, slashed his tires, or even set his car afire. I could hear the glass shattering, the tires deflating, the flames roaring. I felt the muscles in my body tightened. At that very moment, I could have done those things without hesitation. I could have gotten even and settled the score. I began sobbing harder. I wanted to kick myself for not having that plan at the time. Surely, if Roland's car was anywhere in my vicinity during the time of the flashback, I don't doubt what my actions would have been. Thank God it was only a flashback.

# 23

# Oops, You've Got the Wrong Family

Nothing can be compared to a family vacation—unless, of course, it's with the wrong family. One day like many others, I called Roland at work. The voice on the other end of the telephone said, "Oh, he's on vacation for two weeks. He left on Monday and is not scheduled to return until such and such date." Humiliated, I choked as I said, "Thank you" and hung up. Every year after the first year of marriage, he secretly planned his vacations. I didn't know when he scheduled it or what he'd planned to do. Considering a family vacation was completely out of the question. However, this time was worse than all the others.

In the sixth month of our marriage, we planned our first blended-family vacation. Roland, my two girls, his youngest son and daughter, and I were headed to South Carolina so that he could meet my family. We would return by way of Alabama to attend his family reunion. I'd hoped driving would enable our children to become acquainted so we could function smoothly as a family.

The car was overloaded with luggage. We had to place stuff inside the car—I'm talking a fully packed car. The stuff inside was placed in the front with Roland and me. There were six of us in a car made to transport five people comfortably. We knew we had to adjust. The adjustment was difficult because his children wanted to have everything their way. Even in that constraining situation, Roland made sure his children had their way. Four children in the back seat automatically meant that bodies would touch. However, if his children didn't want to be touched, they were not going to be touched. If they wanted to lie down and sleep comfortably, they had the right to do so. No questions asked. Claudia told Roland that James should sit in the front with us. I responded there was no room. A few minutes later James asked to sit in the front and I said, "All of you will sit back there because the bags are up here. There's no room." My response was disregarded. Roland told James to come and sit in the front. All the fussing, fighting, and complaining came from his children. My girls seemingly accepted things as they were. The entire trip revolved around what his children wanted—when they wanted it, how they wanted it, and where they wanted it. We had no voice. It was a family vacation from hell.

When we reached South Carolina, my girls and I dreaded the thought of getting back into the car with them. When we left South Carolina en route to Alabama, hell enlarged itself. The hotel room arrangements were as Claudia wanted them. The food we bought for the room was what Claudia wanted. There was one thing after the other. Nothing ceased. When Claudia and James were not making demands on Roland, he was calling Illinois every night talking with Viola. When we went shopping, it was not whether I wanted anything. It was what should he buy and take to Viola. It was a "living hell." Despite the misery, when the vacation was over, I still hoped for a better day. I convinced myself it wouldn't be this way the next time. Since this was our first blended-family activity, difficulties should have been expected. Expected or not, I failed the test. While I was contemplating a better "next time," Roland had made a different decision. He told me he would never again go on vacation with my girls and me. He said the best thing for us to do was take our children on separate vacations.

I did not accept Roland's suggestion. I concluded he was angry and did not mean it. I could not believe he would not change his mind. I had never met anyone so stubborn and spiteful. Each year that followed, I asked him, "Roland, when are you taking your vacation?" Every year his response was the same, "Why do you need to know? I don't know when I'll take it. I may even put in to be paid for my time, rather than take off." I said I needed to know so I could request the same dates from my job. I soon realized his decision was made in blood. From that day, he kept his word. We were  never a part of his family vacations. Roland, his children, his sister, and her family would go on vacations together. He and his family would plan and attend their family reunion in Alabama. It was the best kept secret, until the day of their departure. My girls and I were outcasts. We were not invited or welcomed to the family reunions. Nevertheless, the way I found out Roland was on vacation was my call to his job.

This time was different. I remember it as if it were yesterday. It was a Friday. I came home, and there was a van parked in front of our house. I went inside. Roland had just finished packing. I asked him where was he going. He said he and his children were going to their family reunion. I asked whose van was parked out front. He said it was a rental. I thought to myself, *A rental? We never have money to do anything I need to do around the house. Yet, he has money to rent a van? I asked him why he was renting a van. Couldn't he and his children fit into his car?* He said he rented a van because he wanted to. The defensive response caused me to ask another question. I said, "Roland, are you and your children going alone?" Further irritated, he said, "Raven, I'm going to my family reunion and I'm only taking my children." Normally, that would have been enough if the irritation level was not so high. So I dared to ask again, more specifically. "Roland, which ones of your children are you taking?" He responded, "Claudia and James." Unbelief controlled my heart. It just didn't seem logical. My heart pained within me. Yet, I began to get dressed to go to church. My husband was on his way to his family reunion. I accidentally found out, but I still didn't know for how long. No one in the family ever mentioned it to us. As I left for church, he left to pick up his children.

On the way, the pain in my heart became so severe that tears began to gush down my face. Years earlier, I had promised God I would be a vessel of strength and love for His name. I promised Him no matter what it took, I wanted Him to receive glory from my life. I told Him if I had to cry about any situation, trial, tribulation, or temptation, I would cry out to Him. He was the only one who could help me. I would not let people or the church see me disheartened or discouraged. I wanted to represent Him in the fullness of His character. The weight of the situation was too heavy. I decided to go back home for God to minister to me.

As I pulled up in front of the house, I noticed Roland had returned also. He had forgotten something. In the meantime, God allowed me to return home. In front of my house was the van. It was filled with Roland and Jezzy's children. Despite the situations I had endured with Roland, one thing I held dear was that I thought he would always be truthful. I figured he was too stubborn and mean to resort to lying. I learned if a person's heart is not truthful to a relationship, their lips would never speak total truth. God unveiled Roland before my eyes. He was a bold liar. I trusted Roland, but I didn't trust Jezzy. When I questioned him about things, it was usually because of uncertainties I felt within. Most times, he would twist my question to say I was implying that he was sleeping around. Other times, he would respond so frankly and curt with answers he knew would result in an argument. Because of his frankness I gave trust. Now it appeared he told me just enough truth to keep me from asking more questions. This situation literally messed my mind up.

I parked the car and got out. My legs were weakening as I walked toward the house. I felt his and Jezzy's children watching me. I heard their voices with some light laughter. I couldn't let them see me collapse. I prayed, "Dear God, let me make it inside the house." He strengthened my legs. I walked up the walkway, then the steps, and finally into the house. I made it. Now I had to be strong as I confronted the man I had entrusted my love to. I could no longer hold back the tears. I was angry. My frustrations came to the forefront. I walked into our bedroom crying, "Roland, how could you? You out right lied. What do you mean by this? Roland, I specifically asked you about the children? Why would you disgrace me like this?" Finally he responded sarcastically with, "There's nothing going on and there's nothing wrong with this. I'm sorry I disgraced you. Why don't you go and find you somebody that doesn't disgrace you." With that he walked out the door, slammed it, and left.

They returned and, as in almost every situation involving his children and his family, all hell burst loose. Days later he mentioned they had videotaped the family reunion. I didn't even realize I had made a mental note of his statement. Until one day, I noticed a videotape in his cabinet over the headboard. I thought it was the family reunion video. I took it out, pulled some of the film off of the tape, and tore it. I damaged it so it could never be viewed. Weeks later when he noticed the damaged tape, he said it belonged to a guy at work. It was the taping of a ball game. He was crushed that it was damaged. He wouldn't be able to explain to the guy how it happened. I expressed my sympathy, but I did not confess I had destroyed the tape. Realizing my mission had not been accomplished, I continued searching for the family reunion tape, to no avail. So I gave up.

# 24
# The "Hit" Team

The doorbell rang and Roland answered it. I heard Viola's voice, "Where is that bitch? I'm coming to kick her ass. I have my backup with me." Her mob squad was her mom, Patsy, Claudia's mom, Rona, her brother, Rufus, and Jezzy. They all came to settle a score, to finish a fight I didn't even know I was in.

Roland's children, ex-wives, and ex-girlfriend were manipulative users. He was available and had no backbone, so they used him. He gave a new meaning to the word "doormat." He was a weakling with them and his family. However, he never had a problem telling me no. Their using him did not directly affect my girls or me. Indirectly it destroyed all of our dreams for a future. Early in our marriage, he made it very clear. He said, "I have my obligations. You have yours. The ones we share will be split fifty-fifty."

The mob squad came because earlier that night I refused to hang up my telephone, so Viola could charge a long distance call to our number. I was on the telephone long distance, talking with my attorney regarding child support. The second line rang and I answered. The operator informed me that Viola wanted to charge a collect long-distance call to our number. The operator wanted to know would I accept the charges. I told the operator Viola would have to call back to speak with her dad. I would not accept the charges. His children would make calls around the city and within the state, and charge them to our telephone number. They knew their dad would pay for it. Yet, when I wanted to do something substantial toward building our future, it was always, "We can't afford it." Those four words took me to a realm of faith I may have never known. I placed my dreams and visions in God's hand and trusted Him for the fulfillment of them.

Even after Viola announced why she had come, Roland still allowed her and her brother, Rufus, to come into our home. I walked out of the bedroom into the dining room where they were waiting. She placed her face directly in front of mine and began to curse me. She called me every unspeakable name. I was a black bitch. I was a MF, a CS, and things even sailors wouldn't dare utter. While she was cursing me, Rufus leaned toward me in a threatening manner, as if he was daring me to make a sudden move. Roland was standing there, not saying a word. I told Viola I didn't allow her to charge that call and neither will she be able to charge any future calls. She started to swear at me again. Then she added, "This is my dad's house. You had nothing when you came. You still don't have anything." I thought, *Such delusion.* Everything we owned I bought or brought with me.

When I decided enough was enough, I turned to Roland and very softly through clenched teeth said, "You'd better get this thing out of my house." He answered, "Don't call my daughter a thing." While he spoke, Rufus moved in closer to hover over me. I became enraged and said, "You stood silently while this thing called me every foul name she could think of. Yet, you forbid me to call her a thing?" I choked as some of the swear words spoken by Viola to me threatened to spew out to him. All respect for him left. I clenched my teeth even tighter and said, "If you know like I know, you'd better get her out of here." I threatened to call the police. She was not moved by my threat because she had witnessed her dad backing her up; therefore, she knew she could do what she pleased.

She got increasingly louder. "This is my dad's house. I'll stay here as long as I like. If you think it's yours, I'll drive by and bust out all the windows in the house and your car." Then as proud as a peacock, she walked into the kitchen and sat down at the nook. We all followed her. My man, my husband, began washing the dishes. She began speaking again, "See. You don't deserve my dad. He's too good for you. Why is he washing dishes instead of you?"

I couldn't take anymore. I allowed myself to sink to her level. I was wearing a nightshirt. I pointed my buttocks toward her face and said, "You are beneath even this portion of me. Have you forgotten that I lived with you? Surely, you don't think I've forgotten the roaches, the unwashed dishes, the filthy refrigerator, the baby diapers, the feces and the food on the floors, in the beds, on the bathtub, everywhere." Pointing my finger at her, I continued, "Please don't forget, I know you. You are filth, filth of the worst kind. The average alley dog is better than you. Let's get to the real deal. You don't want your dad to take care of me because he's taking care of you and all of your bastards, five babies with five different fathers. Let's not forget the one you supposedly rolled over on and accidentally killed. Yea! Right! Some accident! I'll bet! You are simply filth. I will sit here as long as you." I was out of control and there was no stopping me at that point. Then I sat my buttocks on the table directly in front of her face. I began talking aloud in the air regarding things she could relate to—things such as poverty, filth, and lewdness. I stayed there until her mob squad honked for her and Rufus to come out.

The next day after work, I went to the Evanston Police Department. I took out a restraining order against Viola. My complaint stated she had threatened my life, my girls, my home, and my car. I surmised that whatever damages she would have done to the home and car would have affected us. This was my complaint to the police officer. When I finished my account of what had happened, the police officer was irate. He asked, "What are you married to?" With double assurance he said, "If she comes anywhere near you, your children, or anywhere you don't want her to be, call me personally. I'll be there. Doesn't your husband realize his children will be grown and gone. It will be just the two of you?" I said, "My husband said his children will always be his children, but he has no guarantee I will always be his wife." He responded, "The brother has problems." He gave me my case number, my incident reporting card, and his direct telephone number.

I told Roland I had filed a complaint and what the police officer said. I told him never again will his children walk into my house and disrespect me like that. I continued, "I'll see you and all of them under the jail. Even if I have to take it to the Supreme Court." I assured him I was not making idle threats. I told him to tell Viola if any damage occurred to my property, whether she did it or not, I will report it as a result of her threat. I warned him to keep her away. He must have warned her because I never had any more problems out of her.

I would love to say this was the end of the story, but it wasn't.

After the dust settled, I felt terrible about my behavior. God was requiring me to apologize, and I was fighting it. I told God it was unfair. I thought, this must be a joke. I even told God that our versions of what happened apparently did not agree. He said, "Apologize." I made one last attempt to get out of apologizing. I said, "Lord, I would apologize if I knew how to get in touch with her, but I don't." He said get a card and put it in writing. I said, "Lord, you can't be serious. Spend money and apologize too? This is unfair." Yet, I knew I had to obey. I asked Him, "Exactly what am I apologizing for?" He said, "For what you said, not what you did." I asked Him to explain so I could understand. He said, "You had a right to protect your home and to stand for what was acceptable in your home. However, you had no right dragging her nose through the mud of her sinful life. For that, you must repent." Finally, with the enlightenment, I agreed but still had questions. I said, "Okay Lord. I know You are right, but I need an answer. Please tell me why I must always be the one to repent, no matter who else is involved?" Softly and gently He asked, "Do you prefer being a bastard?" I needed no further words from the Lord.

I apologized to Roland. I made sure he understood it was for the things I said. I told him if I had to do it over, I would still defend my home. I never told him the Lord required me to apologize to his daughter also. I bought the card. Wrote in it and carried it around with me. My intentions were to give it to Esther to give to Viola. That was not God's plan, because it never worked out.

One day, unexpectedly, I ran into Rufus. It was the first time I had seen him since he came to our house as Viola's backup. I believe God wanted to free him also. When I saw him and he saw me, he held his head down and sheepishly looked away. I greeted him and asked, "Would you please give this to your sister for me?" He said, "Yes." I thanked him, told him to take care of himself, and said good-bye. I believe he sensed I held no grudge against him. Even though God did not require me to apologize to him, there was a need to forgive and love him. God was there to ensure I did both.

# 25
# The Other Foot

Let the rehearsal begin! The script goes something like this, "IF THE SHOE WAS ON THE OTHER FOOT, WHAT WOULD YOU SAY THEN?" Perfect! With the right amount of inflections and emphasis. It was not a dress rehearsal for a role. It was the theme of my marital bliss. Those words were spoken in almost every controversial situation. I heard them so much, I could predetermine when Roland would interject them. Whenever I approached Roland regarding something that was bothering me, the response was usually the same, "IF THE SHOE WAS ON THE OTHER FOOT, WHAT WOULD YOU SAY THEN?" In retrospect, I should have responded at least once. It would sound like this; "I'll be glad to have the shoe on the other foot. Maybe then things will work to my advantage."

This statement was used when he was wrong and would not admit it, correct it, or deal with it. I often wondered if he understood his own question. Thoughts and images bombarded my mind. Did he really want to experience the hell I was living? Did he really want to receive from me what I had been dealing with from him? Roland didn't have the stamina or the commitment to walk in my shoes.

Regardless of the situation, resolutions were seldom reached because understanding was rarely present. Since the shoe was where it was, I needed a solution from him. I desperately needed one, and he offered none. The two hearts seldom met. Compassion and sensitivity were not present. There were two problems. Roland did not know how to deal with controversies; yet, I believed the more I talked, the better my chances were of correcting things. I had become a nagging wife. It was apparent my nagging was an irritant. I analyzed. I scrutinized. I compiled. I finalized. All for what? To make my point!

Things were bleak. I knew I couldn't depend on Roland for my well-being. Our marriage offered no security. Our future was dim. Roland did not know how to make decisions and stand behind them. He refused to make plans for our future. He refused to establish priorities. Choosing me over his family, his children, ex-wives, ex-girlfriend, and side jobs was out of the question. I was a bottom-line person. If a decision was needed, I was like, "Let's make it and move on." When neither of our responses satisfied the other, we were left frustrated and trapped. What if the shoe was on the other foot? Would I have been given so many opportunities to make things right? Would I have been loved and forgiven? What if I had done or allowed some of the things he did? Would he want to be associated with me? There were times when I desired answers to these questions. Yet, at other times, it really didn't matter. I know Roland's ego would not have endured a "shoe-swapping" life with me. What really mattered was my decision to endure unto the end. Not that I was always right, but rather, I consistently tried to make things right.

Our marriage reached a plateau where we simply tolerated each other. Oddly, we both knew that we still loved each other. My focus and fight became, "I must please

God." It only mattered that I fulfilled my promise to God. He was my only hope. When we got married, I promised God it didn't matter what Roland did or did not do, I would not divorce him. The devil had destroyed my first marriage. I was determined he would not succeed again. My marriage became a fight unto the death. After so many days, weeks, months, and years of heartaches and pain, I thought I would die. What the marriage didn't kill, the stones people threw at me would.

Desperation engulfed me. I suffered many regrets. I should have kept silent and let God fight my battles. I didn't have the right skills for this battle. Each day I lost more ground in my marriage. I found myself falling on my face in slow motion.

Our marriage continued, but I never had the opportunity to wear "the shoe." I forgave when forgiveness was not sought. I held on when everything had vanished. I continued to love when I was no longer being loved. I didn't get a divorce, even though I desperately wanted to.

# 26
# Please Help Me, I'm Falling

What just happened? My world was rapidly falling apart. I was helpless and could not stop it. For weeks, I noticed excitement between Roland and Claudia. The source of their happiness was unknown to me. I tried finding out what was going on but couldn't. Then one day things began to unveil. It began with a telephone call from Roland's former brother-in-law. He was calling to find out the time Roland, Rona, and Claudia were arriving for his wedding. The wedding was the upcoming weekend. I had no idea what he was talking about. I began to ask questions. I was told Roland had planned a weekend trip with Rona and Claudia. The caller needed their arrival information to set up their room accommodations.

When Roland came home he began packing. I acted as if I knew nothing. I asked, "Where are you going?" He responded, "I'm going to Rona brother's wedding." I asked, "Is anyone else going with you?" Without hesitation he answered, "Yes. Rona and Claudia. We'll probably be back on Monday."

I became hysterical and started screaming. "You are doing what? You are going where? With whom? Who are you married to? I am your wife, and you're going away for a weekend with your ex-wife. What is this, *one big happy family reunion?* What am I? Am I stupid or something? If you are going anywhere, to any wedding, it should be with me." To this he simply replied, "You were not invited!" Those were the only words he spoke during my entire screaming episode. I was furious. I was not only trampled on, but my feelings were being ignored.

The flames were hot as I yelled, "You are not going anywhere." He responded, "I'll go any damn place I please." He continued packing. As he placed his clothes in the luggage, I pulled them out. This continued until physical violence erupted. He pushed me. I pushed him. He hit me. I ripped his clothes. He punched me in my face. I scratched him in his face. While striking me in my face, he repeatedly yelled, "You black bitch. You black bitch." I covered my face. So he began kicking me on the leg. Still yelling, "You black bitch. You black bitch." The pain from his kicks made me realize my leg was bleeding. He wore steel pointed boots. I pulled myself up from the floor and ran from the room crying uncontrollably. The mental and physical pain was too much. I did not understand what was happening to me. I needed help, and God was my only hope. I prayed. The only thing that seemed real was my pain, the shame, and the sting from my tears.

I attended to my wounds and returned to the bedroom. Roland had finished packing. He was sitting on the side of the bed. I approached him and asked, "Roland, what's going on? Why do we have to live this way?" He pushed me away and responded, "We don't. As far as I'm concerned, we are not married." With those words, he took off his wedding ring, threw it at me, and yelled, "Don't you ever speak to me as your husband again." I cried while reaching out to him. I begged him not to do this. He stood like a brick wall before me, gave me a long cold look, and walked away. For hours I sat paralyzed.

My world had crumbled. I felt I was losing my mind. My body began to shake and jerk. I moaned and cried helplessly. I covered my mouth so my girls wouldn't hear me. I paced the floor, going from room to room. Oh, the pain. If only someone would stop the pain. I began rocking my body. I was inches from mental collapse. I held my head between my hands, trying to shut out the tormenting thoughts. I couldn't stop them. I stared into space, only to be faced with real darkness—a darkness that led to total blackness. I could not escape the thoughts in my head. I could not control them. I was held captive. They were coming faster and faster. I could not slow them down. I was not myself. I felt like I was drowning, like I was going down for the last time. I had no one to help me. No one to turn to. I was overwhelmed with shame. The disgrace was more than I could bear. Who could I tell? No one would believe me.

I was the new kid on the block. Everyone thought Roland was the nicest man around. He was well-known, but I was a stranger here. I walked into the kitchen and collapsed at the nook. I covered my face in my hands and cried, "God, how much more? How much more can I endure?" I didn't hear an audible voice. I didn't feel the warmth of an embrace. I lifted my head. Next to me was my little pocket Bible. I had left it there earlier that evening. I picked it up and opened it. My eyes immediately fell upon Hebrews 12. I began to read aloud trying to override my thoughts. I read the first three verses,

*Wherefore seeing we also are compassed about with so great a cloud of witnesses, let us lay aside every weight, and the sin which doth so easily beset us, and let us run with patience the race that is set before us, Looking unto Jesus the author and finisher of our*

*faith; who for the joy that was set before him endured the cross, despising the shame, and is set down at the right hand of the throne of God. For consider him that endured such contradiction of sinners against himself, lest ye be wearied and faint in your minds.*

As I read the Scriptures, the tears came with a greater force. I began speaking aloud, "I will consider Jesus, lest I be weary and faint in my mind." I rehearsed that one sentence over and over. I repeated it from about nine o'clock p.m. until dawn the next morning. It was as if God were saying, "Here is the antidote to losing your mind." It was as if He knew I was losing my grip. It was as if He felt what I was feeling. As I saw daybreak seeping through the kitchen window, I laid my head on the nook table and went to sleep. God had washed my mind. He preserved it from being destroyed. When my heart was overwhelmed, He delivered me out of the snares of insanity.

Later that morning I was awakened as Roland left to pick up Rona and Claudia for their weekend celebration. Roland never wore his wedding ring again. I asked, pleaded, and attempted to give it to him. He always refused.

# 27
# What's Mine Is Hers

I remember the marriage vows. I remember the promises to forsake and cling. But for some reason, I can't recall the portion that included the other woman. Maybe the preacher forgot to tell me of the rights of the other woman: Jezzy, the ex-girlfriend and harlot.

When I moved to Illinois, Roland gave me his car to drive and he took mine. His car was newer than mine, and I traveled further to work than him; therefore, we exchanged cars. I thought it was a loving gesture. Having grown up in South Carolina and relocating to Maryland, I was inexperienced driving on snow and ice. En route to work early one morning, I pressed the brakes while on a bridge and skidded on a sheet of black ice. I ran into the back of a bright yellow Cadillac. The damage was minor. The other driver only desired his car to be repaired. It was a reasonable request, and I agreed. I thanked him and went on my way. The accident was not the problem. The problem developed later. I was shaken up and nervous. Thoughts bombarded my mind. *I wish I had stayed home. What if this messes up his insurance? I should have kept my own car.* Then questions followed such as, *When was the last time I paid my car insurance?* I made several calls and discovered my car insurance had lapsed. I immediately told Roland. I explained to him that this was one of the things that fell through the cracks during my relocation. I assured him I had taken steps to obtain insurance. He became very angry. He accused me of deliberately causing the accident, intentionally allowing my insurance to lapse because he was driving the car. I could not believe it. Through tears I asked, "How can you say such evil things?" At the end of the conversation, we angrily agreed to exchange cars. I gave him his car back and he returned mine.

We were married on paper, but we were not one. We did not have a united front. We were living a marriage lie. Our vows to cleave never manifested themselves. If Roland was not at Jezzy's house, his children were there waiting for him to pick them up. Or one of Jezzy's children was at our house. It was a destructive game they were playing. They had joined forces to get him around the corner to her house. All of them participated.

When Jezzy's child came to our house, I told her to go home. She would just stand, stare at me, and continue her conversation with Roland. She called him "Dad." She would walk by his side while he worked in the yard. She kept him company while he worked on a car. She did anything to be near him. I told him I did not want her at our house. I didn't want her pushing our lawn mower or standing in our garage. It didn't matter what I wanted. He told me he was the only father she had ever known. It was not fair for him to cut ties with her. Before we were married, he told me the child was Jezzy's niece fathered by a Caucasian man. If what he told me was true, I felt there should not have been any such ties. I had no proof, but Jezzy's control over him made me think there was a tie. I thought, maybe he was the father of that child with Jezzy's niece. His skin tone was that of a Caucasian. He has been mistakenly referred to as a Caucasian several times.

In general, people did not know we were husband and wife. Tina's friends stopped by the house one day. When I introduced Roland as my husband, several of them said, "Oh, I know him. I see him all the time at the house on Dooley Avenue. He is always with her children." They were referring to Jezzy and her children. I lived in a constant hell of Roland's past and a poisonous den of his present.

One Saturday morning while doing my housework, I received a telephone call from a major department store. The caller said, "Mrs. Hackman, I was calling to confirm the delivery date for your desk set." I said, "I'm sorry, could you repeat that?" She said, "I'm calling to confirm your delivery date for your desk set." I informed her I had no idea what she was referring to. She responded, "Oops. I think I just spoiled a surprise. Apparently, your husband bought you this beautiful desk set. I need to set up delivery." Truer words could not have been spoken. It was indeed a surprise. Roland had bought Jezzy a desk set. How much further can this thing go? When he came home I asked him about it. He said Jezzy asked him to use his credit card to buy it and she would pay him back. Here we go again … another destructive argument. He was rapidly decreasing as a man in my sight. He was pathetic.

One day my church brother called and said, "Sis, I'm going to tell you what Brother Tom said to me." He said, "I see your sister can't satisfy her man because the word is, he's sleeping around the corner." He was talking about the same brother who later said to Tina, "I don't know why your mom is lying and saying she's going out of town on business. She knows she's going to meet a man, especially since she can't hold the one she's got." I ignored what he said to my brother, but I was not going to allow him to disrespect my daughter, nor allow him to cheapen me in her eyes. At our very next meeting, I confronted him and figuratively ate him alive.

I chewed him up and spit him out. I walked away feeling quite proud. From that moment, he stayed away from my girls and me. A long time passed before he felt safe to even speak to me. It was no more than hello and good-bye.

Years later, I faced a job furlough. If we didn't visit the unemployment office and complete the required forms, we could lose our benefits. It was the last date to file my claim. My car was being repaired at the dealership. I had no transportation and no idea how to use public transportation. Roland and I were still living together, trying to reconcile our differences. I asked to borrow his car to go to the unemployment office. I could drive him to work. He said no and left for work. I was devastated. I couldn't believe what was happening. How much more could God expect me to endure? I sat on the bed to figure out what to do. My thoughts were interrupted by the telephone ringing. It was Gloria Miller. I had worked with her at another office. She said, "Raven, I'm calling to see if you want us to go to the unemployment office together." I said, "Praise the Lord, Gloria. I was just trying to figure out what to do." We agreed on the time she would pick me up. We went and completed our paperwork and returned home. I was extremely grateful to her and God, but the mental torment was still present. Roland wanted me to fail. He wanted me to lose money. He didn't care whether I made it or not. It was evident he had evil in his heart against me.

A short time later, the table turned. In the words of Roland, "The shoe was on the other foot." It was his car and his job. His car was in for repairs, and he needed to get to work. He didn't ask to borrow my car. He'd made plans to walk to work. Instead, I offered my car to him and he accepted. Shortly after that, he wanted to apply for a new position at work. It would be a promotion for him. He wanted to apply for a supervisory position but did not know how to formulate his qualifications in writing. Through questions and answers, I thoroughly completed his application. He got the job and was promoted.

The joke was on me. A few months later, I saw Jezzy driving Roland's car. When I asked Roland about Jezzy driving his car, he said, "She had something to do and asked to borrow it. I said yes, because I did not see anything wrong with her using it." I reminded him of the day I asked to borrow it. I asked when was he going to get that harlot out of our lives. I asked many questions, but he offered no response. Nor was any remorse shown. Roland was "The Man" doing his own thing—no matter how much it hurt the woman he once loved.

# 28
# Chopped Liver

Have you ever felt invisible? You said something everyone pretended not to hear. No one bothered to respond. You question your value. Your existence seems meaningless. You have no bearing on the outcome. Your voice is muted. Someone, somewhere coined the phrase, "What am I, chopped liver?" That's how I felt.

It was a brisk fall night. I arrived home just before dark. The chilly evening air caused me to rush into the house. I raised the temperature on the thermostat. I wanted to be warm and cozy. I quickly undressed. Freeing my body was one of the first things that brought me comfort after a hard day at the office. I slipped into my pajamas and robe, then I slid my feet into my warm fuzzy slippers. Then I was ready to search for dinner. I didn't know what was in the refrigerator, but I was starving. On the way to the kitchen my doorbell rang. Immediately after the doorbell, there came a startling pounding on the door. I was headed towards the door, but when the banging started I rushed to see what was happening.

I turned on the porch light and looked through the peephole. I saw a robust Caucasian man wearing a tan coat and hat. I yelled, "Who is it?" He responded, "I'm from the

Sheriff's Department and I'm looking for Raven Hackman. Are you Raven Hackman?" I could feel and hear my rapid heartbeat. A hundred questions raced through my mind. I was scared. What did I do? Who has falsely accused me of something? Is he here to arrest me? I've never been in jail before. What will happen to me? Other questions ran through my head as I yelled, while trying to unlock the door, "Yes, I'm Raven Hackman."

When I finally opened the door, I was face-to-face with a man with a cast-iron expression. As I looked up at him, he said, "I'm from the Sheriff's Department. I'm here to issue you this subpoena for a divorce hearing. Consider yourself served." He abruptly turned and walked away. I don't know where I got the strength to shut the door. I felt as if I had broken the law or committed an unforgivable sin. Was I a common criminal? Is this the only way Roland could tell me he was filing for a divorce?

I returned to my bedroom with my body shaking uncontrollably. My legs became weak. My steps were short. I felt it would be seconds before I hit the floor. I had to get control of myself. Eating was out of the question. I had lost my appetite.

My life was over and I didn't even see it coming. Hello! *Déja vu! Didn't this happen before ... before you knew what was happening... What did you learn the first time?* I knew Roland had said one hundred and one times, "Maybe we should go our separate ways." I knew his children disliked me. I knew he was a part-time roomer at Esther's and Jezzy's houses. Yet, I had no clue this was coming. Every day things continued as normal—normal being an overstatement! We were still intimate. We were still talking. We were still playing marriage. If he had started his divorce proceedings, the least he could have done was tell me. Was that too much to ask? I had so many unanswered questions. What boggled my mind was Roland knew he had filed for a divorce, yet he continued each day as if everything was the same. Ironically, things did remain the same. Sometimes things were good and other times they were bad, while he acted as if all was well. Maybe it was well for him. His light at the end of the tunnel was now in view. When I spoke with Roland about not having the decency or common courtesy to tell me he had filed for a divorce, he simply said, "It's all for the best."

The following day I was so distraught, I could not go to work. I was awake all night. I slipped into bed early morning and fell asleep. Suddenly, I was awakened by voices. People were walking and talking through my house. They opened my bedroom door. I jumped up screaming. I recognized the real estate agent. I began yelling at her, asking, "What are you doing in my house?" She told me Roland had placed the house on the market. She was showing it to potential buyers. I told her and her clients to get out. I threatened to sue her and her realty company. I reminded her that I had an equal share in the property. She had no right walking into my home without an authorization signed by both parties. She was our realtor when we bought the house. When I spoke with Roland, he said the realtor told him she didn't need my signature. One signature was sufficient to place the house on the market.

Roland was moving quickly. I guess he must have learned from Tony. After all, I talked and told too much. He knew all about my life with Tony. Maybe the reality was my life was cursed. There was no For Sale sign in the yard. I had no way of knowing this was happening. Again, there were no signs that I saw. No changes or indications.

It was one thing for Roland to divorce me. It was a totally different ball game for him to sell the roof from over our heads. This was the thin line between love and hate. He had crossed it. It was time for war. When I saw him, I didn't ask questions. I told him, "Hell will freeze twice before I sign papers to sell this house or to give you a divorce." He tried to belittle me. It really didn't matter. He told me how pathetic I was. Fighting to be married to someone who didn't want me. Nothing mattered. I recognized I was at war, and setting my heart to win. Since his insults didn't unravel me, he said, "Tony was right when he said all you want to do is marry a man and take his house." I told him if that were true, they were only paying me a portion of what I was rightfully entitled to. The hell I'd gone through with them should yield some benefits. He said other cruel things, but he could not disarm me. I refused to be distracted. This was my enemy. I had to fight. The fight was spiritual, mental, legal, and physical, if necessary. My eyes were beginning to open and I was ready for battle.

Like Tony, Roland had secretly plotted and planned his escape by negotiating to buy a new home. Claudia boasted many times that she and her dad were moving to either Sheridan Road or one of the new apartments at the corner of Asbury Avenue near Dempster Street. Years later, after my divorce from Roland, Rona confirmed it. She said Claudia told her the same thing. She only shared that information with me because she needed me to do her a favor.

It was Sunday afternoon, and I'd just arrived home from church. I was home alone. The telephone rang and it was Rona. After she identified herself, she began to apologize. She said she was sorry for what she'd contributed to our marriage ending in divorce. She explained how she manipulated her children by telling them what to do, what to say, and how to act when they came to our house. She said she told them not to do anything I asked them to. At the end of her apology, which I accepted, she made her request. She asked would I allow Claudia to come and live with us. Claudia had been institutionalized because Rona couldn't handle her. They'd tried to get her released, but the judge wouldn't release her unless she had somewhere, other than Rona's home, to go to. Rona asked me if Roland talked to me about it, and I told her no. She said he had been searching for a place, but time was running out, which is why she'd called me. We talked a little while, and I even shared the Word of God with her. I gave her my permission. She thanked me and said good-bye. Like Tony, Roland's secret plans were all to no avail; they failed!

Having no choice in two major events in my life was enough to make me feel insignificant.

# 29
# The Invisible Made Visible

Iknew the day, time, and place where the divorce hearing was scheduled. However, I also knew I believed God. My God was greater than a divorce hearing. He is the Almighty. I couldn't begin to imagine the degree of His power. So was I wrong? Did God fail me?

God spoke several times. I heard Him. Each time the message was clear, so what went wrong? Did I hear what He said or what I wanted to hear?

It started one Sunday morning. My pastor called all married couples whose marriages were being attacked to come for prayer. Men from various directions of the church came. They reached for their wives' hands and went into the prayer line. I waited. I hoped. I prayed. Nothing happened. Roland did not come for me. With all the strength I could muster, I stood. I felt a burning from the eyes focused on me. I walked to Roland, reached for his hand and he refused. I placed my hand in his and he pulled it away. Humiliation burned within me. Questions mocked me. *What are you going to do now? Don't you feel like a fool standing here? What were you thinking?* I had no answers. Yes, I felt foolish. I knew I had to do something. I walked to the prayer line alone. The pain was raw within. Suddenly, I felt someone standing by my side. It was Tina. Thanks to her, I made it through. After church someone who I thought was a friend came to me and said, "I can't believe you made such a fool of yourself." Fool or not, I believed God for victory.

The next occurrence involved Mother Duncan. It was Sunday, three days before our divorce date. As I parked my car, Mother Duncan walked up and said, "Sister Hackman, while I was in prayer this morning the Lord laid you heavily on my heart. I saw you and your husband renewing your vows. When you renew your vows, don't tell anyone in advance, not even Sister Roxie." She was unable to finish. Someone walked up and interrupted us. Mother Duncan had no way of knowing we were scheduled to be divorced the upcoming Wednesday. In my heart I whispered, *Okay Lord, another confirmation. Go ahead. Cause me to rejoice in hope!*

After speaking with Mother Duncan, I entered the church. Another word from the Lord came. Brother Moses was leading praise and worship service. He began to testify. He stated that he and his wife were about to get a divorce. The divorce papers were in the glove compartment of their car. He said God stopped their divorce, which would have been a terrible mistake. He continued with, "There is someone else in here in the same situation. You are about to do the same thing. God is saying, no. Don't do it. Work it out. The devil is tricking you. You think you don't love anymore, that it's not worth it. The devil is a liar. I love my wife. There is not going to be a divorce."

Since his days were spent with his family, that night I asked Roland about Brother Moses' testimony. He said he didn't hear it. I told him the entire testimony. God was giving us a witness, an opportunity to reconsider before our divorce hearing. He showed no interest.

My pastor preached a sermon entitled "What If Things

Don't Change." Too many times in my life that sermon became a reality. Many things did not change. Roland was like a stonewall against all "hope" of resurrecting our marriage. Nevertheless, I never stopped believing God for change—even when change did not come.

Weariness gripped me as the date for the divorce approached. I was troubled and filled with pain. I arrived home safely from work. I was strong. I had been through worse things than this. Surely, I'll handle this like a champ, like everything else. Everyone expects it. However, I was limp and lifeless. I was home alone. I didn't know what to do. My body collapsed to the floor. All strength was gone. I couldn't go on. I felt I had no reason to live. If what awaited me resembled the things I had already experienced, I didn't want anymore.

*What if things change? Maybe there is still hope. What if I quit too soon? There really could be a light at the end of the tunnel. Yet, the tunnel seems much too long!*

While lying on the floor, unable to find answers to the questions in my heart, the telephone rang. It was my girlfriend Charlene Wallace. I had to be strong. I sat up and said, "Oh, hi Charlene. How are you?" She responded, "Rae, how are you doing? The Lord laid you on my heart. He told me to call you and pray for you."

As Charlene began to pray, tears began rolling down my cheeks. I didn't want her to know I was crying. Her prayer pierced my heart so deeply, I began to sob uncontrollably. She continued to pray. I felt a Presence in my room. As the prayers continued, the Presence increased. Softly and tenderly I felt two arms go around me. They began rocking me from side to side, until my head rested on the shoulder. I was being rocked into a calm serene state. I had not experienced this level of serenity for a long time. When it really registered that I was being rocked, I opened my eyes.

I wanted to see who was there. No other visible presence was in that room.

Charlene ended her prayer and began encouraging me. She finished and we said good-bye. I lifted myself from the floor. In my spirit I heard, "go to prayer." I looked at the clock. It was almost time for six o'clock prayer at the church. When I arrived, the members were already praying. I knelt at the altar and softly unveiled my heart to God. As usual, prayer ended with everyone greeting each other. When I arose to my feet, Elder Shann was standing next to me. I could not believe what happened next. Elder Shann wrapped his arms around me. He began rocking me from side to side. In the same manner and rhythm as the Presence in my bedroom. My head rested on his shoulder. I wept. The more I wept, the more he rocked. He did not release me until I was strengthened. My knowledge of God being with me increased. My trust in God was renewed. God used the arms of a brother to reveal Himself to me.

The Church of God In Christ (COGIC) Auxiliaries in Ministry (AIM) Convention! This was new for me. It was my first time attending. I was in Memphis, Tennessee. During the very first worship service a woman walked up to me, reached for my hands, and began ministering to me. She said, "I don't know you from Adam, but I know the voice of God. God said the situation back home that you are concerned about, He is taking care of it even now." She began to pray for me. When she finished, I knew God had spoken. There I was, decked out from head to toe, with a smile on my lips, and confidence on my face, declaring I belong to God! Looking good on the outside. I was wearing a gray dress and shoes, with a matching purse, accessorized with silver jewelry. Who, except God, could have known my heart was filled with pain? I didn't look as though I was in despair or depressed. Yet, God sent her to me despite the crowd of thousands. God wanted to speak to me, and He did what was necessary.

After the worship service, I returned to my hotel room and took a nap. I had a vivid dream. It left me saying, "I believe God." In the dream, I saw my home. It was decorated exactly as it was in real life. Everything in it was intact. However, all of my old furniture was broken into pieces and stacked in the middle of the floor. The dream was so real I reached into it and felt the broken stuff. When I woke up, I was troubled. I tried to interpret its meaning. The old furniture in our new home was Roland's past. The broken stuff was the past being destroyed. Our home remaining intact was our marriage surviving the past. It sounded reasonable. Yet, I still couldn't shake it. It lingered as I dressed to return to the evening worship service. As I entered the Civic Center the preacher said, "Turn your Bibles to St. John 6:12."

*When they were filled, He said unto his disciples, Gather up the fragments that remain, that nothing be lost.*

When he read the Scripture, I heard a scream in my spirit. I had received an interpretation of my dream. I kept repeating it.

*Gather up the fragments that remain, that nothing be lost.*

I knew without a doubt God was going to save my marriage. All I had to do was gather up the pieces. I was willing to accept them no matter how small. It didn't matter who was right or who was wrong. I decided not to go to the divorce hearing. I knew God was going to turn this around. I rejoiced in hope. It was settled. What the devil meant for evil,

God was going to change for good.

Did it mean He would rekindle my marriage? Or did it mean I should pick up the pieces and move on? What had I learned from my experience? I had no answers, but I had to trust God. I had received enough confirmations to hold onto. I could stand still and wait for the manifestation, then testify to the glory of God.

As planned, I went to work on the day of our divorce hearing. When I thought the hearing was over, I telephoned home. I asked Roland, "Am I married or am I divorced?" He responded, "I got the divorce." He sadly added, "I started to stop it a couple of times, but I didn't." I said, "I guess you know our living arrangements will have to change." He said, "Yes. I'll move upstairs with Claudia until we can move out." When I hung up, guilty thoughts came instantly. *He may not have gotten the divorce if you were there. You really could have stopped it. You call it faith, but it was just your pride. Pride got you a divorce. You are to blame. It could be different this very minute if you, if you, if you ...* I held back the tears because I was at work. I didn't want anyone to know I had failed again. I called my pastor and informed him and his wife of the divorce. Somehow, I made it through the remainder of my workday.

Afterwards, I sealed my mouth. The words "We are divorced" were not coming out of my mouth. I couldn't bear facing the degradation and shame. Months passed before I forced myself to face the truth. Ironically, Roland kept the divorce more secretive than I did. One thing for sure, Claudia didn't. She went around rejoicing and telling anybody who would listen that we were divorced. Wherever I turned, I heard, "Claudia said ..."

The reality of God in my life was as visible as He is invisible. My faith was not shaken when the prophecies were not fulfilled. God cannot lie. Whatsoever He promises

He performs. However, God will not infringe upon our will. I still believe God would have saved our marriage. However, He would not go against Roland's will. God did not allow me to suffer because of Roland's choices. He has always stood by my side.

# 30
# The Wounded Heart

Listen! Don't you hear it? Someone is sobbing hysterically. Oh, it's me.

It had snowed all week. The temperature was now freezing. The winds were extremely high. Our clothing was not sufficient for the frigid weather. The lake effects made things worse. Although it was freezing, the line was rapidly getting longer. We increased our pace and quickly got into the line. The line would close when it reached the seating capacity.

It was Saturday evening. The Brooklyn Tabernacle Choir was in concert at the Moody Bible Institute. Their first performance was scheduled to begin about forty-five minutes after we arrived. However, the line for the second performance was already outrageously long. Those people were leftovers from the first-performance line.

I had driven to Moody with a couple of girlfriends. As we entered the intersection, we saw a sister and her husband crossing the street. Her husband tried telling me where to park. My girlfriends jumped out of the car to get into the line. They left me alone, knowing I did not know how to get around Chicago. I stayed in the middle of the intersection, yelling back and forth with questions. I didn't understand where he was sending me. Horns were honking. Drivers yelled out of their windows. In anger, I was called ugly names. Shaken up, I asked the brother to park my car while I waited with his wife. He said, "Sure. No problem." I placed my car in park and jumped out. His wife became agitated. She reminded me that he was her husband, not mine. Then she said, "He is only supposed to park our car. If you had looked and listened, you would have known where to park." I apologized and told them thanks but never mind. "I'll park my own car." He was still at the traffic light, so he insisted and drove to the parking lot.

As I stood with his wife, I kept apologizing to her. I said I meant no harm. I assured her I would never again ask her or her husband to do anything for me. I even offered to pay her for her troubles. She refused to be consoled with my peace offerings. I was not used to this level of insecurity within my circle. Exhausted, I became silent. It was total shutdown for me. I couldn't handle another adverse situation. I had to be quiet or else I would lose it. The sister and her husband lined up with us. Everyone became aware of the dissension. My girlfriends tried to hold conversations. I simply said yes or no. I refused to talk with anyone. This was history repeating itself. I was an offense in the least of situations. I was tired of feeling like an outcast. If I had not brought my girlfriends to the concert, I would have left. I was sick of life's situations. I was sick of seeking solutions to problems. I was sick of people thinking they could treat me any way they pleased. Wasn't there someone else life could beat to death?

The sister did not know my life had recently crumbled, that I was fragile and my wounds were open. I'd lost my husband. She did not know the impact of my divorce. I decided to be quiet and enjoy the concert. My girlfriends tried to get us to kiss and make up. We refused.

We were separated and wanted to keep it that way. Those who were talking, cuddled together to stay warm. Finally the doors opened. The crowd from the first performance exited. Then we entered. I decided to sit separated from the others, but my friends would not allow me to, so we all sat together. However, the sister and her husband sat on one end. My girlfriends sat in the middle. I sat on the opposite end. Since we refused to forgive, God took other measures.

The concert was great. Every song was pleasant to my ears. Suddenly, my heart was broken into pieces. The choir began to sing "He's Been Faithful." The songwriter shared her experiences, which resulted in the writing of the song. It involved trials they faced with their wayward daughter. As I listened, tears rolled down my cheek. The more I wiped them away, the more they poured out. I wasn't sure whether I was crying for their deliverance or my bondage. The leader began to sing. It was as if an angel of God came and stood in front of me, to remind me of God's faithfulness in my life. The more she sang, the less I was able to control the tears, which had turned into sobs. I covered my mouth to muffle the sound. It did not work. My hands became a bucket to catch the tears. In the midst of my sobbing, I began feeling a relief. I felt an assurance that God was with me. There was a quiet relief regarding my family situation and the sister. When I stopped sobbing, I reached for the sister and apologized. I closed the book on that small issue because I was being equipped for larger battles.

With great pride the world speaks of the "haves" and the "have-nots." Some have what they need and others don't. My sister had her husband. She didn't even want him to help me. It was her opportunity to help someone in need. Through my sufferings, God made me sensitive to the pain of others. He requires me to reach out. He has transformed my wounded heart into a sensitive and tender heart.

# 31
# Under His Wings

For a while I had been suffering with female problems. Major surgery was now required. I prepared for my hospital stay. Roland took off from work to take me. It was very early when we left. Everything within me shook. I was scared. I didn't know whether I would survive the surgery. I'd had two surgeries in my lifetime—two cesarean births— and almost died both times. All I remembered about this surgery were the risks. Questions about eternity invaded my mind. Roland dropped me off at the main entrance, then went to park his car. Afterwards, he came and sat with me at the registration desk. He grabbed my hand and held it tightly in his. I felt the strength of his support. I needed him and he was there for me. It didn't matter that we were divorced. It didn't matter that we did not live together. The only thing that mattered was Roland's willingness to take care of me.

I was taken to a room, told to remove my clothes, and put on a hospital gown. Roland was still with me. When they came to take me to the operating room, he prayed for me. He assured me everything would be all right. So I relaxed. As the nurses were rolling me toward the door, the telephone rang. Roland answered. It was my pastor. He called to pray with me before surgery. The nurse would not allow me to take the call. We were already behind schedule. I began to panic and anxiety took over. I felt if my pastor did not pray with me, I would die during surgery. Roland calmed me saying my pastor prayed. I calmed myself and the nurses resumed my ride to the operating room. Roland went to the waiting room.

The operating room staff was wonderful. They complimented me on my nails and hair. They made me laugh, so that I would relax. The nurse explained how the medication would make me feel. I told her I felt relaxed and ready for surgery. She touched me and asked whether I felt it. I said, "Yes." She informed me I would fall asleep soon. I said, "But I don't feel sleepy." With that, I went out like a light. The next time I was the least bit conscious, I was lying on the operating table. I remembered opening my eyes and seeing the doctors operate on me. However, I couldn't feel anything. I thought how awkward it was to see the doctors operate and not feel anything. I must have moved because I heard someone say, "Go back to sleep." The next thing I became aware of was the wheels of the stretcher hitting bumps in the hallway. I was told I was being taken to the recovery room.

In the recovery room, I was transferred from the stretcher. I heard myself moan from the discomfort. It seemed an eternity before I was taken to my room. I had a private room. Roland was still by my side. I couldn't see him, but I knew he was there. His hands held mine. I was sedated, but I could hear visitors in my room. I heard the conversations. I felt the emotions. I didn't know everyone who was present. However, I knew Roxie, Molly, Carol, Marie, and Roland were in the room. I could hear Roxie and Molly making fun of me. They were laughing because my hands kept missing my mouth. I had no coordination.

My mouth was not where I felt it was. I wanted to respond to Roxie's comment, but I couldn't. I wanted to tell her I could hear her. I could only laugh in my mind. Later we laughed about how badly they treated me when I was sick.

The next situation was not a laughing matter. A discussion started regarding who would spend the night with me. Roland automatically assumed he would be the one. It was a reasonable assumption. He had been by my side since I entered the hospital. I heard Carol say she would stay the second night. She was working that night. Then Marie said, "I'll stay tonight." Roland instantly got angry. He told of his intentions to stay the first night. I knew Roland's anger extended beyond the struggle of that night. Roland didn't like Marie very much. He never gave reasons for not liking her. I believed it was because Marie was a leaning post for me during our marriage misery. She was the one who constantly reminded me, "Raven, God is still God."

With Roland's low tolerance, I knew it wouldn't be long before his hot temper made him leave and not come back. Marie didn't know what she was dealing with. She was my close friend. I didn't want her to be offended. Neither did I want Roland to get angry. This may be the beginning of our reconciliation. I couldn't risk a wounded friend or an angry ex-husband. Despite my inability to speak, I prayed in my heart. I felt the power struggle increasing. I continued to pray some more. I didn't want anyone to be offended. The Lord answered my prayer. I felt a calmness enter the room. I couldn't speak, open my eyes, or sit up. Marie decided she would wait until I was discharged and needed help. That night Roland stayed and slept on a cot. The next morning he helped me get in and out of bed. He took me to the bathroom. He washed me up. He walked me back to my bed. He fed me. I lacked nothing because he was there to do whatever I needed. If I was concerned about something, he contacted the nurse. He told the nurse when I needed something for pain. When I was resting, he made sure I wasn't disturbed. He verified my meals. Roland took good care of me.

I didn't think he could do any more. To my surprise he did. After my discharge from the hospital, Roland became my resident nurse. He came by every day. If I hadn't eaten, he brought me food. Sometimes the food came from Esther's house. Other times he would buy something for me. Also, Carol and Marie continued nursing me back to health. One day during my recovery, I suffered with so much gas. Roland and Carol came to help me. The gas created so much pain I could only cry. Carol said she would give me a suppository for relief. When she said that, I didn't know she meant it literally. I thought she meant she would supply me with one to use. Instead, she placed gloves on her hands and became my unpaid nurse. I was so embarrassed, but I couldn't help myself. I needed some release. It was no big deal to her; but I was overtaken with emotions, to know she would take care of a friend in that manner. Then Roland stepped in and totally overwhelmed me. When the suppository began to work, I could barely lift myself out of the bed. Roland was there to assist me. He took me to the bathroom. As I sat screaming and crying from the pain, he stood over me rubbing my back and head, and praying for me. As the gas and waste began to expel, the smell offended even me, but Roland acted as if nothing was offensive.

Afterwards, I had more pain than I had at the beginning. I couldn't get up. I could barely move my body. Roland was there to help me. He wrapped his arms around my waist, walked me back to the bedroom, and placed me in bed. He covered me and sat by my bedside. Each time I woke up, he was still sitting by my bed. Roland's caring acts made me love him even more, despite the limbo status he left me in.

Those are some of the memories that kept me forgiving Roland over and over.

# 32
# Mixed-Up Mess

Periodically, I couldn't distinguish the beginnings from the endings in our relationship. I couldn't choose what was best for me. I wasn't even sure any more of what I wanted. I was divorced and caught in an emotional seesaw relationship, which clouded my judgment.

Roland divorced me. He believed I hated his children. I am not convinced he really believed that. It was probably another excuse to avoid making the right decisions. During the divorce we had many fights. We were angry. I'm sure we both felt cheated, disappointed, and betrayed. We went back and forth between anger and friendship. I demanded the keys to the house. A few days later I gave them back. We would meet for breakfast on Saturday mornings and dinner after church on Sundays, then we would stop. Back and forth we went. I visited his apartment to help him out; then I refused. We returned health cards and anything else we had that belonged to the other, and then gave them back. The way we were behaving was a true reflection of our confusion and turmoil. Some couples experience the 'divorce anger' at the onset. Afterwards, things become cordial. We were different. I didn't know what we were doing. It was what my grandparents would call "some kind of mixed-up mess."

After the divorce, Roland and I were inseparable. There was nothing he would not do for me, except make a decision. That was what we needed most. Even though we were divorced, Roland was not relinquishing his position as my husband. He was always at the house. We spent so much time together, he became my shadow. I was lost without him. He again became the reason of my very existence. This stopped my growth. I could not move forward while awaiting his decision, and he was not making one. I knew but didn't want to acknowledge that Roland stayed close to me to keep any one else from getting close to me.

# 33
# Cruising

Almost five years after our divorce, our church sponsored a seven-day Caribbean cruise. We visited four islands: St. Thomas, St. Maarten, Dominica, Barbados, and Martinique. We flew from Chicago to San Juan, Puerto Rico, where we boarded the Inspiration of the Carnival Cruise Lines. Roland did not allow me to carry any of the luggage, even though he was struggling with it.

I did not plan to go on the cruise. I did not ask to go on the cruise. Nor did I pay for it. My girlfriend Carol called and told me someone had paid for me to go, so I should pack my bags. After weeks of asking her who paid for me to go, she finally told me it was Roland. I told her I couldn't go. She encouraged me to go. She did it with such intrigue, I thought she knew something I did not. I decided to go. I got excited, thinking Roland and Carol had secretly planned for us to get remarried on the cruise. I went with high expectations. I asked Carol who I would be sharing a cabin with, and she said Roland. I told her we could not do that. She promised to work out something different for me. When she returned, she told me there were no more rooms. I had no choice but to share a cabin with Roland. I wasn't too concerned because I really believed we were going to get remarried. Carol even registered us on the ship as "Mr. and Mrs."

The cruise was wonderful. It was our first cruise experience. I wanted to see everything. We toured during the day and dressed up every night. We took pictures to capture our memories. When we attended the midnight gala buffet, it was unbelievable. We spent more time taking pictures than we did eating. The people in line became irritated because we held up the line taking pictures. We laughed and went our way.

When we docked at St. Maarten, I bought a piece of jewelry with my birthstone, a 14 carat gold garnet ring and a 1.02 carat diamond ring, marquise cut, in a 14 carat yellow gold band. When we returned to the ship and were asked what we bought, without a word I showed them my fingers. Everyone automatically assumed Roland bought them for me. I did not tell them differently. After all, it didn't matter because we were going to be remarried. While in the jewelry stores, we shared our story. The salespeople excitedly encouraged us to get remarried.

When we docked at Barbados, Roland and I took a long walk downtown. We took an afternoon stroll. I bought a dress and a gold peacock pin.

In the midst of such a wonderful vacation, the inevitable happened. We had a fight! Roland walked out of the cabin. Here I was, dealing with that quick ugly temper again, a long way from home. His childish behavior was wreaking havoc. I regrouped and decided to go look for him. I walked around for hours trying to find him. When I finally found him and talked with him, we walked around the ship talking most of the night. When everyone was disembarking the next morning, we slept in. They assumed we wanted to be alone. The truth was we had not gotten any sleep the night before.

On Sunday morning, there was a worship service. During the service everyone received an opportunity to testify if they desired. Roland and I both testified. We thanked God for the opportunity to rekindle our love and revive our marriage. Someone shouted and others joined in, "Let's get the captain and do it now." We didn't because Roland still had not made a decision.

# 34
# Do It For Love

Three girlfriends and I gathered for our girls' night out. We decided to stay at my house and have ice cream and cake. During our time of fellowship, we discussed the loves of our lives. After all, Valentine's Day was just around the corner. The three of them had spouses, but I didn't. So, they told me since I loved Roland, and he loved me, we should stop the stubbornness and reunite. I knew the truth in what they were saying; but I asked, "How many more times must I try to force love to reveal itself?" All of my creative power had diminished. However, after an extensive conversation, they persuaded me to try yet again. I decided I had nothing to lose.

On the evening of Valentine's Day, I called Roland and invited him over. He accepted and said he would be there shortly. I arose, showered, dressed seductively, and waited for him to arrive. When he arrived, we shared some very special moments together. It was pleasant and promising. Again, we acknowledged our pass mistakes, talked, laughed, embraced, and kissed. Since this was my grand idea, I took the lead and did something I had never done before. Roland always gave me pedicures, but that night I gave him one. I took my time giving him the pedicure;

it took about two hours. We spent the time talking about us: our past, our present, and the future that awaited us. It seems only natural that the next sentence should be "and they lived happily ever after." But sadly it's not. Instead, the evening ended as a lovely song that was soon forgotten.

# 35
# Friends in Troubled Times

There were people who cared about me enough to make me a priority. They loved me through my pain. They wanted things in my life to work for my good. They stood by me continuously. They spoke words of encouragement, gave me borrowed strength. While others stayed away, they came closer knowing an association with me could make them an outsider with "The Family." My situation was leprous. Other than my friends, no one would talk about it or ask how I was doing. However, everyone was watching. I often thought, *If only I could hear their thoughts. Then I would know who was with me and who was not. I would know who was praying and who was gossiping.* Since that power belonged to God, I decided to shake it off. One thing I knew for sure, I had real friends. God gave me a diverse and unique group of friends. I'm not sure I would have made it without them. There are too many to mention, but they were there when I needed them.

Roxie stood by my side continuously. We had history together. We were friends in Baltimore. God used her to introduce me to Roland. I believed God was in control of my life. I told Roxie she was not responsible for my marriage. She was a part of my solution. She appointed herself as my mediator with Roland. On numerous occasions, she tried intervening for me. Sometimes I was present during her interventions. She would remind Roland of his love for me and my love for him. He never denied he still loved me, but he was confused. Condemnation had its grip on him. Roland told Roxie I didn't love him. She assured him I did and was willing to accept him back. He said he couldn't believe I still loved him. She tried to help him see we were destined to be together. A few times she thought she had convinced him, but nothing happened. As the old adage goes, "You can lead a horse to water, but you can't make him drink." Roxie was my American friend.

Mama Anna and Sister Sharon were our only family in Evanston. They were not blood relatives. Yet, they treated us like we belonged. They were also best friends with "The Family," and especially close to Esther. As things got increasingly difficult, I thought they would choose the other side, if for no other reason than the longevity of their relationships. I learned quickly that their love was genuine and strong. They loved all of us. The situation did not change the love for either side. I did not make them uncomfortable by discussing Roland or his children. If the topic came up, everyone felt free to discuss it. They stood firm on what they believed was right. Mama Anna and Sister Sharon were my adopted American family.

During the most difficult time in my marriage, I walked in the mornings with Frances and Marie. Frances and I didn't talk much about my situation, but Marie and I talked constantly. Marie helped me develop an inner strength I thought had long left me. No matter what I told her about the things Roland did, said, or allowed his children to do, she simply said with her Jamaican accent, "Raven, God is still God!" Every time something new would happen, I could hear her voice echoing in my heart, 'Raven, God is still God!'

I was a member of the Prayer Cell group. The Prayer Cell originated out of our church. A group of Christians took the message they received at church to homes in the community. The Cell signified multiplying the work of the ministry. Once a week we visited someone sick or confined to his or her house. It didn't matter whether they were a Christian or a member of a church. During each visit we prayed, sang songs, and shared the Word of God. I became close to the two mothers in the group. One was Jamaican and the other Panamanian. They regularly encouraged me. Mother Mabel always said, "Baby, I don't know how God is going to do it, but one thing I do know, when it is all said and done, you are coming out on top." Mother Duncan always said, "Sister Hackman, acknowledge God and He will direct your path."

One night as I was in the midst of a heated battle within myself, the telephone rang. It was my girlfriend Sheila. Sheila is Belizean. I had seen her faith in action. So it was easy to believe her. She simply said, "Raven, where your faith ends, my faith will pick you up and carry you the rest of the way. God is going to see you through." Sheila was in the midst of planning her wedding; yet, she thought of me. She said she wanted her wedding to be a seed for our reunion. She wanted both of us in her wedding. He and I would accompany each other in the march, a symbol of what would be again. I appreciated everything she said and did. There was an intimacy in her vision. I was excited and activated my faith. Roland and I marched together. We stood together. The evening we shared was a very pleasant one. It was obvious Roland enjoyed the evening as much as I did. However, his pursuit to reconcile was dead. It was like a lovely song sung and enjoyed, but when it ended, it was forgotten!

Then God placed me in the hearts of the Tylers and

placed them in mine. Whenever I became overwhelmed and needed an escape from my prison of pain, I visited the Tylers. Their home became my hotel. They lived in Round Lake Beach. Visiting them was my escape from Evanston. I became a part of their family. Whenever I needed a mental or physical break, their home was open to me. Along with their invitation came a healing salve. They massaged my heart with love and the Word of God. They didn't seem to mind the disruption I caused their family. During my visits, they gave me my own room. I could do as I pleased. I was left alone, undisturbed. If I didn't want to get up, I didn't have to. If I wanted to eat, they had food prepared and waiting for me. If I wanted to talk, they would listen. They were my friends. They ministered to me until I was strong enough to return home. They prayed for me, with me, and taught me warfare prayer. I knew I could go to their home any time I needed to escape. The Tylers were my Trinidadian friends.

Shortly after the release of the movie *The Preacher's Wife*, Meechy called me. She was excited because she believed she had the solution to my problem. She said she had seen the movie and it was excellent. During the movie, she constantly thought about Roland and me. She said there were so many similarities. She believed if we saw the movie together, it would surely help our marriage. Grabbing hold to any ray of hope, I persuaded Roland to take me to see the movie. The movie moved me to tears. The movie could have ministered to our marriage, but all Roland discussed was the negativity of the wife's actions. I was grateful Meechy wanted to help us. Even though our situation remained unchanged, it was worth the effort. I consoled myself. As long as there is life, there is hope. I won't stop trying to recapture the love we once shared. Meechy is an American who thinks she's Haitian.

All of my friends shared one common denominator.

Because they were happy, they wanted me to be happy. Carol and her sister, Georgia, were very special. Georgia and I didn't talk much. However, we knew the love was strong between us. She believed Roland was foolish. She had little or no patience for him. Carol and I talked regularly. She always said, "Raven, I don't care what things look like, feel like, act like, or is, God is working for you, Baby." She refused to call me anything other than Mrs. Hackman. She was not releasing her hope of Roland and I getting back together.

Lis and I were as close as sisters. She loved me and tried to make things right between Roland and me. Lis never referred to the things in my life as "you or yours," it was always "we, us, and ours." We were connected at the heart. My cares became her cares. My troubles became her troubles; and vice versa. Whenever she called or came to the house, she would talk with Roland first. She wanted to maintain peace and make him feel special. She would say things to Roland to build his self-esteem. She would even side with him against me, so he could know how important he was. She did whatever she thought was necessary to make Roland smile. She always made sure she was on his good side. Lis is my "get-down-in-the-mud-if-we-have-to" and "I am-not-leaving-you-to-face-this-alone" friend. She was always there for the good, bad, and the ugly. Because we were connected at the heart, she had liberties no one else had. She tends to be unnecessarily concerned about people's perception of her. So Roland had nothing to worry about. Lis would never see anything wrong with him. She often openly chastised me in front of Roland when she believed I was wrong. Then she privately encouraged me when I was right. It didn't matter what was required to make things right, she just wanted to help. Of all my friends, she had the biggest struggle dealing with Roland after our divorce. Whether real or imaginary, Lis offered to have her "connections" take care of Roland. The care she was referring to was not very tender or healthy. Of course we agreed he was not worth it. Lis is my Haitian friend.

I had a very special friend. She is Jamaican and a very private person. This woman imparted courage, confidence, and assurance into my life. We rarely had a general conversation. We were friends who bonded over the telephone. Our interactions were primarily over the telephone. Every Sunday afternoon and sometimes midweek, she would call me. She exalted the Name of Jesus, encouraged me, prayed for me, and hung up. She had no time for foolishness. I loved her. When I needed it most, the telephone would ring and it was her ready to pray for me. Even after Roland and I divorced, she still proclaimed her belief of our reunion. I felt our relationship was so one-sided because I received so much from her and I'm really not sure what she received from me, except my love.

Ronald was my most trusted male friend. He was a wall for me to lean on. He encouraged me and gave me unconditional love. I met him at church. He was so special to me that he became Tina's godfather. During my hardships and loneliness, he was there. He called himself my "Black Angel." On special holidays he treated us special. He gave us brotherly gifts. He made sure we did not experience void from Roland's absence. He was a pillar of strength for us. His wife allowed him to be my brother and friend. His family became our family. When we faced financial challenges, they helped us. They did this without me telling them I had a need. A place is carved in our hearts, which belongs to them for a lifetime.

After a tornado, hurricane, or any bad storm, there is always a cleanup crew. God gave me such a crew after our divorce. The crew consisted of Molly, Linda, Susie, and

Christina. Each of them deposited into my life a substance that sustained me and encouraged me to move forward. They didn't say it, but their friendship and actions gave me what I needed to move forward.

Molly and I connected because of business. Our friendship developed through our girls. Nevertheless, after Roland and I divorced, Molly shared her happy life with me. When she or her husband cooked something special, she would share it with me. When I needed a man's help around the house, she sent her husband to help me. When I needed to talk, she was there to listen. However, it was one of Molly's statements that totally freed me from my unhealthy love and commitment to Roland. She called me "Roland's Faithful Divorced Wife." I became almost sick realizing that those words didn't even go together. It made me feel stupid. I could not tolerate feeling stupid. I had to do something. I freed my heart.

Linda and I were also connected because of business. Our friendship developed because of her miracle baby. She had a son who became Roland's and my godchild. After Roland and I divorced, Linda used gifts from our godchild to get us to reunite. Linda gave me the joys of a male child, which I had never experienced. She taught him to make me feel special. He still does even as a grown man.

Susie and I bonded in later years. When we first met, it was because her son and Tina had become boyfriend and girlfriend. Although our children did not continue dating, our love for each other grew each day. Susie became a lifeline for me. She was my encourager. She made me feel I was better than whatever or wherever I was. Through her encouragement, I kept raising the bar for myself. When I needed her most she was there, and I didn't have to call.

My heart connected with Christina when I first relocated to Illinois. Our daughters brought us together.

We became friends immediately. My daughter called her Mama Christina, while her daughter called me Auntie Raven. Whenever I needed someone to pray, I could call her. She always gave me words of encouragement either before or after she prayed. Christina carried me in her spirit. She always saw the good in people and situations. I've never heard negativity from her. For no reason she would periodically send me a card, telling me how special I was and how much she loved me. She kept me built up in faith. Those four Americans were my cleanup crew.

The Bible states, *"When the Sons of God came to present themselves before the Throne of God, the devil came with them."* The devil will always try to infiltrate the good things God is doing. One day a minister called me. He said he was concerned about what was happening with Roland and me. He asked to meet with me and talk with me from a man's perspective. I told him I didn't think there was anything he could tell me that I hadn't tried. However, if he thought he could help, I would not refuse the help. So I agreed to hear his revelation. He said it would be missionary work for him, so he was to pick me up on a Saturday morning and we would go to Walker Brothers Pancake House to talk. In my mind, a minister and a meeting in a public place without doubt equal safety. Saturday morning, the minister arrived on schedule. He was dressed in his clergy attire. When the doorbell rang, Roland came downstairs and answered it. Even though we were divorced, and he and Claudia lived upstairs, I told him where I was going and why. The minister and I left in his car. The conversation in the car was all about God.

We arrived at the pancake house, sat down, and ordered. The first thing out of the minister's mouth was, "How can you and Roland live in that house together? It must be hard. How can you stand to see him walk around like that (Roland had answered the door wearing his bathrobe)? Because when I saw you on Sunday in that African outfit, I could have eaten it off of you, one piece at a time. You know I have a problem with my flesh, so pray for me. By the way, if you tell anybody I said this, I will deny it and they won't believe you." Then he added, "Sister Wallace told me you dress the way you do to attract attention to yourself." Even though I did not believe Sister Wallace said that, he spoke with such confidence that I felt defeated. I felt dirty and powerless. I knew he was telling the truth that certain people would not believe, but others would. I had heard too many stories regarding the mothers of young girls. I never dreamt this would happen to me. An older woman, I was old enough to be this whoremonger's mother. My heart sunk. Angry questions crowded my mind. How could he have been allowed to continue for so many years, destroying so many lives? How could he be so bold and strong? I feared unwarranted repercussion. I sat stunned. I was speechless. I became numb to my surroundings. I understood why women who had been violated never came forward to report it. My insides trembled. I didn't hear another word he said. He was no minister. He was a messenger from hell. I wanted to go somewhere and cry. I'd always carried myself in a respectable manner. Why was I faced with such filth? I couldn't eat the food that was delivered to me. I felt like vomiting. After verbalizing his filth, he began to talk positively about Roland and me. His words bounced off of my ears. Without a word, I sat and waited to be taken home. When I got home, I jumped out of the car and never looked back. I told Roland what happened. I had hoped he would physically defend my honor. He only said, "I'm not surprised. That's what he's been doing all of his life."

Years later, when I learned another young lady had been violated by the same minister, I decided to share my experience. The counselor I spoke to asked me, "What did you do? Why didn't you leave? Why did you get back in the car?" Through tear-stained eyes, I said, "I don't know." This was the whole truth. I really didn't know. In my day, women were not taught to report these types of situations. These indiscretions were swept under the rug. So if I, at 38 years old, became helpless, I feared for the youth. They are in serious trouble. We must educate our children, warn them, and provide the comfort needed for them to feel comfortable discussing those types of situations. We must make sure that the extended hand is indeed a helping hand, the hand of a true friend and not an evil predator!

# 36
# Stay with Me

Agirlfriend and I were talking. She said her husband had packed his clothes and left home, not to return. She was upset, but pride wouldn't allow her to follow her heart. She refused to ask him to stay. I suggested she call him and ask him to come home. She responded, "What! You want me to beg him to come home?" I slowly spoke. "Beg? If that's what it takes, yes, beg." She replied, "I'm not going to beg him to stay married to me!" A lump rose in my throat. I choked on my words. I didn't want to reveal my secret. Nevertheless, I knew I had to. I felt pressured to tell her something no one else knew. I spoke almost in a whisper and said, "Beg, huh? You, don't want to beg! Well, if I told you how many times I've begged, I guess you would never respect me again." I told her details she didn't know about my marriage. Although I was not the primary problem in our relationship, I begged Roland repeatedly to stay with me.

When I finished, her response was exactly the response I'd always feared. She said, "And you see what it got you. In the end, Roland still left." Her words were true and hurtful. This hurting, angry, disappointed woman could not comprehend my story. I remembered that begging made me feel like I'd lower my standards. It left me feeling horrible. Why should I expect others to do what I did? I knew she was not trying to hurt me. She was my friend. I hid the sting of her painful words and continued, "Yes, Roland left. He got married and he is free of me, but he is miserable. I don't rejoice in that. I rejoice in the fact that I didn't go under. I wasn't defeated. I wasn't destroyed by or consumed with grief because of his leaving. I rode on the wings of my adversities. I rose to heights I would have never known. Do you know why? Because, I did all I knew to do, in our relationship. I have no condemnation. I am free. I survived because I loved Roland, but I also loved me. There are people running from themselves. They can't live with themselves. They can't live with the reminder of what has happened or who they have become. When Roland left me, I became freer than I had ever been in our relationship."

My girlfriend decided to do the right thing. She repented to God for the wrong she'd contributed in her marital dispute. She asked Him for forgiveness and to help her. She called her husband, apologized, and asked him to come home because she needed him. Her husband came home and they began to work through their differences. God intervened and renewed their marriage. What she may not realize until some time later, is that this little growth will produce a much greater harvest.

Less than a week later another girlfriend called. She told me she had asked her husband to leave. He was leaving but not voluntarily. He was honoring her request. After talking with her, I learned she was asking him to leave for all the wrong reasons. I ministered to her as God led. She was open to God and His Word. She acknowledged her wrong. She said she could not imagine what he's thinking or feeling. I discussed some areas she needed to give immediate attention. Because she had mentioned her husband did not like confrontations, I suggested she write him a letter. We discussed the contents of the letter. She listened and followed through. God intervened for her and refreshed their marriage. Her husband began communicating more.

Marriage-counseling situations arose daily. I was routinely called for prayer and advice. Whatever God told me to say worked for each person who called. So, in prayer I asked, "Lord, why didn't your principles work for me?" The advice I gave to minister to others, more often than not, was the same principles I had previously applied in my relationship, but they didn't work. My resolve was this: Although the Word of God is sure and the advice of God is guaranteed to work, God will not invade the will of anyone involved.

Roland refused to deal with the adverse situations that developed in our relationship. He would shut down in silence, walk out of the door, and go to Esther's or Jezzy's house. Lastly, his defense would be total rage. Regardless of his reaction, I would talk with him, asking him to communicate his feelings, thoughts, and beliefs concerning the things causing us grief and discomfort. None of my approaches received a positive response.

I am a communicator. Good, bad or indifferent, if it isn't right, I want to talk about it. I wanted each of us to understand, so we could apply a solution. I wasn't seeking a selfish solution, even though Roland always believed so. I wanted a solution that would work in our relationship. When the solution wasn't readily found, I kept talking, trying to force a solution. This made Roland even angrier. He would put on his shoes and/or his coat to leave. I would follow him to the door, still wanting to talk about it.

I would position myself by the door to block him from opening it. I would then touch his arm and ask him to stay so we could talk about it. He was not hearing it. Each time I explained my feelings, it was always interpreted as "justification." His response to anything I said was "You don't ever do anything wrong. You are perfect. God only loves you. God only works for you. Your children can make no mistakes. Why don't you find someone who's good enough for you?" Then he would snatch his arm from my hands and walk out of the door. By the time he walked out, the situation had escalated. I said, "Roland, why can't we ever just talk calmly so we can hear what the other is saying? Why can't we work things out? Don't run away from me. That is not the answer." All of my efforts were to no avail. This happened so often even a fool would have given up, but I didn't. I tried for weeks, months, and years. I tried until he remarried and the door was closed on our relationship.

Marriage meant a lot to me. I didn't mind losing my pride to save it. I didn't mind begging if it was necessary. I didn't mind revealing my heart even if it meant I had to cry. Nothing mattered but Roland staying with me and working things out. I remembered my promise to God. I would not seek a divorce this time. I remembered my promise to Roland. I would be with him until death separated us. I also remembered my girls who stood with us as we made our vows of love. I remembered the minister saying, "I'm placing you at the top of the list of marriages I've performed. I believe your marriage will be sustained by the love I feel between you." Periodically, we received a long distance call from her, checking on us. When asked how we were doing, my answer was, "All is well." When asked about Roland, I said he is doing fine, but he was not at home. She would rejoice and ask me to give Roland a big hug and kiss from her. I didn't have the heart to tell her the faith she had placed in our marriage was wasted. What made it worse, with each telephone call she recalled the memories of our wedding day and the love it contained. I thought, *Eventually I will have to tell her.* I decided to do it later. However, Mother Foster died and I never told her of the dissolution of our marriage.

Some would say I was in denial. I'd decided whatever it took, I would do it for the survival of our love. I believed that God could and would work things out. I believed we could and would find a way to make it work. We needed a plan from the innermost depth of our hearts. We needed to commit and recommit. We needed to stop evaluating and judging each other. We needed a plan to encourage each other, one that would give us hope of staying together.

Roland didn't stay with me, but the story doesn't end there. There's a message to be told and a lesson to be learned. So often a wife expresses to her husband things that are troubling her. If the husband chooses to ignore her concern, it becomes an unresolved issue. This unresolved issue will surface with every new controversy. It will attach itself to every new issue; thus, creating a snowball effect. Each issue raised in a relationship must be given the attention or solution needed. Otherwise, it comes up time after time. From the husband's perspective it becomes nagging. From the wife's, it remains an unresolved issue. Just as the husband needs to address the issue, the wife needs to be sensitive to timing when presenting a concern.

# 37
# Pursuit and Purpose

A woman should never reject being treated like a lady. It was a day like any other day in my life. I had worked hard and was exhausted. For whatever reason, I drove to work instead of riding the train. I dreaded the drive home because I sometimes fell asleep at the wheel. Normally, I took naps during my lunch period, but that day I did not. I had to get a package ready for mailing, and it had to be mailed that day. I had also prepared my bills for mailing. Even though I was exhausted, my mind was peaceful. I turned on my music, hoping to become more energized. I decided to go to the post office before going home. I was on my way to the Evanston post office when I remembered I would pass one on Devon Avenue in Chicago. So I decided to stop at that one.

It was a pleasant but cold winter evening. The absence of snow made the cold bearable. I parked my car, got out, locked the doors, and began walking across the street. There was no traffic going north. I crossed the street halfway. There was heavy traffic going south. I anticipated standing at the halfway mark for a while. Cars were speeding by. They didn't even slow down as they passed me. Then all of a sudden, a black car came to a complete stop in the middle of traffic. The person lowered his window and beckoned me with his hand to go across. I lifted my hands in thanks and ran across. The car did not move until I was completely on the other side. During the time it took me to get across the street, the post office closed. However, there was a mail truck with a carrier out front. Playfully, I explained my situation, and he was quite understanding. Nevertheless, he could not help me. I was not surprised. I knew my package needed to be weighed to determine the postage. I became very dramatic, telling him how desperately I needed his help. We were having some lighthearted fun, laughing. I told him I would leave him to do his work. Then I felt someone watching us.

I turned slightly and saw a man laughing as if he were a part of our conversation. It was the man in the car who had stopped and allowed me to cross the street. As I was returning to my car, the man leaned his head out of the window and asked, "Is it Miss or Mrs., and is there a Mr.?" I prayed silently but fervently, *"Tongue, don't fail me now! Speak!"* Billy D. and Denzel didn't have anything on the image I beheld at that moment. I softly and shyly responded, "It's Miss and there is no Mr., but my question is, is there a Mrs.?" He continued, "There's no Mrs. My name is Romeo Knight. What's yours?"

"Raven Hackman."

Romeo was Haitian. When he repeated my name, time stood still. "Raven" spoken with a French accent weakened me. His voice captivated me. He asked how I spent my spare time. I answered with a question, "Why do you ask? You are a kid compared to me." With a half smile in the corner of his lips, he responded with a question, "How old do you think I am?" I answered, "I would guess you are about 35 years old." He responded, "You are wrong. I'm 38." I said, "That's still younger than me. I'm 40." He asked, "What does age have to do with anything?" I responded, "Age doesn't have anything to do with it when there is a level of maturity that exceeds the age." His smile widened and he said, "It does!" He handed me one of his business cards. He was self-employed. He owned a car wash. He invited me to his place of business. Umm, thirty-eight, single, self-employed, and good-looking too, I was impressed. He made me promise to call him and visit his car wash. This was one promise I intended to keep.

Romeo came into my life like a whirlwind. It was at a time when I needed a boost. I felt I had lost my appeal as a woman. We began to talk on the telephone every day at home and at work. His conversations left me speechless. I didn't want to talk. I just wanted to listen. He had so many stories to tell. We started going out to dinner and to the beach. The first time we went to dinner, he took me to Indiana. It was one of his special restaurants. It was unbelievable. I was being treated special. I had forgotten what special treatment did for a woman. We only went to the movies once. He believed it was a time waster. I didn't mind since I was not really a moviegoer either. The more we went out, the more he consumed my heart. In as much as I wanted to believe he was sent by God, he was not a Christian. I could not get him to go to church. When I talked about God, he always rationalized and explained away my faith. I was not discouraged. With time, I could change his unbelief.

We were together so much that it felt awkward when we were not together. I'd told him of my living arrangement with Roland. He'd told me about his "girlfriend," who was in and out of his life. According to him, she wasn't sure what she wanted. She periodically stopped by his place, stayed a few days, and she would leave again. It was obvious: We were company and consolation for each other.

Since Roland and I were divorced, I allowed Romeo to

call and pick me up from home. Each time we went out and had a long, intimate conversation, he would say, "You still love your husband. If he says today or tomorrow, 'Let's get back together,' you would do so without a thought." I disagreed with him, but deep down I knew it was true. Romeo was very creative. He did things on impulse. Yet, he was level headed. One night out of the blue, he asked me to move in with him. I told him he was crazy and I would never do that. He said, "If you move in with me, you can have half of what I own." I smiled and said, "That sounds good, but it's not complete. There is no salvation or commitment connected to your offer." Even though I knew he was not a Christian, and there was no real commitment, it just felt good dating. On a regular basis he worked 12-14 hours a day. Since his shop opened early morning and closed late evening, we normally went out late.

One night after dinner, when Romeo brought me home, I noticed Roland looking out of the upstairs window. I was not the least bit concerned. He and Claudia went out every day of the week. They went to Esther's house or Jezzy's house or wherever. They returned when they wanted to, usually around bedtime. However, Roland would always watch me through the curtains, unmoving, as Romeo dropped me off. A few days later, Romeo was parking in front of the house to walk me to the door. I looked up and Roland and Claudia were driving up. I asked Romeo to drive off. I explained I didn't want Roland knowing my business. He did as I'd asked and drove off. We returned later. Again, Roland stood in the shadow of the curtains, looking out the window. It was amusing. He was having a problem dealing with me moving on with my life. Yet, he was doing what he wanted, with whomever he wanted. He came to me one day and said, "Why do you think Romeo is going out with you? He's just trying to get into your pants. I know you go to his car wash located at 1234 Market Street. He is just using you." I asked where he got his information. Without hesitation, he said, "I have friends in the police department." I said, "Roland, if he's trying to get into my pants, then I'll be the one to decide if he does or does not, not you! Hello? Remember? We are divorced! At least I waited until we were divorced before I started seeing someone else."

Then one Sunday morning after I had left for church, Romeo called. Roland answered the telephone. Romeo asked to speak to me. Roland said, "She's not here. This is her husband. Would you like to leave a message?" Roland didn't know with whom he was dealing. Romeo was strong and confident. He politely gave Roland a message for me.

When Roland came to church, he had the message in his shirt pocket. He flipped the piece of paper out, and handed it to me. As I reached for it, his face was red with anger. He said, "Your nigger called. When I told him I was your husband, it didn't seem to matter. He said to tell you Romeo called." I said, "Thank you" and walked away. I was not creating a scene in the vestibule of the church. After church, he went his way as he always did. When I got home I returned Romeo's call.

When Romeo and I were out, people often commented on how good we looked together. How much we seemed to enjoy each other. He was playful. We talked and laughed a lot. One night after he closed his shop, we went out to dinner as usual. However this night, he decided to finish his paperwork while we waited for our meal. While he diligently worked, I propped my face in the palm of my hands, smiling and admiring him. While looking at his baby face, I decided I needed proof of his age. I took my wallet out and pretended to look for something. I faked a confused look. Then I softly asked, "Romeo, may I see your driver's license a moment?" Unsuspectingly he looked up, reached into his wallet, and handed me his driver's license. He continued working. I looked at it and burst into a loud laugh. I laughed until tears were streaming down my face. He stopped his paperwork and started laughing just because I was laughing. Then he so sweetly and innocently asked, "What's funny, Raven?" Through my laughter I said, "You liar! You big liar! How old are you? According to your birthday on this license, you are 35 years old. You are such a liar!" With his captivating smile, he said, "Has it made a difference?" I said, "No, but I was correct when I guessed your age. You said I was wrong, so you could increase it. You knew if I frowned on thirty-five, you had to make it more, and thirty-eight sounded better." Then I said, "Romeo, you don't have any idea what people have been thinking. Seeing me with you, especially, if they guessed you to be thirty-five also." He responded, "Who cares what people think?" This was the topic of our conversation the rest of the evening. We laughed and talked about the difference in our ages.

Romeo and I had been dating for months, and we were getting closer and closer. One day, I asked him to stop by the house to meet my daughters and soon-to-be son-in-law. He did. We sat at the dining room table talking for a long time. Then he took all of us out for dinner. I felt myself falling for this guy. He was a great companion. He was fun and he was focused. When I felt myself weakening, I said, "God, I can't help myself. If there was ever someone who would cause me to utterly fall, this is he. Help me!"

God didn't waste any time answering that prayer. A short time later, Romeo and I were talking on the telephone. His girlfriend was at his house. He found out later she had eavesdropped on our conversation. We were reminiscing over the months we had spent together. Romeo made a point that he thought it was interesting we had not been together sexually. As it was told to me, this conversation pleased his girlfriend. She was glad to know we had not been sexually active. This brought them back together. I couldn't help but think, *If only she knew what I knew.* This was true only because of my fighting him off. She didn't know I was invited to move in. She didn't know the times I visited his place. I could describe intricate details of his place. My thoughts were running wild. I knew it was because I was jealous.

A few days later, Romeo called. He was upset. We had never exchanged strong words, but I could tell he was angry. I didn't have a clue what caused the anger. He said, "Raven, what gives you the right to call here and be disrespectful to my girlfriend? She is so upset over what you said to her." I was finally able to get a word in. "Romeo, what are you talking about? When did I talk with your girlfriend? I've never spoken with her." He said she told him I called, cursed her out, and told her to stay away from him. I asked him had he ever heard me curse? I pointed out the time the call was supposed to have been made, and where I was. I concluded my conversation with, "You can believe what you want. I really don't care. It just shows you don't know me at all. I am offended that you would jump to conclusions and approach me in that manner. I understand that your girlfriend is Haitian and I'm American, and you want to stick with yours ... so good-bye." I was hurt and angry. The nerve of him. The nerve of her to use me to manipulate him. I wondered how someone could tell bold lies like that.

After a few days passed, Romeo called to apologize. After our conversation, he spoke with his girlfriend. She decided to tell the truth. I accepted his apology. However, my weakness for him had vanished. I became direct and somewhat cold. His humor was not cute anymore. I no longer desired his conversations. He had hurt me. I was not available to be hurt anymore. We agreed to remain friends. I told him I would be leaving for South Africa within a few days. He said he would be glad to take me to the airport. I explained that it would be Roxie and I. He said okay. I told him I would let him know my final decision.

Roland knew I was seeing Romeo. He also knew I was going to South Africa. Suddenly, he started coming home a lot earlier and hanging around downstairs longer. He started asking more questions. One day he came home without Claudia. He asked to talk with me. I consented. He invited me to dinner at Davis Street Fish Market. When we arrived, our name was added to the one-and-a-half-hour waiting list. While waiting, we decided to walk around downtown and talk.

It was beginning to get dark. Little by little the streetlights began shining brighter and brighter. It was a cool evening, but we were dressed warmly. We walked and talked. We cried and apologized. We reminisced over the good times and agonized over the bad. We discussed things that could have been done differently. We briefly held hands to comfort one another. Sporadically, we embraced and held each other tight. We expressed our fears of tomorrow, where would they find us. I said I was willing to work through the fears if he was. He said he was not sure. He needed more time. I didn't say it but couldn't help thinking, *After all the time he'd already had, he needs more time?* He asked me to give him until I returned from South Africa, then he would let me know what he wanted to do. Roland was asking me to place my life on hold again, until he decided what was best for him; not us. Nevertheless, I agreed. I was scheduled to spend fourteen days in South Africa. In fourteen days I would know whether my current life was over permanently or beginning anew. As we walked, cars passed and drivers blew their horns at us as they yelled joyous sounds out of the window. They were people we knew from church. There were always people praying and encouraging us to recapture our love.

After an hour had passed, we headed back to the fish market. Within a short time, our name was called. We were led to our table. En route to our table, I saw my dentist. She was seated at a table next to ours. I introduced her to Roland saying, "This is Roland, my boyfriend, my husband, my ex-husband, my date tonight, and possibly my future husband." We laughed and ended our conversation. While Roland and I ate, we continued the conversation about our future. Certain times I was thinking Roland's concern was more for Romeo than for me. He said he knew Romeo was taking me to the airport. I assured him Romeo was not. I told him Roxie was going to get someone to take us.

After dinner we returned to the house. I was leaving the next morning. I had to review my checklist one final time. I called Roxie and told her to go ahead with our travel arrangements. I was not going to ask Romeo to take me. She agreed. Roland didn't know Romeo and I were not seeing each other anymore. Neither did he know Romeo was not taking me to the airport. Roland began pacing back and forth. He went upstairs and then downstairs. I could feel the restlessness. It seemed fear and depression were overcoming him. He repeatedly said, "I know Romeo is going to be at the airport. Even if he doesn't take you, he will meet you there." It was getting late. I needed some rest. So finally I said, "Roland, do you want to take me to the airport?" He said yes. I thought that would end everything, but it didn't. I called Roxie and told her Roland was taking us to the airport. I gave her the time we would pick her up. Roland continued pacing. He was so restless I felt sorry for him. I worried about his sanity. I invited him to sleep on the opposite side of my bed, on top of the covers while I slept under the covers. He welcomed the invitation and laid down. He slept in that position all night.

The following morning, when we arrived at the airport, Roland refused to drop us off and leave. He wanted to go to the gate and wait until we departed. That was his way of making sure Romeo wasn't there. I was a little uneasy because I wasn't convinced Romeo would not show up. Romeo did not come, and I was relieved. As Roxie and I were boarding the plane, Roland assured me of an answer when I returned.

During our layover in Florida, I called Romeo. He told me to hang up and call him back using his calling card number. I did so. He asked how I got to the airport and I told him. I also told him what Roland had promised me when I left. He said, "I told you this would happen, but I want you to know you could have had half of my kingdom." I laughed and said, "Romeo, you have been good for me, at a time when I was feeling so unloved. Even though we are not going to be together, I believe this was a "win-win" situation. It took your coming into my life to cause Roland to take a closer look; and it took me coming into your life for your girlfriend to appreciate you. I'm going to miss you."

Upon arrival to South Africa, I lived with Evangelist Ford and his wife. I had met Evangelist Ford at my church in Evanston; however, this was my initial meeting with his wife. Yet, they had become like "family" to me. Over the years we had communicated over the telephone.

While getting acquainted with all of my African brothers and sisters, questions regarding family constantly came up. In shame I responded, "I'm divorced, but I have two daughters and a soon-to-be son-in-law. At dinner one night, I shared with Evangelist and Mrs. Ford that Roland told me he would let me know his decision about our marriage when I returned. Mrs. Ford spoke up very quickly. "That's not right. Everything is not about him and what he wants. He's stopping you from living. You don't know whether you will have a life afterwards." I felt stupid as I agreed. I said I didn't know what else to do.

When we returned home, Roland picked us up. When

Roland and I talked later, he told me it was best if we went our separate ways. He further stated he didn't think it would work. I was instantly filled with pain. However, I mustered up a smile, as I realized the purpose of Roland's pursuit. He didn't want me, but he didn't want anyone else to have me either.

# 38
# The Buyout

After our divorce we still shared the house. He and Claudia lived upstairs. My girls and I lived downstairs. Our financial situation had finally reached a point where we could settle our affairs and sever ties. When Roland filed his divorce papers, he alleged all the down payment on the house was his money. Therefore, he wanted to be reimbursed for his down payment. This would be taken off the top of the appraised value of the house. Then, we would equally share the difference between the balance owed and the balance of the appraised value.

I spoke with a minister and his wife about my financial situation and Roland's expectations. The wife was very direct. She said Roland owed me a place to live. She also said she would not agree to return down payment monies because this was something done in our marriage. He can't just take back previous care he provided for his wife because of a divorce. That helped me tremendously. Anxiety and stress had me confused and a little hopeless. I was not thinking logically. I was fearful and weak. I gained strength from her encouragement. Then I remembered, I also gathered all of my funds to help with the down payment. I searched my records and found receipts of my contribution. When I totaled them, it was a little less than a thousand dollars different from what Roland had contributed. I also remembered what Viola said the night she came to our house. She said our house was her dad's house and I had nothing. She probably said it based on information he gave her. He believed he had paid the entire down payment. So enlightening!

I remember one night when we were having our differences, Roland was so angry. He said, "I see why Tony said what he did. He is right! You just marry men so you can take their property." His statement hurt deeply. I swallowed, held back the tears, and said, "You can say and believe anything you want. Because it doesn't even matter anymore."

After the tension subsided, Roland agreed to sell me his interest in the house. I applied for a mortgage, refinancing the house. Since I'd never bought a house alone, I asked Roland to go with me to the closing. He agreed. Here we were four years after our divorce, finally getting closure. I believe the most important document we signed was a Personal Undertaking Agreement. The agreement contained all the critical information. For example, it contained the facts from the divorce decree, our agreement regarding the house, each person's equity share, and my gaining sole ownership of the property. Roland was required to quit claim his interest in the house to me, and I was required to pay him the balance after the closing.

We never agreed on how many installment payments had to be made, neither on the deadline for payment in full. I was grateful. I wanted to do the right thing and pay him. Since he was still around all the time, I didn't feel rushed to pay. After a while, I started coming out of the red. I would go to church and testify how God had blessed me to do this or that. Every time I testified, Roland would come to me after service or call me and say, "How would you feel if I owed you money and did everything but repay you?" I told him he was right and I was going to pay him in full real soon. Within a year and four months I'd paid him in full, plus interest.

# 39
# Nothing Hidden

Time passed and we remained amiable. We agreed to resume our five-mile walk. Every morning before work we walked. It was beneficial to both of us. I even hoped it would heal our relationship. We walked during the wee hours of the morning. One morning we returned from walking, and his car was gone. It had been stolen. We called the police, filed a report and waited. Roland accused me of having someone steal his car. He said it was probably my boyfriend. I couldn't win. I thought, *Doesn't he remember his car was stolen before?* Shortly after we were married, I walked out to go to work and his car was gone. Someone had stolen it. So how could he blame me? What causes him to see me as this evil person? For my own sanity, I dismissed the whole situation. I concluded, *this man has real problems. He may even have a mental disorder.* While the real truth is, I should have been the one classified as mentally disturbed. Because even after he accused me, I prepared all the paperwork he needed for his insurance company. I even researched the prices for the trunk full of tools, which was in the car when it was stolen.

One Sunday afternoon a girlfriend asked me whether I still had my life on hold, waiting for Roland. I answered,

"No. I've met someone, but I'm not sure it's going anywhere". She was happy for me. Then she asked whether my new friend was ever married. I said, "Yes, but his wife died a year ago." Then she said she had not planned to tell me, but since I was moving forward with my life, she would. She said Jezzy called her and the caller ID showed the caller as Jezzy Hackman. She asked had Roland married Jezzy. I told her I did not know. I also told her Roland swore to me he would never marry Jezzy. He said he never had a desire to marry her, even when they were together. We agreed I should ask Roland about the name situation. When I asked him, he said, "No, I'm not married to her and you would never understand." I told him to try me. He repeated, "You would never understand." I guess he was right. I never understood Jezzy's control over him.

One day like every other, information just fell in my lap. I heard a rumor that Roland had bought Jezzy a house. I was told his name was on the house, and it was located in Gurnee. I ached as I faced the embarrassment and disrespect. One Friday night after church, I asked his sister Jennifer if I could drive her home. I needed to talk with her. Jennifer was a God-fearing woman who loved God and people. She would do anything for anyone, without an expectation of a return. She agreed and I took her home. We sat in the car in front of her apartment and talked. I asked about the rumor. The words that followed shocked me. She didn't address my question. Instead she immediately responded, "Roland wanted to talk to you about that situation, but he knew he could not talk to you without you getting angry. He said you were hard to talk to." Totally agitated, I said, "What you are saying is that it is my fault my husband bought his whore a house?" She quickly answered, "He didn't buy her the house. She needed to use somebody's name with an income. She asked him and he did it. Anyway, he's in the process of getting his name off of it. He has already talked with a lawyer." When she paused, I jumped in and said, "He wasn't satisfied until he got every penny that I owed him from the house. Yet, he can buy a whore a house and I'm the problem because I'm hard to talk to? Give me a break! Roland and everything he represents can go to hell, because that's where all of this mess is going. I've taken all I plan to take." After a heated period, things calmed down. We talked for a long time, prayed, and said good night. I asked Roland about the rumor. He said, "I did not buy her a house. It's a long story." My mind was tormented. I needed answers. I called him repeatedly, asking him to tell me the long story. His answer was always the same, "It's a long story and you wouldn't understand." If I did not understand, it would not have been anything different ... because I had never completely understood anything about his family.

# 40
# Memories

Memories are lasting. You must control how they affect your life. Memories can creep into your life during daily activities or places visited. The people you see. The social and recreational things you do. Memories! I didn't realize Roland and I had shared so many good memories. Most of them occurred during the first two years of marriage. After that, turmoil covered the good memories.

When we were first married, we were inseparable. We did everything together: We went to church, socialized with others, did household chores, went grocery shopping, walked through the malls, frequented the raceway, went to the theater and the movies, went out to dinner, visited family and friends. He visited me at work and brought me flowers. Such memories left an indelible impression in my heart.

I remember the days when we walked hand-in-hand around the block, down the street to Roxie's house. We regularly strolled around the beach, sat on the rocks, and watched the waves roar. We took blankets and lied on the beach. We attended the Independence Day fireworks celebration. We watched and enjoyed the city parades together. On special occasions we had dinner at our favorite restaurants. When Roland and I went shopping, he was so patient. He would sit and wait as I shopped. Other times we went shopping just for him. We totally changed his style of clothing. Roland was distinguished looking, but his wardrobe was a little antiquated. He gave me the freedom to change his style. The change improved his self-esteem and confidence level. I saw a new Roland. He felt good about himself. I felt good for him. He smiled as he admired himself in the mirror. He began overcoming his inferiority complex regarding his buttocks and legs. I regularly reminded him that I loved them and that he should not be concerned.

I remember the surprises for special and non-special occasions. One evening we had a fight. The next morning he showed up at my job with a dozen of red roses. It created a big stir in the office. Every whisper brought me joy. This was special because Roland was not one to apologize. Sometimes he was so sensitive and loving that I forgot his quick temper, his jealousy and his stubbornness. He would routinely buy me roses, even if he couldn't afford them. If he couldn't afford a dozen, he bought a half dozen. If not a half dozen, then one rose. If not one, an artificial rose. The thought was what mattered.

We revisited places we frequented when we were dating. Once, we spent an entire day at the Great Lakes Raceway. We sat watching one car after the other race, predicting which one would win. I'd never been to a car race before. Roland knew I'd dreamt of driving a race car, so he allowed me to experience my dream secondhand. It was a sunny day. The heat was uncomfortable, but we stayed and watched the races all day. While we watched the cars race, we gave each other manicures when there was down time in the races.

Scroll down to the perfect family photo-shoot. Claudia and James were over for the weekend. The six of us got dressed for church. We decided to take some pictures before leaving. This was the first opportunity to function as a family. I asked Robert to take some snapshots of us. Robert was not attending church with us. As he took each snapshot, I noticed a trend. Claudia's demeanor changed with each snapshot. If the picture included her and Roland, she smiled brightly. If it included her, James, and Roland, she again smiled excitedly. However, if the snapshot included my girls or me, her look was distorted. I guess I should have seen what was to come from that first interaction, but I didn't.

The memories that dominated me most were the ones within the walls of my home. There were so many good and bad memories. The walls contained a distorted mirage of memories. It was painful.

One day God spoke to my heart. He said He would remove the pain from my heart. I didn't know how he would do it, but I knew He would keep His promise. After a while, I experienced an urgency to remodel my home. The projects kept me busy. It kept my mind off of my troubles. I started with the bathroom and kitchen. It was very costly. Nevertheless, the satisfaction of my accomplishments made it worthwhile.

I completed one project after the other. I had new windows installed throughout the house. I had new gutters, downspouts and a new roof installed. The house was a brick bungalow. However, the back of the house was a frame extension. So, I had vinyl siding installed. When we bought the house, the basement was not finished. One small area was paneled. There was an old 1940 octopus-type furnace. It sat in the middle of the basement. The gigantic ducts extended all around the basement. We had to bend our heads to avoid hitting them. My next project was to remodel the basement. It took months to complete it: new plumbing, electricity, waterproofing, sump and ejection pumps, and plastering. I also had a new efficiency furnace, new water tank, and a clean-air unit installed. When completed, I had a large family room, with a large closet that covered the entire back wall, two bedrooms, an office area, enclosed laundry and furnace rooms, and a new bathroom.

I had no time for old memories, good or bad. Next, I bought central air conditioning. I had ducts installed to reach the attic bedroom so the heat and air could be distributed there. Next, the living room, dining room, and bedrooms were remodeled. I removed the drop ceilings. Refinished all walls and installed new ceiling fixtures. Then the enclosed back porch was insulated, plastered, and converted to a library. Built-in bookshelves and a utility closet were added. Finally, I made it to the garage, which should have been condemned years earlier. Nevertheless, I had it refurbished.

Along with all the remodeling, I filled the rooms with new furniture—the type of furniture I'd always wanted. I had no one to box me in. This was between God and me.

Finally, I sat down and breathed. It was a breath of satisfaction. All of my work was completed. I loved what God had allowed me to accomplish. I was happy in my new home. It represented me. It was a dream come true. Then God spoke, "I promised you I would make you forget the pain of your past." God allowed me to rebuild an entire house in less than five years, so the reminders of my past could be erased.

It didn't matter which room I walked into. There was nothing to remind me of Roland, his children, his ex-wives, Jezzy, or her children. He had nothing to do with anything that existed in my home. God had enabled me to control my memories and prevent them from consuming me.

# 41
# The Cobra

Approximately two years after the cruise, I had a frightening dream. It was so terrifying I began to cry. As the dream unfolded, Roland and I were standing in a house that looked like Mama Anna's house. We were standing in separate rooms, but we could see each other. I stood near the stove and he was near the front door. Between us was a cobra curled up, with its head raised high and ready to strike. The thoughts of the cobra echoed through the house. They could be heard as if they were orally expressed, saying, "I'm going to bite you, and it's going to be a bite of death."

Panic stricken, I began shouting, "Roland, don't you hear what the cobra is thinking? It is thinking it's going to bite you, and it will be a bite of death!" The yelling and commotion did not distract the cobra. Its attention was focused on Roland. It had a look of determination to accomplish its mission.

Hysterically, I shouted again. "Roland, don't you hear what the cobra is thinking?" My voice trailed off and in almost a whisper I said, "Roland, it's going to bite you, and it's going to be a bite of death." Roland never responded. He just stood there, motionless. Then suddenly, without warning, the cobra's head went swiftly forward; its teeth penetrated Roland's left arm, and a flow of blood gushed out. In a robotic motion, Roland caught the blood with his right hand, wiped it on his pants, and took small steps toward the door. He repeated the same actions over and over until he faded out of the front door. The cobra, satisfied, curled up and relaxed in the middle of the floor. I stood at the stove crying and muttering, "He didn't even try to resist. He didn't even try to fight it. It didn't have to end this way." I awoke in a cold sweat. I was scared. I was afraid for Roland. My body was trembling. I couldn't explain what I was experiencing, but I knew Roland needed help. I also knew he would never find the strength to help himself.

Later that morning, I called Roland. I told him about the dream. As tears rolled down my face, I said, "Roland, this is not about you and me. This is about you. The devil is trying to destroy you. Whether our lives ever reunite, you need to know that the devil has a trap set to destroy you; and sadly, you are not even fighting back." I begged him to pray for God's help and to resist the devil. He lived with his sister Esther, who was an intercessor, so I shared the dream with her also.

After I had the dream about the cobra, I learned that Mother Duncan had a similar dream when we were still married. In her dream, Roland's arms were tied together behind his back. A rope was around his neck. Someone at the end of the rope was leading him around like a zombie. Mother Duncan said she could not see who the person was at the end of the rope. However, when she told Esther about the dream, Esther immediately said it was me. She also said, "Raven is holding Roland in bondage." Mother Duncan said she immediately stopped Esther's accusation against me by saying, "The person at the other end could not be seen."

# 42
# Lurking in the Dark

During the same month of my dream, an incident occurred. Our New Year's revival meeting was ending. The speaker was Bishop Marshal Conner. The service was great. Afterwards, I assisted in giving our guests guided tours of the church. Roland, who was ushering, agreed to hold my coat until I was finished. When we finished touring, I approached Bishop Conner, took him by the hand, and asked him to come with me. He followed me. I took him to Roland, who was standing at the front entrance. He was still holding my coat, waiting for me to return. When Bishop Conner and I reached him, I briefly explained our marital situation. I asked Bishop Conner to pray for us. While I was explaining things to Bishop Conner, I noticed Roland was distracted. He was looking over my shoulders, shrugging his shoulders in an I-don't-know gesture. I turned and saw Jezzy standing behind me. The expression on Roland's face was one of fear and confusion. He was like a child who knew chastisement was coming from a parent. I turned and looked at her and said, "I bind this demonic spirit that's always lurking in the dark." She gave me a catty smile and stood there, unmoved by my prayer or me. Bishop Conner was ministering to Roland. So, I blocked her view of him.

She stayed there, undaunted by my actions, patiently waiting. Before Bishop Conner prayed, he reminded us of how God had placed Roland in his heart during the last revival. He said he had been praying for him. The three of us held hands as Bishop Conner prayed. When he finished praying, he turned to me and told me to leave Roland alone, and just pray. He didn't speak a prophetic word, but "leave him alone and just pray" was enough.

To my amazement, Jezzy was still waiting when our prayer ended. To stop any foul plans she may have made, I asked Roland for his help. I told him I had parked over three blocks away and since it was dark, I needed him to walk me to my car. He refused. I saw his eyes meet hers. Filled with pain, I began to walk away. Just then, Brother Alexander walked through the doors and said, "I brought Mother Thomas' car to the front for her." I said, "Does that mean you will go and get mine also?"

"Yes," he said. He made two trips before he could find it, because it was extremely dark. The car was further than he had expected. After that night's episode, I wasn't sure whether Roland was even worthy of me. My question remained, *God, is this the end?*

I guess not. A few weeks later pie was in my face again. That night was like every other Sunday night. It was normal for the members to gather in the vestibule and dining hall to fellowship after service.

It was also normal for everyone to march out of the sanctuary. The lights were turned off and doors closed. What was not normal was what I saw as I walked toward the main door to leave. I saw Roland through the glass doors. He was standing in the back of the dark sanctuary. When I looked closer, I saw he was not alone. Facing him was Jezzy. Scene or no scene, I didn't care. As he walked out, I said, "Roland, what's this? Why are you in the sanctuary, in the dark, with that whore? Don't you even respect the House of God?" He answered angrily while waving his hand at me, "Raven, it's nothing. You are always making something out of nothing." Then he walked away.

# 43
# Breaking the Link

I was humiliated by the things I allowed in the relationship I embraced with Roland. I finally realized that I was in a prison and I had the key! I was the one who wouldn't open the door and let myself out! That night I told God if He gave me the strength, I would use the key. I made a decision to release myself from my prison cell.

The first order of business was to discontinue the help I was receiving from Roland. All of the following had to stop. No more calling him to fix things. No more asking his advice on things. No more calling him to come and pose as the man of my house during my business transactions. No more telling him about my next endeavors. No more washing my hair or giving me a pedicure. No more asking him to pick me up when I was stranded. No longer would he maintain the keys to my house and garage. No longer would he escort me to events. No more will I accept his volunteered favors. No longer would I appear helpless before him. No more would I allow him to accompany me to the hairdresser. No more would we walk the five miles together. The list would go on and on if I told all the good things he did for and with me as a former spouse. No more! The link had to be broken. It had to be an immediate and clean break. We had nothing that linked us. When I couldn't do it, the Holy Spirit helped me.

Shortly after my liberation, I needed the keys to my house and garage. I called Roland and told him I needed my keys. Molly and I drove to Esther's house, where he lived, to pick them up. He reluctantly surrendered them. With confusion on his face, he asked, "Why?" I said, "I just need them." He asked if he would be able to use the keys to get his things out of the garage. I said, "Yes, just let me know when you want to get them" God knew my future, and He began breaking ties I couldn't.

# 44
# Dressing for Battle

In September of the same year, the Lord said, "I want you to start going to the church at 6:00 p.m. to pray." I said, "Okay, Lord. I'll leave work, go by the house, change clothes, and then go to the church." I wanted to do it that way because I perspired so badly. I didn't want to perspire in my work clothes. He said, "No. You will leave work and go directly to prayer. If you go home, you'll start doing this and that. The telephone will ring and any other distraction the enemy can send, he will send." I said, "Okay, Lord."

I obeyed the voice of the Lord. I took extra clothes to work to change into before leaving for prayer. For a change, I was immediately obeying God. If I had not, the enemy would have consumed me. My disobedience would have been my destruction. God knew what the enemy had plotted against me. He wanted to fortify my strength.

Each day in prayer, I felt a unique working of the Holy Spirit. Even though I couldn't understand or explain it at the time, I knew He was doing something special in me. I couldn't wait to see the completion, because the process was strange. Often during prayer, I wailed, mourned, cried, sobbed, and laughed. I prayed in my heavenly language. I prayed the Scriptures. I sang songs. I traveled back and forth across the altar. I pulled my clothes from my chest and my abdomen as if I were pulling something out of me. Other times, I collapsed in His Presence. I tried to understand what was going on. I wasn't sad. Things were not going bad for me. To the contrary, things were going extremely well. I concluded the Spirit of God understood what type of war I was engaged in, because I didn't. The prayer sessions were consistent until the day of what would have been the devil's victorious attack.

The days that followed cannot be understood in the natural realm. The workings of God can only be discerned by the Spirit of God. One day I heard in my spirit "wedding/ marriage." I began to analyze what it could possibly mean. After all, I was an analyst by profession; I was paid to analyze. My analysis maintained an excellent accuracy rate. So I concluded, since Jezzy's daughter was getting married, it probably meant Roland would give her away at the wedding. Using my intellect totally confused the issue. I missed what the Spirit was saying to me. Even though I had missed the real message, I was still troubled by my analysis. I ached because of the unknown and the troublesome possibilities.

# 45
# The Stuff

I was still struggling with breaking the ties. I kept going
back and forth. One day I was confident that the ties were
broken. Then the next day I wasn't sure. I was living such an
unstable life. Yet, God patiently waited for me.

A few weeks later, I smelled gas in the house. I knew
God was breaking the ties, but this was an emergency. I
called Roland. Of course, it never occurred to me to call
the gas company. I repeatedly called him but never got an
answer. Then I called Esther's number. She was evasive
regarding his whereabouts. She said she would send her son
to help me. I thanked her and said good-bye. Her son came,
checked the stove, and lit the pilot light. I thanked him and
he departed. The next day Roland stopped by to ask about
the gas smell. Esther told him I'd called the previous night. I
told him it was taken care of. However, he asked to check it
again. While checking the gas line, he pulled the stove out,
washed it down, cleaned the sides, and placed it back—all
without my asking.

Later during the week he called and asked to get his
things out of the garage. I agreed to let him in on Friday.
As agreed, he came and gathered his belongings. While he
was present, I kept hearing those words again, "wedding/

marriage." Again, I analyzed it away. Thinking, *He wouldn't dream of giving Jezzy's daughter away.* Considering, he had continuously denied any current dealings with her. On the other hand, I questioned, *Why is it suddenly so important to get his stuff out of the garage? It had been there this long, so why now?* As he finished packing his things into his niece's car, I reminded him he had promised to check my ceiling light. He removed it and took it with him to repair. He also promised to return it by Friday. I thanked him and he left.

Friday night after church, Roland came to replace my light fixture. While getting out of our cars, his grandson rode by on a bike. He stopped and said, "Hi, Granddaddy," and talked with him for a while, then began riding away on his bike. I called to him jokingly, "So Junior, you don't know me when your grandfather is around?" Before the child could answer, Roland chimed in, "He didn't see you." How did he know what the child saw or didn't see? His grandson turned and said, "I didn't see you." I said, "I know you didn't. Because you had no way of knowing this was my car." I chatted with him a little while and he went on his way. As I walked toward the house, I thought, *Roland has not changed yet.* We entered the house. He repaired the light. I thanked him and he left.

That night, I had a very comforting dream. It was quite vivid and most intriguing. In the dream, the trauma of a death had just occurred within my family. I was feeling overwhelmed. In the midst of the trauma, a tall slender man walked out of the shadows into my life. I could not see his detailed image, but the aura of his presence captivated me. He was suave. With a smile he said, 'You don't look like the type of lady who would fall for a man saying, "My search is over. You are who I've been looking for." With raised eyebrows, I smiled at him. He continued, "And you don't look like the type of lady who would believe a man who says, 'I know we just met, but I think I'm in love with you.'" I watched him as he came closer with each flattering statement. I was consumed by his tenderness. When he started his third statement with "You don't look like ..." with a half smile, I interrupted him and said, "Since you know what I don't look like and would not fall for, could you tell me what I do look like? What you would say? Let's see whether I would fall for you." We began to laugh. The scene returned to the trauma. I felt weighted down. Everyone was depending on me. As we reentered the mourning scene, I noticed that the man's presence remained and brought me calmness. I whispered to myself, this is what I need. He began to take charge, controlling everything that concerned me. All the things that troubled me, he took them and handled them without my assistance. Tears of relief filled my eyes. My heart was lifted. Then I heard a voice saying, "This is the man for you. He is your husband. He is compatible with you. He will appreciate who you are and give you what you need." I began to experience a joy and a fulfillment I had not known for a long time. As I looked at the man, I heard myself say, "Oh no, not another light-skinned man!" From the beginning of the dream until the end, I was not able to see the man's face. However, I felt his presence. I heard his voice. I experienced his laughter. From this dream, I knew I would be married again.

Also, my dream confirmed a previous dream that one of the sisters at church had. One Sunday morning, I was walking through the vestibule of the church and Sister Gwen Cooper stopped me to tell me she had dreamt about me. She was reluctant and apologetic about telling me. I thought she had received a rebuke from the Lord for me. I told her, "If God told you to tell me something, just do it." She said, "I'm not saying this is from the Lord, because it might even offend you. I dreamt that you got married again, *but* I don't think that's what you want because you seem to have it all together and so complete with yourself." With tears in my eyes, I told her I received her dream as prophecy, because only God knew the desires of my heart. So, it was easy for me to grab hold of the interpretation of my dream. I would be married again!

# 46
# The D-D-D

Saturday, October 17, 1998, was the devil's defeated day in my life. The devil intended evil, but God transformed it into good. The events of this day propelled me to my expected end. This would be the day all questions regarding my divorce would be answered. All questions concerning what was going on with Roland would become meaningless. I woke up early that Saturday morning. I was accompanying Tina in search of a dining hall for her husband's surprise birthday party. I arose excited. I told her and Joni about my dream. I told them the Lord had shown me my husband. There was a man out there who was compatible with me. They laughed at me. Nevertheless, I felt an assurance the Lord was preparing a husband for me and me for a husband.

Tina and I were out all day. When we returned early evening, there were three messages from Esther. Puzzled that she had called so many times, I started to return her call. Then Tina asked to call her husband first. She made her call and left for Wisconsin.

I returned Esther's call. She began by asking, "Did my brother tell you anything?" I said, "No. What was he supposed to tell me?" She responded with another question, "Didn't you see him last night?" I answered, "Yes.

He came by and fixed my ceiling light." She asked again, "And he didn't tell you anything?" I said, "No. What's going on?" She said, "Roland married Jezzy today." I responded, "Praise the Lord." She continued, "Jennifer said she would tell the pastor. I decided to tell you so you could hear it from 'The Family.' I didn't want you to be caught off guard. With someone from the outside coming to you with it." I said, "Thanks. God bless. Good-bye." I felt absolutely nothing. I did not feel hurt, anger, or betrayal. I felt nothing!

Until the day of their marriage, Roland had been by my side. He took care of the maintenance in the house. He did more for me during our time of divorce than he did during our entire marriage. Whatever I wanted to be repaired, he repaired it. Whatever I needed added or taken away, he did it. Whatever I desired to change or improve, he did it. During our divorce he completed tasks I'd begged him to do when we were married. Ironically, while divorced he fulfilled my requests after my asking only once.

I picked up the telephone and began calling my friends, the friends who had believed God with me, the ones who had prayed with me and expected God to deliver. To my surprise, friend after friend was shocked. Some were not only shocked but also hurt, and at the point of tears. Unbelief overwhelmed them. I had to abruptly end some of my conversations because they were refusing to believe it.

Afterwards, I called Tina and Kevin. Tina had not arrived home. I told Kevin and asked him to tell Tina. Joni was the last person I told. I knew it would be difficult for her. I called her into my bedroom and quickly told her. She stood motionless. A look of dismay formed on her face. Tears filled her eyes. When she finally spoke she said, "Why did he keep coming around here? Why did he keep acting like he cared? Why did he keep pretending like you were going to get back together?" Feeling her pain, I said, "Joni, don't cry for me. I am fine. God has it all in His control. Rejoice with me because God has vindicated me. You may not see it now, but trust me, you will." I told her to get dressed because we were going to church. The Sanctuary Choir was celebrating its anniversary. We dressed and left for church.

En route to church, the Holy Spirit said, "Raven, I want you to shut the mouths of the whisperers." I responded, "I don't understand." Then, Esther's message echoed in my mind. "So no one can come to you with it." With a chuckle the Holy Spirit said, "Shut the mouths of the whisperers by telling it yourself. If you tell it, there's nothing for anyone else to tell." I did as the Holy Spirit had instructed. I told everyone I passed as I entered the church. I enjoyed every moment of it. It was hilarious. When I finished, I took my seat in the Sanctuary and smiled with contentment. I sat waiting for the worship service to begin.

The worship service began. It was unbelievable! The first song sung was "I'm Free." The words were:

*I'm free, praise the Lord, I'm free.*
*No longer bound, no more chains holding me.*
*My soul is resting, it's just a blessing,*
*Praise the Lord, hallelujah, I'm free.*

I could barely control myself. God was sending me a coded message. He was celebrating me. My liberty was being proclaimed from the rooftop. If that wasn't enough, when the song ended, another unbelievable thing happened. The testimony leader, of all the people in the audience, asked me to stand and give a testimony about the wonder-working power of God. It was hilarious. I could hardly believe it. I stood up and testified. I proclaimed that God had my back covered, even from the foundation of the world. Mother

Duncan said my testimony was a mini-sermon. Surely, you would think all this attention would be enough, but God didn't stop there. During the sermons, one of the speakers used Joni as her main point of reference during her entire message. Joni was being encouraged also. I said, "God, you are too much." He whispered, "Didn't I say my love would remove any shame?" I smiled and said, "Yes, Lord!"

God wasn't finished yet. At the end of the service, Meechy gave me a gift. It was a book she had bought for me. Get this, the book was titled *Don't Sweat The Small Stuff*. When Meechy bought that gift, she had no way of knowing the day's events, but God did. Everything was a coded message to me. What happened was truly small stuff next to my Big God and what He had in store for me!

On Sunday, Roland came to church with his new wife, Jezzy. The message was on marriage, divorce, and remarriage. It was a soul-searching message. The preacher talked about doors left open after marriage, the influence of unhealthy ties to ex-girlfriends, the ungodly control of family members, and repeated failures in marriage. Sometimes the Word of God was so piercing, I cringed. I had experienced from Roland everything the preacher was sharing. Roland came to church dressed in his usher's uniform. As he ushered, I caught him staring at me several times. There was a sick longing in his eyes; it was almost frightening. When I caught him looking at me, I looked straight ahead as if he were invisible. From that moment, my prayer to God was this: "God make them invisible. Cause me not to see them." God answered my prayer. As time passed, they became less and less visible as I rejoiced in the Lord.

On Monday, I called Roland at work. I asked him to pick up the remainder of his belongings. I said, "Unlike your new wife, I will not be calling you ever again. Neither will I pursue you, as she did, in an attempt to get you back." I couldn't help myself. I had to ask. "Roland, didn't you respect me enough to tell me of this disgraceful affair?" He began with, "I told Esther I was going to tell you after church on Sunday, but the word got out like wild fire." I smiled as I remembered the Holy Spirit's instructions. Roland didn't have a clue I was the one who started the wild fire. He attempted to continue his conversation, but I stopped him saying, "Please don't go there. You told Esther? This is not about Esther. This is about me. Don't tell me what you told Esther." Then I said, "Better yet, don't explain. You don't owe me an explanation." He quickly agreed, "Okay." I started wavering. I wanted the explanation, yet I didn't. I couldn't believe he was still hiding behind his sister's skirt. Then I heard myself say, "Go ahead, finish what you were saying." He responded, "No. You said I didn't owe you an explanation." We confirmed the time for picking up his belongings. While awaiting his arrival, I remembered things I had forgotten, things that belonged to him. I gathered them all, ready to give them to him when he arrived. The doorbell rang. I told him to wait on the porch, and that I would bring his things to him. I told him as a married man, he would never walk over my threshold again.

When I returned with his stuff, I reminded him of the "Cobra" dream. I told him his adulterous new wife was the cobra. I expressed my sympathy, telling him his marriage was cursed and that I pitied him because he was about to experience the ride of his life. I also told him that I pray God extends him mercy for the saving of his soul. We never spoke privately again.

I checked around the house again to make sure nothing remained that belonged to Roland. I found nothing. However, Lis noticed a two-piece outfit Roland bought me for my birthday after our divorce. She snatched it out of my closet and threw it to the floor. Then she told me to get rid of it. It was a very nice outfit. I didn't really want to throw it away, so I gave it to someone.

The following month, God blessed me with a brand new Mercedes Benz. One of the ushers told me that Jezzy said, "Raven may have the Mercedes, but I have the man." I smiled and thought, *I'm sure this adulterous woman doesn't know the God I know, the Righteous Judge.* I believed her statement revealed the feebleness of her mind.

God was blessing me in ways beyond my imagination. He blessed me to pay for my car in full within sixty days. That was one of many miracles God gave me. Ironically, a few weeks after I bought my car, Jezzy showed up with a new SUV. Bless her heart because she didn't even know she was competing with God, and not me.

A short time later, after worship service one night, Esther came to talk with me. She told me about the sorrow and pain the family was suffering because of Roland's marriage. She said Jennifer had been crying since it happened. Then she said, "It will not last. It won't work. I was talking to my niece Wanda, and she said the marriage was demonic and it won't last." I shrugged my shoulders and raised my eyebrows. I had nothing to say. I really didn't care. I felt nothing.

The real test came when she asked me to pray for "The Family." I promised to do so. However, I had some heavy afterthoughts. The nerve! They were hurting and grieving because of their shame and humiliation! What about the shame and disgrace I suffered? Do they even remember how they judged, isolated, and treated me poorly? Her request gravely impacted my emotions. I started talking to myself. "Which one of them cried or prayed for me, or cared about the hell I was going through when I was married to him?" The Lord answered, "I did." He continued,

"You will earnestly pray for them, even as Job prayed for his friends." I prayed and asked God to help them. I asked God to send deliverance. I especially asked for mercy for all of them because there was a portion of my hell to which they contributed. Nevertheless, I knew that *"Whatsoever a man sows, that shall he also reap."*

Weeks passed, and I remained unshaken by the recent events. However, I did not understand my peace. I prayed and asked God whether I was in a state of denial. I knew I loved Roland. I knew in his sick way he loved me. Yet, I had not experienced any heartbreaking emotions. Yes, I'd had situations that triggered an emotional breakdown, but not the kind the situation dictates. Being the emotional crybaby I am, I said, "Lord, please help me not to live a lie. Don't let me deceive myself. Please tell me what's happening." The Lord spoke and said, "Raven, do you remember when you were praying, moving back and forth, pulling your clothes from your chest and your abdomen, wailing and broken before me?" I said, "Yes, Lord." He continued, "That was a symbolic demonstration. You were removing all the residue of Roland and your past from your Spirit. Raven, you are free to live."

God is so awesome! His conversation did not stop there. He continued with another reminder. He said, "Raven, do you remember when you were talking with your friends and you decided to release yourself from your prison cell?" I told the Lord I remembered. He stated, "You did it. You released yourself from your prison cell. Raven, once a warden opens the prison doors, the prisoner walks out. However, he can only go as far as the prison grounds. It takes a higher power to release him to walk off the prison grounds and experience total freedom. You released yourself from your cell. However, you were still on the prison grounds. It took a higher power, Me, to release you from the prison grounds.

Roland and Jezzy did not do this against you. I allowed it for you. You are off the prison grounds. You are free to live."

On two other occasions, Esther came to me about two dreams she had concerning me. Each time, it was after worship service. We were standing in the church dining hall. In the first dream, she said I was dressed in all black, a long black skirt and a doubled-breasted black jacket. I was very happy, going from person to person sharing joy. (Unknown to both of us, she was describing the outfit I would wear to her funeral a year or so later. And my going from person to person talking occurred at her funeral.) She said one thing stood out to her. As I was talking with someone, Roland walked up and said something to me. I very sweetly turned to him and answered him. Then I continued doing what I had been doing. Just as she said that, she whispered, "Don't turn around now. He's walking up behind you this minute." I smiled at her. My back was toward him. In my peripheral vision, I saw him approaching. Not far behind him was his new wife. He said something to Esther. I turned to them and said "God Bless Y'all." That was another step closer to total victory for me.

The other dream Esther shared was simple but powerful. She told me, "I don't know why I keep dreaming about you. This time, God showed me your heart. God showed me your heart was pure and clean." I said, "Esther, I don't have anything against Roland." She stopped me and said, "No, no! It was not just Roland. God said your heart was pure. There was nothing in your heart against anyone." I said, "Praise God! That's good to know. However, I really need to know it for myself." We laughed, kissed, and said good night.

When Esther died, the saving of my life was illuminated. During her funeral, I scanned 'The Family' and softly uttered thanks to God for His grace. Roland was sitting with his fourth wife, Jezzy. The other two Baltimore women's ex-husbands were sitting, one with his third wife and the other alone. All the lineages of ex-wives were present and accounted for. They marched in with "The Family." As I continued scanning "The Family," I saw a sadness. It was not their bereavement. It was their loss of wholesomeness. I closed my eyes and worshiped God. This was one Baltimore woman who was glad to be a Baltimore woman, rather than a member of "The Family." I finally saw the blessedness of being excluded.

Sunday after Sunday, I caught Roland staring at me. I thought, *He's married, why won't he stop looking at me?* His eyes were sad. It disgusted me. He walked around like he was spaced out. He looked like the zombie Mother Duncan dreamt about. A few times he waved at me from afar. I had no desire to respond and didn't. God was always reminding me of lessons I should have learned. He said, "They didn't do it against you. I allowed it for you. If you really believe I allowed it, then you will do what's right."

# 47

# How Is it Spelled?
# H-A-W-A-I-I

Four months later, on February 1, 1999, Tina called. "Ma, if you had an opportunity to go to Hawaii, who would you take with you?" After a few moments of going back and forth, trying to understand why she asked. I said, "Joni." Then she said, "Praise the Lord, that's confirmation." I said, "Tina, what are you talking about?" She said, "In my hands I'm holding an itinerary with your name on it. You and Joni are going to Hawaii for eleven days and ten nights. Flying first class on United Airlines. Staying in a hotel suite with an ocean view. Visiting four islands. You will depart on August 4, 1999, and return on August 15, 1999." This was Tina and Kevin's anniversary celebration. All they asked was to be left alone for three of the eleven days. We could handle that with ease. I could hardly believe the level of love God was showing me.

# 48
# Italy Awaits Me

Two months later, on April 4, 1999, I was leaving my footprints in the sands of Italy. Months earlier, Kevin called and invited me to go with Tina and him to Italy for a week. It was an all-expenses-paid trip, including spending money. All I had to do was to accompany Tina on her shopping sprees in Rome, Florence, and Venice. Life was good! I rejoiced over the miracle-working power of God.

# 49
# Time for Hawaii

August 1999! Who would have thought Hawaii would be my charted course for this hour? Oh well, it had to be cancelled. While we were in Italy, Tina learned she was pregnant with her first child. I purposed in my heart that when that child got older, I would tell him how he interrupted my Hawaii vacation. All was not lost! In 2002, for my 50th birthday, Tina and Kevin took me to dinner on the lake in Wisconsin. They gave me a replacement Hawaii vacation: an all-expenses-paid eleven-day, ten-night Hawaiian cruise. From May 20, 2002 through May 31, 2002, I was aboard the Celebrity Cruises Infinity Ship. They shared with me that Roland wanted to help them with my cruise expenses. So, he gave them $500. The thought turned my stomach, and I demanded they give it back. I said, "He's a married man." They didn't want to hurt his feelings. I said, "Okay, this one is for me." If Roland thought that was the price of freedom, he was sadly mistaken. I wrote him a letter and returned his $500. I decided to write Tony a letter too since he had not stopped his pursuit of me.

*February 6, 2002*

*Roland,*

*I thank God you came into my life when you did. I thank God for the good times we shared. I also thank God for the benefits of the bad times. Roland, those times are over, all of them. Our lives will never again be as one. Don't let life pass you by, just because what we had is dead. Life doesn't always progress the way we hope; nevertheless, we have to live with it. Please close the book on you and me, because we are no more.*

*Roland, when I learned you had voluntarily contributed $500 towards the Hawaiian cruise my children gave me for my birthday, I was confused. God strengthened me to face reality and do the right thing. Accepting that money from you would be the same thing your new wife did to me when we were married. If it was wrong then, it's wrong now. I have enclosed a check in the amount of $500 to reimburse you for your contribution to my birthday gift.*

*Roland, go in peace and seek the fullness God wants to give you in your current life. Remember this one last thing. I want you to know, with all of my heart, I FORGIVE YOU! I forgive you for everything. GOD FORGIVES YOU. Now, FORGIVE YOURSELF and move on. There is nothing for you to hold onto. Nothing can be changed about our past. Everything that is, and everything that has been done, is past. Forget the past and move on. I also hope that you have forgiven me.*

*Enjoy the years you have remaining. I wish you well and pray that God's best comes to you.*

*My heart's greatest desire is to see God in peace!*

*God Bless You,*
*Raven*

*February 6, 2002*

*Tony,*

*I thank God you came into my life when you did. I thank God for the children produced from our union. I thank God for the good times we shared. I also thank God for the benefits of the bad times. Tony, those times are over, all of them. Our lives will never again be as one. You can only hope to be the best daddy you can be to your adult children. I encourage you to do all you can to develop a healthy relationship with your children, son-in-law, and grandchildren. Don't let your life with them pass you by just because what we had is dead. Life doesn't always progress the way we hope; nevertheless, we have to live with it. Please close the book on you and me, because we are no more.*

*Tony, go in peace and seek the fullness God wants to give you in your current life. Remember this one last thing: I want you to know, with all of my heart, I FORGIVE YOU! I forgive you for everything. GOD FORGIVES YOU. Now, FORGIVE YOURSELF and move on. There is nothing for you to hold onto.*

*Nothing can change our past. Everything that is, and everything that has been done, is past. Forget the past and move on. I also hope you have forgiven me.*
*Enjoy the years you have remaining. I wish you well and pray that God's best comes to you. Let's live peacefully as parents of two beautiful daughters.*

*My heart's greatest desire is to see God in Peace!*

*God Bless You,*
*Raven*

While Tina and I were cruising, being adventurous on excursions, I noticed her sleeping and eating patterns. We were having fun, but I saw signs of pregnancy. She'd already had two sons, whom she had left at home. Do I dare ask, "What's going on now?" Yep, her third son was on the cruise with us. At least he had the decency not to interrupt my Hawaiian vacation.

\*\*\*

Raven reached the end of volume two of her diary. She felt she'd been on an emotional roller coaster ride that came to an immediate stop. The jerk caused her to have a quick flashback of Tony and Roland. Tony has remained unmarried because he is "waiting for his family to return." He still believes Raven is coming back to him. Despite the plans, plots, and voodoo practices Jezzy used to get Roland, he divorced her for a younger woman. She is a scorned woman. Raven shook her head and released a heavy sigh. Wow! She asked herself, "What resulted from all of this?" She smiled as she thought of her "knight in shining armor." The husband she'd dreamt about years earlier, has been a reality for the past eleven years. His name is John. He is indeed tall, slender, and light skinned as she had dreamt. He is as sensitive and tender as the man in her dream. He covers and protects her as the dream portrayed. He is a strong black man who leads with integrity and trust. He supports and appreciates her in a way she has never known. He challenges her to be all that she was meant to become. They are best friends who live in their own private world of love. They laugh with and at each other. They laugh at life and love. They live for God together and apart. Raven knows that John was sent to her by God, and John has the same sentiments. She sweetly refers to him as her, "Strong Black Man with Soft Tender Feelings," which was written on a card that he had given her years earlier, while dating. John and Raven travel extensively, enjoying one another, alone in their world. All Raven can say is, "Wow, what a love life!"

She forces herself to snap out of her daydreaming to answer her initial question. "What resulted from all of this?" She answered, "A Better Me!" All of these situations had helped to develop a better Raven. With that, she rose up and wrote a poem to celebrate her life.

# 50
# A Better Me

There's a dream in the heart of every little girl;
Reflecting her desires in this big-wide-world.
A dream to be loved, by everyone we know,
Even though we realize, this could never be so.
We accept the thing called "Life," and live the best we can;
Even as it forces us, to follow its unrevealing hand.
Life brings us experiences we would rather reject,
resisting the truth that "God's not finished with me yet."

As truth collides with life, let us be real.
No one wants pain to be the primary emotion they feel.
We congregate in the 'zone,' where we comfortably exist.
Because becoming 'A Better Me,' seems such a great risk.
We avoid the rough roads, destined for us to trod.
Not realizing, these roads lead us directly to God.
This is a dilemma, each of us must settle;
Or we'll delay our opportunity to become better.

The day Jesus Christ came and set me free,
Was the day I truly became the "Real Me."
The "Real Me" was the path for the 'Better Me' to come
forth.

Now the 'Better Me' is expanding, at a very rapid growth.
I boldly declare, I have become "A Better Me."
Seeing clearer the person God intended me to be.
I am a "Me," that no one else can become.
I am the past, present, and future Me, and there's only one.
I was who I was then. I am who I am now.
I will be who I will be.
As ... I continue becoming "A BETTER ME!"

# Why "No Scars"

Why "No Scars"?

You may think it is not possible to go through the things contained in this book and come out with no scars. Allow me to disagree as you walk with me down *Memory Lane*. Coming out with no scars is dependent upon who's covering you. God was with me, He was on my side, He was my rearguard, and He went before me. He is the very essence of a "Body Guard!"

It was New Year's Eve, 1998. We were within a few hours of a new year. All of my life I was in church when the new year came in, and this year was no different. However, this year the service was being held in the gymnasium of the church. The decor was festive. Parishioners were excitedly gathering. We were invited to wear formal attire, but as always, welcomed to wear whatever clothes we had. I'd found just the right seat. It had a good view and was somewhat close to the front. The chair next to me was empty. Within a short time, a voice said, "Sister Rena, is someone sitting here?" I looked up and responded, "Yes, you are. It has your name on it". We laughed, she sat down, and I embraced her. It was Sandra Ham. She had recently become a member of our church. We talked as we waited for the service to begin.

In the middle of our conversation, she looked me in the eyes and said, "You are such a beautiful woman, inside and out." I was taken aback. Graciously accepting a compliment was one of my weak areas. Rather than just saying, "Thank you," I said, "Girl, you are looking at someone who has been through hell and high waters." She simply responded, "You can't tell it!" This time I embraced her and whispered, "Thank you" in her ear. I was glad the praise team started to sing because I was choked with emotions as tears welled up in my eyes, remembering what God had brought me through. It was great to know I did not look like what I'd gone through.

The next day, Lis and I were talking on the telephone and I told her what had happened at the service. When I told her the story, instead of saying Sandra said, "You can't tell it," I said, "No Scars." Lis began to laugh and yelled, "Re, that's the title for your book, "No Scars." I immediately knew that she was correct and this was a God-ordained book title. I was so excited. To further show that it was God, I explained to Lis that Sandra did not say, "No Scars," she said, "You can't tell it." We rejoiced as we marveled at God's doings. The service being held in the gymnasium rather than the Sanctuary was another assurance that God orchestrated my receiving the book title. In the sanctuary, Sandra would probably not have been sitting next to me. Like most parishioners, we had seating preferences; mine was in the front, while Sandra's was in the back. We had never sat together in the Sanctuary. To God be the Glory!

Here we are on Memory Lane, where the unrevealed is revealed. We will walk slowly and deliberately, allowing God to speak to our hearts.

You've probably heard them before, words spoken to keep from looking foolish. Have you spoken them? Those famous last words, "If I knew then what I know now, I would…" do what? The same thing?

When I was about 25 years old, Missionary Margaret Solomon, a speaker at the Women's Aglow Fellowship in Baltimore, Maryland, said to me, "Thus saith the Lord, 'Hold fast, don't give up, because I, the Lord thy God, am on thy side. I will uphold you and no evil shall destroy you.'"

That evening, during a service at Little Tabernacle in Baltimore, Maryland, Missionary Ray Solomon (not knowing that his wife had prophesied to me earlier that day) said to me, "The light of the Glory of God is shining upon your head. Receive the burning of the Holy Ghost upon you now. God said that many obstacles have come your way, but you shall not be destroyed, because the same things that the devil used to try to destroy you, I will use to bring you up again."

In March 1977, the pressure of my mother's illness sent me into a tailspin. I felt I was losing my mind. I was in South Carolina trying to take care of the business surrounding my mom's hospitalization. I felt so alone because I was away from the spiritual support of my friends. Nevertheless, back in Baltimore, Maryland, my friends had attended a service where God spoke to the evangelist about me. While preaching, he stopped and told the church that they needed to pray for me because I was in trouble. After service my friends called and told me what had happened. I received strength and hope.

On July 19, 1979, I dreamt that I was walking with others on a road made of solid ice. While walking on the road of ice, one other person and I decided to walk on the side of the road. After a while, we realized that the ice on the side of the road was soft. It was melting and began to drift away. The person and I decided to get back on the solid ice, but as we attempted to do so, the realization of helplessness hit us and we cried for help. The others who were on the road tried to help me first, but to no avail; so they proceeded to help the other person. Just in the nick of time they caught her and pulled her up as the ice gave away. All of them, including the person they pulled up, returned to help me, but they still could not pull me back onto the solid ice. As my ice began to give way, they threw up their hands, acknowledging that they couldn't help me.

As I was falling, I saw a sea of roaring waves waiting to swallow anything that dared to enter the sea. As my body reached the tip of the tallest wave, almost touching the sea, there suddenly appeared a door out of nowhere. The door was not there when the people were trying to pull me up. Yet, it reached from deep within the bottom of the sea to far above the solid ice road. With no efforts of my own, almost robotically, I reached for the door. My strength was fading fast, but I managed to catch the doorknob. The door was made of rubber, and the waves caused it to spring my body upward like elastic. As I was coming up, I cried, "Lord, you waited until I almost died before you helped me." Then there I was, back on the solid ice road, safe and sound.

So many of the situations in my marriages were like that solid ice road experience. I felt that I was almost dead before the Lord helped me.

In December 1980, at the age of twenty-eight, I left home to commit suicide; instead I ended up at a church on Biddle Street in Baltimore. I had never been there before and I cannot explain how I found it that night. Broken, weak, and filled with pain, I entered a service with a prophetic anointing in the midst. The young preacher called me out into the aisle and said, "God said the devil desires to destroy you. Many ditches have been dug all around you, but God said if you would turn your face like flint toward Him, He will cause your enemies to fall into the ditches that were dug to destroy you." He continued prophesying for a long while, regarding things that only God knew about. When it was all said and done, all I knew was that God had spoken to me and given me hope in my paralyzed state.

A few years later, Rosalie Edwards said to me, "The Lord has called you into a work for Him that when you touch the sick they will be healed. This night God hath anointed your hands to bring life. With your touch, gently rub your hand over the person's back and head and pray silently. God will heal and set free through your hands. Your house shall be called a "Sanctuary of Prayer".

At the onset of my move to Evanston, Illinois, until this day, Dr. Randolph Moore of Chicago, was used by God to change my whole spiritual persona. His ministry changed my faith, my vision, my expectations, my goals, my dreams, my thoughts, and my decisions. The ministry of Dr. Moore affected literally every area of my life. God used him to open my eyes to behold a BIG GOD. At the beginning of each new year, he came to our church to conduct a New Year's revival. He ministered to me in almost every service of every year. His prophecies to me were of such magnitude that they seemed impossible. However, today I can tell you that almost every one of them has been manifested.

Once he told me, "Sister Rena, you don't even know or realize the power that you have with God." I began believing that I had power with God. I began living like I had power with God. Another time he told me, "God said that you have the power to do and become even greater than Pastor Jennifer Cooper (fictitious name). Pastor Cooper was a renowned pastor residing on the south side of Chicago. He continued with, "Not to do what she's doing, but the power to achieve what she achieves through influence." There is one prophecy that I replay in my mind constantly because it assures me of God's presence and His love. Dr. Moore said, "Sister Rena, I see you driving in your car. You are crying and talking to the Lord. You are saying you didn't think things were going to be like this. You'd promised yourself that you would never go through anything like this again. It is more than you had bargained for and you are tired. God says dry your eyes for He is with you to bring you to an expected end."

In December 1997, during the Christmas holiday I visited my children in Milwaukee, Wisconsin. While out eating, at approximately 1:00 a.m., we saw Brother Johnny at the restaurant. He was from one of the churches in Milwaukee. We greeted one another and suddenly he began to prophesy. He said, "Your prosperity is in your hands. God is waiting for you. Your prosperity is waiting for you. God is going to elevate you in the Word. He is going to give you a new level of revelation of His Word; without a title. Your pastor won't even understand what is happening with you. People shall give into your bosom, not monetary or materially, but they are going to give into YOU and as they give into YOU, they are going to be blessed. Businesses shall come out of them because of what they impart into you. You will be a mentor for young people. They will cling to you. You will take them into your home. There is going to be a breaking. God is going to break you and it will not feel good, but trust God. God will be with you as he was with Joseph and Joshua.

Saturday morning, October 3, 1998, I was in a deep sleep. I heard a voice prophesying. The prophecy kept repeating two sentences over and over. **"Stand. You must focus your eyes upon me. This is the day of war."** I wiped my eyes, trying to determine where the sound was coming from. It was coming out of my spirit and I heard the voice say, "Arise and write." I sat up on the side of the bed and began to write what I'd heard. After I wrote the two sentences, the rest came forth:

*Stand. You must focus your eyes upon me. This is the day of war. You are in the heat of battle. Don't be deceived. It is not calm! There is a rumbling in the earth. There is a moving and a shaking. You may not be able to see it with your eyes, or hear it with your ears, but be aware and know, it is happening.*

*Arm yourself. Build yourself up. Bind your hearts together. Uphold one another. Strengthen one another. Encourage one another. Let none be lost. Stand together! Fight! Focus! You need each other more now than ever before. Put your backs to backs! Shoulders to shoulders! Hearts to hearts! Fortify your walls and strengthen your gates. Don't let the enemy win. He is defeated. He cannot win, if you stand together and fight. You are the Victors.*

*I desire to do a work in you. I am in the midst of you. Focus on me and see my hand. See my heart. They are with you. I am doing a quick work, if I spoke it, I shall bring it to pass.*

*Move, Move, Move Forward! Walk in Faith. Do the things I have told you. I am with you to keep you, and to bless you. Get what I have reserved for you. Your name is on it. Get it. It's yours. Saith the Lord of Hosts. I hid this word in my heart.*

The following year, I believe it was 1999, one of "Those Baltimore Women," Sylvia Hicks, returned to Illinois for a visit. She had previously moved back to the east coast. She began to share a vision that God had given her concerning me. She said, "There are large doors opening to you! You must be ready to walk through them because there are great things God wants to do with you. Ooh, you just don't know, but the doors are there."

I was continuously comforted with the promise that

God was with me. Without that, I had nothing and would have gone under, but He was my sustainer and keeper.

The second greatest truth that sustained me during my marriage was this: "The steps of a good person are directed by the Lord." The most difficult decisions were made because I received strength from God. The decisions I could not make were worked out by God. The unknown and unfamiliar things were welcomed because God was with me. He was the one I ultimately looked to for an answer, for a decision, and for understanding; and, each time I looked for it, I received it. However, they came with sweat, tears, and near blood.

One of my most difficult decisions was the decision to "FORGIVE." With each new occurrence of wrongdoings the pain caused my heart to grow harder. Even though I knew it was critical for me to forgive my husbands and everyone involved, I just couldn't. I eventually started praying for them in hopes that God would enable me to forgive. After a l-o-n-g struggle, I forgave because I needed help. I had gone through too much to end up stuck in a rut because I refused to forgive. I'd learned that forgiveness was not for the people who hurt me—forgiveness was for me.

We will never become all that God desires us to be if we don't forgive. Unforgiveness stunts our growth and development. Forgiveness releases us to soar. It doesn't even concern itself with who was right and who was wrong. Learning to forgive is not a 1-2-3 step and you've conquered it. It is an act of our will, a choice, a decision. Forgiveness affects our spirit, soul, and body. It is a heart's decision, a mind's acceptance, and a physical execution. This process applies to every occurrence of wrongdoing. Some say it is easy because there is nothing to it but to do it. You just make the decision to forgive knowing that it frees you and places you back into the vulnerable arena. Others say it is not easy to forgive because there is so much to consider. Easy or not, I failed often.

Whenever I retaliated or sought revenge against Tony or Ronald, it always came back to haunt me; in one way or the another. I suffered many "should've, could've, would've" regrets. However, that made me sensitive to my actions, because I knew I would face them again. I was s-l-o-w-l-y learning to live a life of forgiveness. Operating in the knowledge and revelation of forgiveness freed me to move forward.

The secret of my survival can be summed up with Psalm 73:23, which states, "Nevertheless I am continually with thee: thou hast holden me by my right hand." God was always by my side and he never released my hand. Though I fell, he did not allow me to be utterly destroyed.

So many times God preserved my mind. He broke the grip of insanity off of me. So often I was wearied and felt like giving up, but God kept me. He was my strength. The love of God kept my heart and mind stable. God, through His love, wiped away all of the shame that accompanied my sufferings. He is a keeper, and a mender of the brokenhearted. I learned that I couldn't always expect Him to change my situations, but I could always depend on Him to cause me to triumph in any situation. Even in the ones where He had to change me.

One real truth I had to settle within myself was that, God moves in His own time. When I thought my situation required emergency attention from God, He said, "Be still and know." When I thought my situation had to be handled 'yesterday' or I would die, He said, "Not yet." I had to resolve that nothing really mattered except my decision to endure until the end. I was not always right in my painful situations, but I consistently tried to make things right, wherein resting my hope in God.

One Sunday morning I went to church weary. I was tired of always being the one trying to make things right. I was ready to throw in the towel and call it quits. My pastor, Bishop Moody, began preaching; and it was as if he was speaking directly to me. He said, "God puts things in your heart to fulfill, but He needs your faith to get it done". Then he said something that caused my Spirit to leap within me. While expounding on the biblical account, from the book of Daniel, of the three Hebrews who were thrown in the fiery furnace, Bishop Moody said, "God said, 'Believe Me while you are bleeding'." When I heard those words, I received comfort and strength from the Word of God. I knew that in the midst of my sufferings, trials, and temptations, I had to trust God. I knew that God was trustworthy. I knew that I believed God, but I had to believe Him enough to continue holding on.

I have not yet attained, but I am working to attain. We can overcome any lack in our spirit, soul, and body, if we trust God and obey His Word. God not only saved me from two murder attempts, a suicide attempt, and insanity, He saved me from myself.

Despite all of the things I suffered, I can't help but thank God for the things He kept me from experiencing. One sunny day, while driving on the expressway with very few cars, I began to worship God. As I thanked Him for His work in my life, I asked Him why I had to endure so much pain in my life. God so sweetly and fatherly said to me, "Rena, what you went through was not about you, as much as it was about Me. I chose you, you didn't choose me. I wanted others to see Me in you." I was speechless as He continued, "You were used so others could see My Glory." In our sufferings, God is not always testing us; rather, He wants to show Himself great through us.

Don't misunderstand me. The scars were there. They

were present all the time, like lumps on the body. The scars were my constant companion, where I went they went. I felt the impact of them long after the incidents. I relived the pain. The shame and embarrassment caused me to hang my head. I rehearsed the accusations and blame. I could not erase the memories associated with the scars, but the one who covered me could. God erased the scars and I was left with "No Scars."

The premise of "No Scars" is supernatural forgetting. God took care of everything that concerned me and the painful memories associated with my situations. He cleansed the agony of the painful situations from my mind and made me free from scars. I can now recall my experiences as testimonies, and not as sufferings. Although I may still cry, my tears are now tears of joy as I stand in awe of what God did for me. It was good for me to have suffered. I am in a place now where I can see the good in what I've been through. I have learned that the rewards of God are incomparable with anything in life, good or bad. In Romans 8:18, the Bible states, "…the sufferings of this present time are not worthy to be compared with the glory which shall be revealed in us." God took away all of the evidence of my suffering. He eradicated me with a dramatic deliverance. All things—mentally, physically, socially, spiritually, and financially—have worked together for my good. The excellence of God's Spirit was superimposed over my spirit, covering my scars. I was released to be Me!

# Order Today

**Walking Softly I** $12.95

A book of poetry designed to help keep love alive. It creates an intimate ambiance to discuss ugly issues and helps men and women express their feelings. It brings warmth to ice cold settings. This book is a must read…(June 2003)

**Walking Softly II** $12.95

Part Two of the Walking Softly Book Collection reveals new ideas to invigorate your relationship. It is for anyone who is "in love", waiting "for love", and those who are not sure "about love". (August 2004)

**Jehovah, It's All About You Book** $7.95

Have you ever been Center-Stage with God? Use this book during your devotions and it will move you into a powerful worship experience with God. (September 2004)

**Jehovah, It's All About You CD** $15.00

This CD contains the Jehovah worship book PLUS several worship songs intermittently sung by renown artist Kenneth L. Daniel. Allow this CD to move you into a powerful worship experience with God. (June 2005)

**"If Only" Motivational CD** $7.00

Have you ever made excuses you knew were unacceptable? After all, self-preservation is all about excuses; our reasons and justifications for "doing" and "saying"; what we do and say. Listen to this CD and stop allowing excuses to stunt your growth. (June 2005)

**Walking Softly Calendar** $12.95

This calendar contains 12 poems surrounding love-walking. The power to feel love, find love, and experience love are on every page. The monthly challenges are designed to create an atmosphere of sensitivity and warmth. (October 2005)

**Humility Before Honour**                    **$19.95**

This hardcover book is a must-read. It is a "keepsake" for generations to come. Bishop Carlis Lee Moody, Sr.'s biography will reveal a man of faith and integrity. He has travelled the globe fulfilling the great commission in over 42 countries. He is an international symbol of hope to those he serves. (October 2005)

**Walking Softly for Everyone**                **$14.95**

This book contains a special message for everyone. It encourages the discouraged, cautions the singles, massages the heart of the divorced, and prepares the married for a life of challenge and love. (April 2007)

**Hopes, Dreams, Visions**                     **$9.95**

This motivational handbook revitalizes the heart and provides the strength to conquer obstacles in life. It contains 60 scenarios designed to elevate the readers' expectations of themselves. (August 2013)

**MONEY, The Master or The Servant**          **$8.95**

This book is a must-read! However, you may find yourself laughing and crying at the same time. It may even feel like a roller coaster ride, but I assure you there's a safe landing. You will experience a liberation and a thirst to assume control of your money. (August 2014)

Just Writers Publishing Company
"Where Fingers Write From the Heart"

*Prices do not include Shipping & Handling.